CHUMLEY'S GOLD

A Western Duo

Other Five Star Titles
by Wayne D. Overholser:

Nugget City
Riders of the Sundowns

CHUMLEY'S GOLD

A Western Duo

WAYNE D. OVERHOLSER

Five Star
Unity, Maine

Five Star Western
Published in conjunction with Golden West Literary Agency.

May 1999

First Edition

Five Star Standard Print Western Series.

The text of this edition is unabridged.

Set in 11 pt. Plantin by Minnie B. Raven.

Printed in the United States on permanent paper.

Library of Congress Cataloging in Publication Data

Overholser, Wayne D., 1906–
    [High Valley]
    Chumley's gold : a western duo / Wayne D. Overholser. — 1st ed.
      p. cm.
    "A Five Star western" — T.p. verso.
    High Valley — Chumley's gold.
    ISBN 0-7862-1571-2 (hc : alk. paper)
    1. Frontier and pioneer life — West (U.S.) — Fiction.
2. Western stories. I. Overholser, Wayne D., 1906–
Chumley's gold. II. Title.
PS3529.V33A6 1999
813'.54—dc21   98-54653

Editor's Note

Nearly forty years separate the writing of the two short novels by Wayne D. Overholser to be found in this volume. "Chumley's Gold" was among the last fiction this author wrote in a career that began with publication of "Wanted Man" in *Popular Western* (12/36) and concluded with the writing of THE OUTLAWS, the last novel he completed before his death in 1996 and the next Wayne D. Overholser Five Star Western. "High Valley" was published previously only in magazine form and that was nearly fifty years ago. It is this short novel that begins this Western duo. "Chumley's Gold" appears here for the first time. Wayne D. Overholser was an author of the Western story who rarely disappoints with his narratives of characters about whom his readers come to care deeply and who confront the dire complexities of life on the American frontier in such a way that they embody universal themes of the human condition. Taken in tandem these two short novels aptly demonstrate the range and development of this author's extraordinary imagination.

Table of Contents

High Valley

I

It was cold for September, cold even for Rainbow Basin, and the wind that funneled down from the Big Bear range to the west had quite a bite that gave the morning a January feel. Grant Talbot, tightening the cinch on his buckskin, glanced at the mountains and shook his head. It had snowed up there again last night, and it would still take several days of hard riding to finish gathering the steer herd that was to be delivered in Placerville early in October.

"Grant."

It was Mrs. Dexter, standing on the front porch of the Wagon Wheel ranch house, the wind tugging at her red hair, her right hand holding the collar of her maroon robe tightly around her neck.

Grant thought angrily: *She's aiming to send me on some errand a chore boy could do.*

Bruce Mayer grinned at him with taunting insolence. He said: "The widow wants you, boss."

Grant glanced around at the Wagon Wheel crew. They were all grinning, even Dick Sharples, Grant's *segundo* and the steadiest of the lot. They knew as well as he did what Linda Dexter would say. "Shake the range down, will you, Grant? It just won't draw this morning." Or: "Cut some kindling, won't you, Grant?" Or: "Ride into town for me, will you, Grant? I'm out of perfume."

Well, it hadn't been quite that bad, but Bruce Mayer would make out that it was. A lot of good it did to ramrod an outfit and have the owner use him for an errand boy.

9

"Might as well marry the woman," Mayer had said a dozen times. "She couldn't boss a husband around no more than she does you."

Grant stepped into the saddle. "Get moving." He swung a hand toward the aspen-covered foothills to the west. "You don't need me along to tell you what to do."

Mayer tucked his chin against the back of his clasped hands, looking coyly at Grant. "But I need to tell you what to do, Granty," he said in a falsetto voice. "I lost my hanky. Won't you look for it in the pile of dresses that's underneath my petticoats?"

"Bruce," Grant said in a low tone, "so help me, one of the these days I'm going to knock so many teeth down your throat you'll be gumming your grub for the rest of your life."

Mayer threw back his head and roared with laughter. "I'm scared, Grant, I'm scared." Wheeling his horse, he let the animal pitch a few times. Then, cracking steel to him, he rode toward the foothills, Sharples and the rest stringing out behind him.

"Grant, are you coming?" Linda Dexter called again, her voice edgy.

She was still there on the porch, looking cold enough to crack if she took a step. Grant said — "I'm coming." — and turned his horse toward the house.

For the life of him Grant could not understand why old Joe Dexter had married Linda. She'd been twenty-five and Joe had been over sixty. It hadn't worked from the first because Linda was out of place here on the Wagon Wheel as a canary with a flock of crows. Old Joe had done his best to make her happy, but he had missed by a cow country mile.

Now Joe was dead. Broke his neck when he'd fallen from the trail to High Valley, or so the sheriff, Steve Ollard, said,

10

a conclusion with which Grant did not agree. It had happened three months ago, and Linda had been leaning on Grant with steadily increasing weight ever since.

Linda waited on the front porch until Grant dismounted in front of the house and stepped up beside her. He said harshly: "You know how much work we've got to do, Linda. I can't be running errands for you all the time, if we're going to get Ira Connors off our necks this fall."

She shivered as a stronger blast of wind struck at her. Grant thought she was about to cry, and that always got him. He said hastily: "All right. What is it?"

"Come inside," she said, and led the way into the house.

Grant followed reluctantly. It didn't look right for Linda to start chasing a man so soon after Joe had been killed. It wouldn't have bothered Grant if it had been some other man, but he was woman-shy, especially when the woman was a pusher.

Linda waited at the kitchen door until Grant came through, then closed it behind him. "It's warm in here," she said. "I just about froze to death outside. Isn't this a terrible country, Grant? September would still be summer anywhere else."

"I don't think it's a terrible country," he said.

She looked at him gravely. "It's a good cow country, so you like it. What it does to a woman isn't important."

He thought about Mamie Dolan who owned the Seven Bar Seven on the other side of Bell Creek. Three years ago she had been bucked off a horse, and the fall had injured her back so that her legs were paralyzed. She spent every waking hour in a wheelchair, usually on the front porch of her log house where she could look enviously across the valley to the rich grass that belonged to the Wagon Wheel, look and hate Joe Dexter's widow with all the intensity of a

11

violent nature. The country had not dampened Mamie's spirit, but there was no use pointing that out to Linda.

"I might as well be riding, if that's all you wanted."

"No. Sit down." She motioned to the table. "I'll pour you a cup of coffee."

"Don't want one," he said brusquely, and was ashamed of his tone of voice.

He sat down and took the makings from his vest pocket, noting that Linda's breakfast dishes were still on the table, and it didn't look as if she'd eaten much. She sat down across from him, her blue eyes on him.

Linda's red hair hung down her back, gathered by a small, blue ribbon at the base of her neck. Her robe had fallen open below her chin. He could see the top of her nightgown and the upper swell of her breasts. He lowered his gaze to his cigarette. She had no business running around in her nightgown. He wondered what Bruce Mayer would say if he knew about it.

"I don't understand you, Grant," Linda said worriedly. "I've tried to be nice to you, and you've treated me like dirt."

"I work for you." Grant still stared at his cigarette. "That's all. I just work for you."

"It could be a lot more," she said. "At least, I haven't got in your way. I mean, I don't know the cattle business. You do, and I've been smart enough not to tell you how to run the ranch."

"Thanks," he said.

"I'm thanking you for being loyal and working as hard as you have. I know you ought to be with the crew, and I know that, if we don't pay the bank off this fall, Ira Connors will make it rough on us, but there's something I've got to tell you."

12

He fired his smoke, glancing at her briefly. Pretty enough, he thought, with her bright red hair and blue eyes and full, rich lips, pretty enough to have nailed old Joe when he'd gone to Denver for a good time. Neither Joe nor Linda had said where they met, but it had been respectable enough. Grant was sure of that, for he didn't believe the gossip Mamie Dolan had started. But it didn't make any difference. Linda wasn't for him, and he would probably wind up telling her so straight out.

"Go ahead," he said. "Tell me."

"I don't know why Joe asked me to marry him," she said miserably. "Of course, I wanted a younger man, and I told him I didn't love him the way a woman ought to love her husband, but it didn't make any difference. He wanted me, Grant. I tried to make him happy. I tell you, I tried."

He looked at her taut, worried face, thinking he could argue with her about how hard she'd tried, but he let it go. He said: "I never claimed you didn't. I reckon Joe was happier after you came than he was before."

"Thank you, Grant. It makes me feel good to hear you say that." She lowered her eyes. "What I wanted to say was that I can't stand it here any more. Nobody to talk to. Nowhere to go. Living through one day that's just like the one before it. Nothing to do but scrub and dust, and no one to see the house after I get it clean."

He rubbed his cigarette out. "I could get a Mexican woman in town. She can do your housework. And about going somewhere. There's dances. . . ."

"I know," she broke in. "After a widow mourns so long, she can go to dances and maybe get another man. Owning the Wagon Wheel would make me a pretty good catch, I suppose."

"You're a good catch several ways. You're pretty. Take a

little more time and you'll have every man in the basin camping on your front steps."

"Except Grant Talbot," she said in a low voice.

"I work for you," he said again. "I don't know why I have to keep saying it."

"It doesn't bother Bruce Mayer. He's asked me to marry him."

"I ain't Bruce Mayer."

"I've found that out." She put her hands on the table. "There's no use to keep fooling myself. I don't belong out here. I made a mistake marrying Joe and leaving Denver. Now the best thing I can do is to go back. I'm selling the Wagon Wheel."

So that was it. He rose, automatically reaching for the makings again, and walked to the window. He had been afraid this would happen. He felt the hammering of his temple pulse; he fought down an impulse to turn her over his knee and spank her as he would have disciplined a willful child.

He stood looking eastward across the broken floor of the basin. In the distance he could make out the vague shape of the town of Rocky Fork. Not much of a town, but it had survived through good years and bad years, through hot summers and cold winters, and it would continue to survive.

He thought of Ira Connors, the banker, who would walk across town for a penny but was absolutely honest to the letter, if not the spirit, of the law. He thought of Sheriff Steve Ollard who, when he was younger, would have followed a man to hell and back if convinced the man was wanted by the law, but now had become lazy with nothing to do, and of Marty Reem who owned the Mercantile. He remembered a story Joe Dexter had often told about Reem.

It had happened years ago, long before Grant had come to the basin, but Joe often told it because he liked Reem. The valley folks were starving, and Reem's shelves were empty, and, just as Reem's hired man was about to take the freight wagon to Placerville for a load of supplies, a late spring storm struck the basin. The hired man refused to go, so Reem took the wagon and made it back, although, when he had started, several men in Rocky Fork had offered ten to one odds he'd never get to Placerville.

To Grant that story about Reem symbolized the basin and its people. It was a tough country, and it took tough folks to live in it, a fact which was beyond Linda's understanding. It was not her country. She did not understand the people, and they did not understand her. She could not change herself, and she could not change the basin or the people here.

It was a shame, too, because the West had need of women, strong and energetic, with wills of their own. And no one would deny Linda Dexter was that kind of woman, but something was wrong, because she seemed out of place in the country that needed her.

II

Grant had not really considered the possibility that Linda might sell. Now it struck him like a blow from an unseen fist. If he talked an hour, he could never make her understand what the Wagon Wheel had meant to Joe Dexter, and did to himself.

There was this long period of silence, and then Linda

cried: "Haven't you got anything to say, Grant, anything at all?"

"Nothing you want to hear."

She came to him and touched his arm. "Listen, Grant. I told you I did all I could to make Joe happy. Holding onto the Wagon Wheel won't make any difference to him now, one way or the other."

He looked down at her pale, anxious face, a faint stirring of conscience in him. She didn't like Bruce Mayer. Perhaps that was why she had thrown herself at Grant. If she hadn't done such a complete job of throwing herself — no, it would have been the same anyhow.

"All right," he said tonelessly. "What do you want me to do?"

"I had a letter from a man named Cole Fenton. He said he'd heard Joe had died, and he wanted to know if the Wagon Wheel was for sale. I wrote back and told him it was. He's coming to look at it."

"I'll break his neck," Grant said.

She shrank back as she often did when the strange streak of violence that was in him came to the surface. "He'll be on the stage today, Grant. I want you to meet him and bring him out. Please don't do or say anything that would keep him from buying the Wagon Wheel."

"How did he find out about Joe?"

"He didn't say. He just said he had made a fortune in mining and wanted to get into the cattle business. He was in the basin several years ago, and he liked it here. He made me a tentative offer of fifty thousand."

"You mean over and above the mortgage?"

She nodded. "I explained that to him."

There was a strong smell about it, the kind of smell that a man gets when he has an unexpected meeting with a

16

skunk. The Wagon Wheel wasn't worth fifty thousand, not with Ira Connors holding the mortgage on it that he did. Somebody had put Cole Fenton up to this, Connors maybe.

"Have you thought about what would happen if somebody got the Wagon Wheel who wasn't as square as Joe always was?"

"What do you mean?"

"I was thinking about the High Valley folks. Like Red Johnson. Some fellows might figure High Valley belonged to the Wagon Wheel. We could use it for summer range all right."

"Wouldn't make a difference," Linda said. "Joe was too easy with them. They're an outlaw pack, from all I hear."

"He knew how to handle them," Grant said. "I know there's been some talk about 'em being rustlers and bank robbers, but they've never bothered anybody in the basin."

Linda backed away, her lips tightly pressed. "I know, Grant. You're in love with that Rennie Johnson. I guess that explains a lot of things. Like the way you've treated me."

"Rennie's just a kid," he said indignantly. "Of all the damned fool notions!"

"Go ahead and deny it. It doesn't make any difference. Not really. I just want you to meet Cole Fenton and bring him here. You show him the ranch, and I'll get the best price I can. I don't care one way or the other about High Valley, Grant."

"I'll meet him," Grant said.

Picking up his Stetson from the table, he walked out, mounted his waiting horse, and rode off.

Directly north of the Wagon Wheel buildings the sandstone wall separating the basin from High Valley rose a sheer thousand feet, dotted here and there by the dark green of tenacious footing in the sandstone. A mile to the northeast Grant could see the thread-like trail that worked its way up the side of the wall. It was the only route into High Valley from the south and was seldom used except by the valley men who visited Marty Reem's store in Rocky Fork occasionally for salt or gunpowder, or any of the few items they could not produce themselves.

As Grant rode out of the Wagon Wheel yard, he remembered how often Joe Dexter had said that he could run twice the herd he did if he could use High Valley for summer range. By September, grass was belly-deep on a cow, and, since none of the valley men owned more than a dozen head, most of it went to waste. But whenever Joe had approached Red Johnson, the accepted leader of the High Valley settlers, Johnson would say, no, not for any amount of money. They were getting along, they were happy, and by damn they didn't want any Wagon Wheel cowhands getting underfoot.

So Joe had let it rest, getting along with the inadequate summer range in the Big Bears which he shared with five other basin ranchers. Someone like Cole Fenton might look upon the matter in a different light, but if someone did force the issue, Johnson and his boy, Bugeye, and their neighbors would fight.

Then, for no reason except that Linda had mentioned her, Grant thought of Rennie Johnson. Linda's saying that he loved Rennie was ridiculous. The kid wasn't more than seventeen. Cute enough, Grant thought, the way a wildcat kitten was cute.

Grant had never quite understood the situation in the Johnson home. Rennie was supposed to be Red's daughter, but Grant had a notion she had been adopted. She was small-boned and fine-featured, and mild except when she

18

was aroused, whereas Red and Bugeye were big, with coarse, repellent features, and there was no mildness about them.

Grant's idea that she was an adopted daughter was based, moreover, on more than looks or manners. He had been eating dinner with the Johnsons and Joe Dexter the spring before. Rennie had been standing at the stove when Bugeye, getting up for more coffee, had patted the girl on her behind. She had promptly picked up a stick of stove wood and hit him over the head. She had almost knocked him out, and Red had laughed for five minutes.

"She told you the other day to keep your paws off her," Red had said. "Now maybe you'll remember."

Afterwards, it occurred to Grant that he had sensed fear in the girl. He felt sorry for her because Red never let her out of the valley, and she was always dressed in men's clothes, probably some that Bugeye had outgrown. But for Linda to say he, Grant Talbot, was in love with Rennie was just plain crazy.

Living close to the High Valley people was a good deal like living next door to a colony of grizzlies. Joe had often expressed it in those words, and Grant agreed. The best way to get along with them was to let them alone. Besides, as Joe used to say, even grizzlies have a right to their homes.

The road had swung south to the creek, and now Grant's thoughts were turned suddenly from High Valley and its people. Ben Piper was sitting his saddle on the other side of the stream, a cigar cocked at a jaunty angle between his molars.

He called: "Mamie wants to see you, Talbot."

Grant pulled up and let his horse drink, his eyes on Piper. The man was about thirty-five, big and shaggy-haired, and his yellow eyes always seemed to be

19

grinning at a man even when his meaty lips were without a trace of humor. He was the only rider Mamie Dolan employed. Apparently he suited her, but he was the last man in the basin Grant would have hired to ride for the Wagon Wheel.

"That's kind of funny," Grant said. "The last time I dropped in on Mamie, she showed me the business end of her scatter-gun."

Piper shrugged his thick shoulders. "I don't know what's got into her. Sometimes I think she's the smartest rancher in the basin, and then there's times when she seems to have less sense than a day-old calf."

"You been waiting for me to come by?"

"Yeah," Piper said sourly. "Mamie sits up there with a pair of glasses and watches the Wagon Wheel. Hell, she can tell you what kind of underclothes the Dexter widow woman wears. Don't miss a washing, Mamie don't."

"She saw me leave?"

"Yep. Saw you head down the road and sent me to stop you. Well, I've got to go to town."

Piper turned downstream. Grant hesitated. He didn't trust Ben Piper, and he wasn't sure he could trust Mamie. Now the thought occurred to him that this man Fenton might have heard about Joe's death through Mamie. In any case it wouldn't hurt to find out what she wanted.

Grant rode across the creek and took the steep road leading to the bench on which the Seven Bar Seven buildings were located. He had not been here for months, and it seemed to him that the spread looked a little more run-down every time he came. Ben Piper was lazy, and Grant wondered how Mamie, who had been a tireless, hard-working woman before her accident, could put up with Piper.

20

He dismounted in front of Mamie's log house, calling: "Howdy, Mamie!"

Mamie Dolan had been a handsome woman, but the frustration that being bound to a wheelchair had brought to her was beginning to show in her pale, lined face. Her hair, once a dark, lustrous brown, was thatched with gray. Now, sitting on her front porch in her chair, she held her blue eyes on Grant for a moment without speaking. He found it hard to believe that she was only thirty, but he was certain of her age because he knew she was only three years older than he was.

"Sit down, Grant." Mamie motioned to a rawhide-bottom chair. Lifting a whiskey bottle from under the blanket that was spread across her knees, she held it out to him. "Have a drink."

Grant dropped into the chair. "No, thanks."

Mamie shoved the bottle back under the blanket. "So you won't take a drink from a woman. Well, now, I'm wondering what you take from other women, like that chippie Joe left the Wagon Wheel to."

"She's no chippie, Mamie."

"Got her out of a sporting house, didn't he?"

"If you sent for me to talk about Linda. . . ."

"Aw, don't get your fur up." Mamie produced a cigar and bit off the end. "Real touchy when it comes to what you call good women, ain't you?" She shrugged indifferently. "I want to hire you away from the Wagon Wheel. What'll it take?"

It was a morning of surprises for Grant, but the surprise he had felt when Linda had announced she was going to sell the Wagon Wheel was nothing compared to the surprise he felt now. He stared at Mamie while she fired the cigar and blew out a cloud of smoke. He wasn't sure he had heard her right. She had hated Joe Dexter for years, she hated the Wagon Wheel, and she hated Linda. Like everyone else in the valley, Mamie knew that Grant Talbot went with the Wagon Wheel.

"Damn it!" Mamie snapped. "Are you deaf, or did you hear me ask you a question?"

"Yeah, I heard," Grant said, "but it didn't make sense. You don't want me."

She took the cigar out of her mouth, grinning a little, one hand coming up to brush back a vagrant lock of hair. "I want you, all right. I want you bad enough to let you write your own ticket."

"Why?"

"You're the best cowman in the valley, that's why. Beginning in the spring, you're going to see this end of the basin chuck full of Seven Bar Seven cows. I want a ramrod, a good one, and I'll pay for him."

"You've got Piper."

Mamie snorted. "So I've got Piper. He's all right when all I've got is a shirt-tail full of cows, but he never was big enough to run a spread, and he never will be." She leaned forward. "Grant, we both know the Wagon Wheel is finished, but what you don't know is that the Seven Bar Seven is moving in. I tried once before, and I got knocked flat on my back. Well, I won't miss this time, not with Joe Dexter dead." She paused, watching him closely, then she asked: "Want to know the real reason I'm offering you a job?"

"You said you wanted a ramrod."

"It's more'n that. When you go to work for an outfit, you take your heart along with the rest of you. Call it loyalty if you want to. Ben Piper wouldn't even savvy if I explained it to him."

"I ain't so sure the Wagon Wheel is finished."

"I am. You know what I thought of Joe Dexter." She slapped a leg. "I hated him for that. I hated him for corralling me like he done between the creek and the south wall on a ten-cow range. Grant, there's one job I'll pull off if it's the last thing I ever do. I'll flatten the Wagon Wheel so there's nothing of it but a memory!"

While Mamie raved, Grant tried to be conciliatory. "The Wagon Wheel is still a big outfit," he reminded.

"Hell, I got off the subject," she broke in. "I meant to say I didn't hate Joe so much that I was blind to the fact he was a big man. When a fellow like that dies, he leaves a vacuum. I'm moving into that vacuum."

"It was Joe who died," Grant said. "Not the Wagon Wheel."

Mamie's cigar had gone cold in her hand. With a sudden violent gesture she flung it into the yard, her head thrown back, her eyes on the Wagon Wheel ranch house at the foot of the north wall.

"You're blind, Grant," she said. "The Wagon Wheel died, when Joe died. That frothy collection of buttons and bows he married won't do anything with the spread, and you know it! She'll sell, or take what she can and walk off and leave it. You're in love with a ranch, Grant, but I think you're too smart to love one that's dead."

He shook his head. "I'll stick till they bury it."

She brought her gaze to him, her face filled with sudden malice. "Is it that floozy who's holding you there?"

"No."

"I didn't think so. It'd take a real woman to satisfy you, and there's nothing real about her." Mamie turned her head to stare across the basin again. "There was a time when I would have gone for you. You didn't know it, but I did. You couldn't see me, Grant. Too much dust in your eyes, dust that old Joe Dexter kicked up because I'd tried to lick him. But maybe I'm wrong about you, Grant. Maybe you don't want a woman. Maybe a ranch is all you need."

She was trying to tell him she had been in love with him. He couldn't believe it. It was a simple matter with Linda. She wanted a man who would give her some sense of security. But it was different with Mamie. Even crippled as she was, she was still the proudest and most independent woman he knew.

"I've got to stick with the Wagon Wheel," he said finally. "Joe done a lot for me. I drifted in here when I was a kid. . . ."

"I know," she broke in. "Not even dry behind the ears. Just a kid with a horse and a gun and a notion he was as big as all hell. That was after Joe had settled my hash. He taught you everything you know and he made you foreman, so now you'll stick with the outfit because you're sentimental about what you owe a dead man. Forget it, Grant. Throw in with me and we'll be running this basin inside of five years. No, make it three."

"I can't, Mamie."

She shrugged, hiding her feelings behind an expressionless mask as she so often did. "I'm sorry, Grant. That red-headed hussy will sell the Wagon Wheel, and the new owner will fire you. Just remember one thing. If you don't take my offer now, you'll never have another chance."

"I'll remember." He fired a cigarette, cupping the flame with one hand, then flipped the match into the barren yard. "I'm supposed to meet a fellow in Rocky Fork named Cole Fenton who wants to buy the Wagon Wheel. Did you send for him?"

"Sure," Mamie said. "He's old friend of mine."

He couldn't tell if she was lying, or whether she even intended for him to believe her. He said — "Thanks for the offer, Mamie." — and walked to his horse and mounted.

She raised a hand in a masculine gesture of farewell. "So long, Grant. Best wishes in hell if I don't see you alive again."

"What do you mean by that?"

"When you turned me down, you asked for a lot of trouble, more trouble than any man born of woman ever had."

III

Below the Seven Bar Seven the road followed the south side of Bell Creek, a slow-moving stream that murmured faintly between the close-growing rows of willows. In the spring and early summer it was a white-maned, brawling torrent, but at this time of year it was low, and Grant was only faintly aware of its sound.

He rode past the Double O, set on the bench to the north; he passed the Horseshoe Bar to the south. Then the road swung away from the creek to make a wide turn over a ridge so that it kept an easy grade instead of taking a steep pitch alongside a fifty-foot fall in the creek.

From the crest of the ridge Grant could count ten ranches, for at this point the basin widened. Some were so distant they were mere dots in the early fall haze. There were others he could not see, small outfits tucked out of sight in the bottoms of innumerable cañons that were ragged openings in the red sandstone cliff surrounding the basin.

Grant reined up. It was a scene at which he had gazed more times than he could count, but it always impressed him. He remembered that Joe had often stopped at this point just to look, and he had never failed to say: "Now there's a sight that'd please the eyes of the Lord." Grant didn't know about the Lord, but it pleased him, and it had pleased Joe.

He could see a few dark patches of timber that knifed out into the basin floor from the bottom of the cliff, and there were willows along the creek, but generally this was open country with a fine carpet of grass. The basin had never been overgrazed, largely because Joe Dexter, knowing what had happened on other ranges, had organized the Rainbow Basin Cattlemen's Association and had been its president from the day it had been organized. Through the association Joe had been able to control the number of cattle that were kept in the basin. Aside from Mamie Dolan, there was not a rancher in the country who had not counted Joe as a friend.

It had been nearly ten years since Grant had ridden into the Wagon Wheel and asked for a job, and during that time there had been no real trouble in the basin. Grant had never heard the whole story of the trouble between Joe and Mamie. It was something Joe had refused to talk about, and Grant had never been inclined to ask Mamie about it. But he knew there had been at least one man killed, and that all of Mamie's crew except for Ben Piper had left the Seven Bar Seven. Grant could not be sure, but he had a notion that Joe could have run Mamie out of the basin if he'd wanted to.

It would have been better, Grant thought, as he rode on toward town, if Joe had made Mamie leave the country. She had refused to join the association; she had seldom left the

Seven Bar Seven; and, although she had been young and attractive when she'd had the fight with the Wagon Wheel, she had lost all interest in social gatherings after her defeat and had even quit going to dances. She had become bitter and vindictive, and now she promised trouble.

It didn't make any sense, doing nothing for ten years and then, after Joe was killed, starting to talk about moving into the vacuum that Joe's death had brought about. Or maybe it did make sense. She had been afraid of Joe, but she had never forgotten her old dream. The more Grant thought about it, the more it worried him, because he didn't see what she could do. But he did not doubt that she was up to something. Idle talk was not one of her failings.

It was not yet noon, when Grant reached Rocky Fork and stabled his horse. The stage was due at one. He loitered for a moment in front of the stable and rolled a smoke, a lanky figure in the bright sunlight. It was warm now, and the wind had died.

A thought occurred to Grant, as he glanced along the deserted street. Maybe Linda would like it here in town where she could see other people and visit with them. It was possible that she could buy a small house. Usually the Wagon Wheel showed a sizable profit. There would be enough left this fall after the herd was sold to give her a good living in town for a year, if it wasn't for the money that had to go to Ira Connors.

Grant crossed the dust strip to the bank, the only brick building on Main Street. Marty Reem and Sheriff Steve Ollard were talking to Connors when Grant came in. They said — "Howdy." — and he spoke to them, and then there was a moment of awkward silence.

It had been different when Joe was alive. If Joe had come in instead of Grant, Connors would have looked up, and

27

they would have gone across the street to the Silver Dollar and had a drink. But today no one suggested it, and Grant knew how it was. He was young, and they were old. Now, looking at Grant, they felt their age, and they resented his youth.

"Got your herd gathered?" Connors asked, after a moment of silence.

"No." Grant poked his thumbs under his belt, an impulsive idea gripping his mind. "Suppose we don't meet that loan next month, Ira?"

Connors was a thin, pale-faced man who had stomach trouble. Now he bent forward, a hand on his middle, looking pained as if Grant's question had started his stomach hurting. He said it in a low tone. "That's a hell of a question, Grant. Nothing to keep you from raising the money, is there?"

"Maybe we've got other use for the *dinero*."

"Like what?"

"Like buying a town house for Linda."

The pained look on Connors's face deepened. Steve Ollard laughed and slapped his leg. He was a big man with a sweeping white mustache of which he was inordinately proud, and he had grown lazy and a little fat with the peace that the basin had enjoyed for ten years. He winked at Marty Reem, saying: "That'd be a hell of a good investment for the Wagon Wheel, wouldn't it, Marty?"

But Marty Reem saw nothing funny in it. He was a bald, pudgy man, mild-mannered and polite, and he possessed the sharpest and most penetrating mind of the three of them. He said: "Something's biting you, Grant. Let's have it."

Ollard sobered, looking as if he regretted having laughed, and Connors straightened up, green eyes searching Grant's face.

Grant said: "You were all Joe's friends. I was a little more than that. He was the nearest thing to a father I can remember. Now that he's dead, I savvy what a hell of a big man he was."

"We know that," Reem said softly. "Something's happened. Let him talk."

"Big or not," Grant went on, "Joe had his faults. He was soft when it came to women. Or maybe he just didn't understand them."

"Never figured out he was getting old," Ollard said with deep malice.

Ollard had a young wife, and Joe used to hint slyly that she was too much for him. Apparently Joe had overlooked the fact that he had put himself in Ollard's position, when he married Linda. Grant pinned his gaze on the sheriff, suddenly realizing that he disliked the man. He wondered if these three were as good friends as they let on.

"I didn't mean it that way," Grant said. "He should have run Mamie Dolan out of the country a long time ago, and he should have fixed Linda up with a town house where she could see other women and gab over the back fence. She's lonesome."

Ollard grinned. "You're out there."

Reem said softly: "That's enough, Steve. You're taking a long time to get at this, Grant."

"I know," Grant said. "I keep asking myself a question, and I'm afraid of the answer. You see, I'm wondering if you three are big enough to hold the lid on when the big blow-up comes, now that Joe ain't around."

Red-faced, Ollard sputtered: "What's the matter with you, Grant? You're as ringy as hell today."

"I'm just asking," Grant said.

"And I'll give you a damned quick answer," Ollard

snapped. "I'll keep the lid on if a blow-up comes, and I'll do it alone."

"You ain't man enough," Marty Reem said wearily. "Me and Ira ain't, neither. No use trying to fool ourselves, Steve. We all leaned on Joe. The Wagon Wheel had always stood for something in this basin because Joe threw a big shadow. Now the shadow ain't here."

Reem was scratching his bald head, eyes on Grant, acting as if Ollard didn't exist. He said: "We've got trouble, Grant. That it?"

"Linda's figuring on selling the Wagon Wheel to a gent named Cole Fenton," Grant said. "He's coming in on the stage. Did you send for him, Ira?"

"No," Connors said. "I'm satisfied the way things are."

Grant nodded, believing the banker. "Looks like somebody wrote to Fenton about Joe dying. I'm wondering who it was."

"Not me," Ollard said. "Suppose she does sell. That won't make no never-mind to any of us except you. This Fenton jasper might fire you."

Grant nodded. "I figure he will, and I don't like it. Joe would have wanted me to stay on the Wagon Wheel, and, as long as Linda has it, I will. I was thinking that if she had a town house, she might be satisfied."

"You'll pay the bank when the loan's due," Connors said. "Business is business."

"It is with you," Grant said heavily. "There's one more thing. Mamie offered me a job on the Seven Bar Seven. She says the Wagon Wheel is done, and she's moving in on our range."

Ollard snorted derisively. "You've got no reason to worry about her. She's broke, and she's crippled. What the hell could she do?"

"She may be crippled," Reem said slowly, "but I don't figure she's broke. I've wondered about that for years. She don't buy anything to speak of at the store, and every fall she's had a few steers to sell. I'm guessing she's saved her money."

"Why?" Ollard demanded.

"She'll be hiring gunslingers," Reem said. "But you'll hold the lid on even if she brings in an army, won't you, Steve?"

Ollard jammed his big hands deep into his pants pockets. "Sure," he said. "Sure, I'll hold it on."

"It don't make any difference to us," Connors said thoughtfully. "With Joe gone the Wagon Wheel is just another ranch."

"Not to me," Grant said.

He looked at the banker, and then at Ollard, making no effort to hide his dislike for them both. They were tough enough in their own way, but it was a small way, and now he thought they had never been Joe's friends. Not real friends. He had overshadowed them completely, and Grant sensed that they had resented it more than they had let it appear.

"If Linda's going to sell," Connors said, "nobody can stop her."

"I aim to," Grant said, "and not just because I want to save my job. If she sells, I've got a hunch you'll be combing Red Johnson and the rest of the High Valley bunch out of your hair."

Wheeling, Grant stalked out of the bank, knowing that he would say too much if he stayed. He stopped when he reached the boardwalk, for Marty Reem called: "Wait, Grant!"

The storekeeper had run to catch up with him, and now he puffed a little, stopping beside Grant and looking up at his lean, dark face.

"You thinking like them other two?" Grant asked.

"No," Reem answered. "Ollard don't never think of anything but women, and Ira thinks only of dollars. I know how you feel."

"I wonder," Grant said.

Reem rubbed his bald head, eyes sweeping the street. "Even this little old town don't seem the same with Joe gone. When he was alive, his ranch was a sort of balance wheel in the basin. He had a way of putting down a little pressure here and some there, and everything rolled along peaceful-like. Given a little time, you could do the same. Mamie knows that, or she wouldn't have tried to hire you."

Grant waited, knowing Reem had more to say. The things Reem had just said had been in his mind, things that neither Connors nor Ollard would admit.

"I know how you feel, I tell you," Reem went on, "but it ain't something you can put into words. You and the Wagon Wheel belong together. We'll stop Linda from selling some way. Got anything saved?"

"Not much."

"Nothing to do now but stall Linda." He rubbed his bald head some more, eyes thoughtful. "This house in town idea might work. Tell her she can rent mine. I'll move into the back of the store."

"I'll tell her," Grant said. "Thanks."

"Don't thank me," Reem said. "It's for all our good, which Ira and Steve ain't got sense enough to see. Once the ball starts, there'll be a hell of a lot of grabbing for Wagon Wheel range. Mamie won't be the only one."

"Stage is coming," Grant said. "I'm supposed to meet Fenton."

"Go ahead and meet him," Reem said. "One more thing. I know what you meant about the High Valley bunch. Go see Red Johnson. Maybe you can get Rennie to stay with Linda. It'd give Linda somebody to talk to."

It wouldn't work, Linda feeling about Rennie as she did, but Grant didn't tell Reem that. He said — "Might be a good notion." — and moved down the street to the hotel where the stage would stop.

IV

The instant Grant laid eyes on Cole Fenton he knew he would not like the man, although the knowledge was tempered by the realization that he was prejudiced. Fenton was the only passenger, a medium tall, florid-faced man with a small, neatly trimmed mustache, the kind a vain man would wear. He was about forty, Grant judged, with dark eyes and black hair that needed trimming.

Grant held out his hand as Fenton stepped down from the stage. He said: "I'm Talbot, the Wagon Wheel foreman. Missus Dexter asked me to meet you."

A quick smile touched Fenton's lips. "That's fine, Talbot. I appreciate the courtesy."

Fenton gave Grant's hand a quick grasp and turned to the coach to wait for his luggage. Grant said: "If you're hungry, we can go put the feed bag on. The driver'll leave your bags in the hotel lobby."

"Good idea," Fenton agreed. "Been hungry for an hour."

"Leave the valises in the lobby, Butch," Grant called.

The driver nodded. "Sure thing, Grant."

They walked across the lobby into the dining room, took a table near the door, and now Grant saw that the man wore his hair long, that it was not a case of needing a trim. Fenton was wearing a brown broadcloth suit and a flowered waistcoat. There was a heavy gold chain across his chest from which dangled an elk-tooth charm. A dude, Grant thought, the last man in the world that anyone would expect to go into the cattle business.

"Missus Dexter said you'd made some *dinero* in mining," Grant said.

"That's right," Fenton said. "Cripple Creek. I'm not a miner, you understand. I bought and sold claims, and I've been lucky. Funny thing about mining. It's not what you'd call a solid business. You can drop a fortune down a shaft in about five minutes. A dozen things can go wrong. It's not that way with cattle, is it, Talbot?"

"Not if you run a spread right, although a bad winter can break you." Grant rolled a smoke and sealed it. "I believe she said you'd been in the basin before."

"Several years ago. I met Joe Dexter. At the time I understood he was a big man hereabouts."

"The biggest. How'd you hear of his death?"

"Saw it in the papers."

It was a quick answer, a little too quick, Grant thought. He pondered this a moment, thinking there must be some way to discourage Fenton, and knowing that he would have no scruples about doing exactly that regardless of how Linda felt. Their steaks came then, and they ate in silence.

Later, when they had finished their pies, Fenton said: "I'm a greenhorn, Talbot. I'll need a crew. I mean men I can trust who know their business. I assume you'll stay on?"

"Maybe," Grant said. "I was offered another job today by Mamie Dolan."

Fenton's brows lifted. "Mamie Dolan? Does she own a spread in the basin?"

"The Seven Bar Seven across the creek from the Wagon Wheel. She said she knew you."

Fenton laughed shortly. "She's got the best of me." He rose. "Bring a rig in from the ranch?"

"No. I'll get a livery horse for you."

Frowning, Fenton put on his derby. "I have several valises. I don't believe I can handle them on a horse."

"I figured you'd be staying at the hotel. I didn't know. . . ."

Temper showed on Fenton's face. "Look, Talbot. If I buy this ranch, it will be a big transaction. I don't aim just to take a look at the buildings and sign the papers. I'll live out there and see what kind of an outfit it is, or no deal."

"I'll get a livery rig," Grant said.

"I'll be in the saloon," Fenton said. "Give me a holler when you're ready."

He would be right at home with his belly up against the bar, Grant thought. He said: "I'm looking out for Missus Dexter. The Wagon Wheel is all she's got. Naturally I'd like to know if you're in a position to swing this deal. She said you were offering fifty thousand."

"A tentative offer, my friend." Fenton shoved his hands into his pants pockets. "Are you questioning my ability to raise fifty thousand?"

He was close to blowing up. Anger showed in his red-flecked eyes, in the tight set of his mouth.

Grant said: "It ain't a proposition of questioning. Just strikes me that it'd be fair if you had the money on deposit here so when you make up your mind. . . ."

"When I make up my mind, I'll have it on deposit," Fenton said, and strode out of the hotel.

Staring at his back, Grant thought: *I'd play hell working for a man like that.*

35

It took a few minutes to get a buckboard from the stable, tie his buckskin behind it, and load Fenton's valises into the bed, minutes in which a nagging sense of irritation grew in Grant. Fenton was loading up on whiskey, while Grant did the work. If he hadn't clung to a small hope that he could say something that would sour Fenton on his proposed deal, he would have ridden out of town and let the dude wait on himself.

Grant tied in front of the Silver Dollar and went in. Fenton and Ben Piper were bellied up against the bar at the far end, talking amiably as if they were old friends. They were the only ones in the saloon except for the apron and a 'puncher from the Box B in Shadow Cañon. Nodding at the Box B man, Grant went along the bar to where Fenton and Piper stood, their heads close together.

"Old friends?" Grant asked.

Fenton wheeled, startled. "Hell, no. I just don't like to drink alone."

Piper stepped away from the bar, lurching a little as if he were too drunk to stand up. He said thickly: "I reckon you're quitting the Wagon Wheel. Reckon you're going to work for Mamie."

"I didn't take the job," Grant said.

Piper took a step toward him, his big hands fisted. Whiskey always made him proddy, and he'd had enough to make him hunt for an excuse to fight. He said: "So you're too damned good to ride for Mamie! I'll tell you something, sonny. She's a better man than old Dexter ever was."

"Ready to travel, Fenton?" Grant asked.

"No hurry." Fenton fixed amused eyes on Grant's face. "Looks like this cowboy ain't done talking to you, Talbot."

"You're damned right I ain't!" Piper shouted. "Got a lot to say. A hell of a lot. Old Dexter thought he was God. Ran

36

everything in the basin, Dexter did. Now Talbot here thinks he's big enough to wear Dexter's boots. Even sleeps in the same bed with Dexter's. . . ."

"Shut up," Grant said sharply. "If you wasn't drunk, I'd beat hell out of you."

Piper laughed. "Hitting pretty close, ain't I? Hitting right where the hair's short."

"You're a liar!" Grant said. "Come on, Fenton."

"You know, Talbot," Fenton said as if the thought pleased him, "strikes me you're afraid of this man."

"Sure he is," Piper reared back, meaty lips pulled away from brown teeth. "I ain't no liar, Talbot, and I don't cotton to being called one!"

Piper drove at Grant, a big fist swinging for the face, and in that instant Grant realized that the man was not drunk. He had wanted a fight and had set himself to provoke one. Grant side-stepped Piper's rush, catching him on the side of the head with a punishing right. Piper grunted and, swinging sharply, nailed Grant on the point of the chin with a sledge-hammer left.

Grant was knocked off his feet. He never fought well unless he was angry or hurt, and he had not been angered by what Talbot had said because he had thought the man was drunk. He rolled to escape a swinging boot that Piper aimed for his ribs and came to his feet. He was both angry and hurt now, and convinced that this had been rigged, that for some reason Fenton wanted him licked.

Grant waded in, rolling his head as Piper landed a right, then he was close, and he hit the Seven Bar Seven man with a short, punishing blow that made him give ground. Grant caught him in the stomach, a driving blow that jolted wind out of him; he nailed him on the mouth and cut a lip, and hit him on the nose. Piper, crazed by pain, left himself wide open and grabbed Grant around the middle. Grant hit him with a downswinging right on the side of the head. The blow knocked him loose, and Grant stepped back.

Piper fell flat on his belly. He lay there a moment, apparently half stunned, then he raised himself to his hands and knees and shook his head. He came on up to his feet and lunged at Grant, a knife in his right hand.

The barkeep yelled. The 'puncher from Shadow Cañon bawled: "Put that up, Piper!" There was no time for Grant to pull his gun, no time for anything except to jump clear as the six-inch blade slashed at him in a sweeping blow that would have disemboweled him if it had connected. Then Piper fell flat on his face again, and it took a moment for Grant to realize that Fenton had tripped him.

The barman came running from behind the mahogany, a sawed-off shotgun in his hand. "Damn you, Piper!" he yelled. "Drop that knife, or I'll blow your head off!"

Piper tossed the knife behind him and wiped a hand across his bloody face. This time he was slow in getting up, so slow that he seemed almost out on his feet. Grant moved in fast, bringing a right through that snapped Piper's head back. Piper went down again, and this time he lay motionless.

"That snaky, no-good son-of-a-bitch!" the barman barked angrily. "I've worked here for three years, and I've seen more fights than I can count, but this is the first time I ever saw a knife pulled."

"Must have been out of his head," Fenton said. "Or too drunk to know what he was doing."

Grant looked at Fenton. He said: "You wanted this fight. Why?"

Fenton stared at him as if this were beyond his comprehension. "You're loco. I just came in here for a drink. Why

38

would I want a fight between two men I'd never seen until today?"

"I don't know," Grant said, and drew his gun. "I wish I did."

"I don't take that kindly," Fenton shouted in an outraged tone. "I figure I saved your hide, tripping this fellow, and then you claim I wanted a fight. Hell, I should have let him cut you to pieces!"

The barman said: "Grant, put that iron away. If you're aiming to kick up a smoke ruckus, get outside."

Piper was sitting up, his eyes glassy.

Grant cocked his gun. He said: "Piper, did you ever see this man before?"

"Put that iron up, Grant!" the barman shouted.

"How about it, Piper?" Grant asked, ignoring the barkeep.

Piper stared at the gun in Grant's hand. He got up and staggered to the bar. He poured a drink and gulped it, then he looked at Grant. "No, never saw him before."

Grant holstered his gun and, wheeling, stalked out of the saloon. He realized it had been a foul play, for he should have known that Piper would not admit anything. He was untying his buckskin from the back of the buckboard when Fenton came out of the saloon.

"What are you doing?" Fenton demanded.

"Riding home," Grant said. "You can do what you damned please."

"You're going off half-cocked," Fenton said. "I had nothing to do with Piper jumping you. I don't know how to get out to the Wagon Wheel. It's up to you to take me."

Grant hesitated, the violence of his fury dying, but he was still obsessed by the suspicion that there had been something between Fenton and Piper. It would do no good,

39

he thought, to leave Fenton stranded, and it might destroy any faith that Linda had in him if he showed up at the Wagon Wheel without the man.

He said: "All right. Get in." He tied his buckskin again to the back of the buckboard.

"Looks like a hell of a country," Fenton said in a complaining voice as he stepped into the buckboard. "And I thought Cripple Creek was wild."

Grant was silent until they were out of town. Fenton had lit a cigar and was looking around when Grant said: "I don't get it. I don't get it at all. This morning Mamie said she knew you, but you claim you don't know her. Then you go into the Silver Dollar and get chummy with Mamie's man. When I show up, he starts a fight. Don't try telling me he was drunk. I know better."

"I don't get it, either," Fenton said blandly. "Look, Talbot, if I buy the Wagon Wheel, I want you to run the outfit. You must be a good foreman, or Dexter wouldn't have given you the job. Is it a deal?"

"No," Grant said. "I don't want Missus Dexter to sell, and I'm thinking she'll change her mind."

"Not for fifty thousand," Fenton said. "We've corresponded for a couple of months now. I take it she don't like the country and she's anxious to sell. I should think you'd want to keep your job. If it's a matter of wages. . . ."

Grant shook his head. "Let's put it another way. Fifty thousand is too much for the Wagon Wheel. What's more, you're going to have trouble with Mamie. She told me this morning she was going to flatten Wagon Wheel till it wasn't nothing but a memory."

"Forget it," Fenton said. "I never ran into a woman I couldn't handle. As for the price, why, if I like the ranch, I don't mind paying more'n it's worth." He drew a cigar from his pocket and lighted it. "Have you got a good crew?"

Grant was silent for a moment. It was a good crew with the exception of Bruce Mayer. The man was a top hand, but Grant had felt an instinctive dislike for him from the first. He would have fired Mayer weeks ago, if Linda had let him. The rest of the crew had been with the Wagon Wheel a long time, but he had no way of knowing whether they would stay under a new owner.

"Yeah," Grant said finally. "It's a good crew."

"Then we'll keep them," Fenton said. "We'll go right on running the Wagon Wheel the way Joe Dexter did. I try to get along with my neighbors, so I see no reason why this Mamie you talk about should make trouble for us."

Grant said nothing. When they reached the falls, they swung away from the creek, climbing steadily, and at the ridge top Fenton pointed to the north wall of the basin.

"What's up yonder?" Fenton asked. "I mean, on the other side."

"High Valley."

Fenton pulled on his cigar a moment, eyes on the cliff. "As I remember it, when I was here before, there's a shortage of summer range. That right?"

Grant nodded. "Too many of us using the Big Bears."

"Anyone live in High Valley?"

"A few families. They run a shirt-tail full of cows."

"Kind of a rough outfit, aren't they? Seems to me I heard something like that."

"Good people to let alone," Grant said.

"But the Wagon Wheel could use that valley, and Dexter never went after it. I'm wondering why."

"He got along with his neighbors," Grant said.

"Hell, if the grass in High Valley is going to waste and we need it, it just ain't smart to pass it up."

41

"It's smarter to pass it up than to go after it. Them *hombres* up there don't want nobody bothering 'em."

"Take me up there tomorrow," Fenton said, "and I'll talk to them. I'll pay 'em, if that would do any good."

"It wouldn't," Grant said. "They just want to be let alone."

Fenton grinned. "Sounds like the old yarn about the dog in the manger. Only thing to do in a case like that is to kick the dog out of the manger."

If there had been any doubt in Grant's mind about working for Fenton, there was none now. Fenton would be looking for a new foreman the instant he closed the deal with Linda.

Grant glanced up at the north wall, thinking of the Johnsons and Gib Lane and the others who had lived there for a long time. Through all those years there had never been any trouble with the High Valley folks, largely because Joe Dexter had insisted that the basin ranchers leave them alone. Now Fenton was talking about kicking them out, talking as coolly as if they had no rights at all.

For a time Grant's mind lingered on Rennie, and he thought: *I've got to get up there tonight.*

V

Up in High Valley it was nearly dark when Rennie Johnson returned to the cabin, a string of trout in one hand, her fish pole in the other. She had hurried along the creek, not knowing whether Red and Bugeye were back or not. If they were, she'd get a tongue lashing from Red for not having supper ready.

A sense of injustice grew in her. She never knew when they would be home. They were gone every day when the weather was good, fishing or hunting or playing poker in Gib Lane's cabin down the creek. They were typical of the High Valley men — lazy and careless and expecting to be waited on by their womenfolk.

Like other valley women, Rennie was little better than a slave. It was a situation she had accepted when she had been younger, but now she was nearly eighteen, and with the years a feeling of rebellion had grown in her until she knew she could not stay here any longer.

Relief swept through her when she saw that there was no light in the cabin. Red and Bugeye might not be back for hours. Possibly for days. They never told her where they were going or when they'd be back, but they expected her to be here when they did return.

Rennie laid the trout on the table and lighted a lamp, her eyes sweeping the kitchen. It was a barren room as all the rooms in the cabin were — a homemade pine table, two benches, the range, and some shelves along the wall that held a few pans and dishes and the supplies that were left from the last trip Red had made to Rocky Fork. That was all.

She was a small-boned girl with fine features and dark brown eyes in a tanned face. Her hair was jet-black, holding a bright sheen from the lamplight. She raised her hands to it, tightening the pins that held it, a feeling of discontent growing in her.

She would leave right now if she had any place to go, but this was the only world she knew. It had been her home since she had been a child, but she had some remembrance of another, distant place, a ranch where she had been born and had lived her first two years. She seldom prodded her mind about it, for it was vague to her and shadowed by nightmare memories she wanted to lose.

Now she wondered about the outside as she did every idle moment. She could leave the valley and go down into the basin, but she had no idea what she would do then. She had never been to Rocky Fork. She had no money, no friends except Grant Talbot, and the only clothes she had were Bugeye's shirt and trousers that she had cut down so she could wear them.

The sound of a horse coming downstream over the rocky trail reached Rennie Johnson. She whirled to the range and started a fire. She made biscuits, working frantically because she knew what Red would say when he came in. The feeling that she was trapped brought her close to panic. This was no way to live. She had to do something! She had told herself that over and over. She would not stay here, growing old and dowdy and beaten as the other women were, marrying Bugeye as Red had told her she would have to do.

The horse had stopped in front of the cabin. She wondered about that as she slid the pan of biscuits into the oven and filled the fire box with pine. If it were Red or Bugeye, either would put his horse in the corral and come tramping into the kitchen. Bugeye, always demanding, would bawl: "What the hell you been doing all day? I'm hungry."

For a moment fear touched her. It was someone else. Maybe Gib Lane, who sent a chill down her spine every time his lecherous eyes were on her. She was afraid of Bugeye who let her alone only because Red made him, but she was far more afraid of Lane who was a bachelor and had a strange, slinky way of moving that reminded her of the slithering passage of a snake.

She picked up a knife from a shelf and laid it on the back

of the stove so it would be handy. She stood motionless, her slim body rigid, eyes on the open door. Then she knew it wasn't Gib Lane, for a man called: "Hello the house!" Relief was a weakness in her when she recognized the voice. It was Grant Talbot.

Rennie stepped to the door. "Come in!" she shouted.

Saddle leather squeaked as Grant swung down, and a moment later he stepped into the finger of light that fell past her. He asked: "Red here?"

"No." For a moment she was afraid he was going to turn around and walk back to his horse, and she added quickly: "Come in, Grant. He'll be along."

She moved back to the stove. He followed her, reluctantly she thought, as if he wasn't sure this was what he should do. She looked at him, his bronzed face with its gray eyes and wide mouth and square chin. Her eyes moved down his lanky body, a little slack as if he were very tired, and she thought how different he was from the valley men she knew.

There was none of the animal furtiveness about him that characterized Red and Bugeye and Gib Lane. It was not a definite thing she could put her finger on, but she always had a feeling that he was not afraid of anything, for the simple reason he had done nothing he was ashamed of.

"I was getting supper," Rennie said. "Sit down."

"Don't fix anything for me," Grant said. "I ate before I left the Wagon Wheel." He motioned to the trout on the table. "Looks like you had luck."

"They were biting tonight," she said. "I'll fry some for you. I've got biscuits in the oven."

He shook his head. "I ain't hungry." He sat down on a bench and rolled a smoke. "Got any idea when Red will be back?"

She hesitated, not wanting him to go, and yet knowing she had to be honest with him. She could lie to Red or Bugeye because they lied to her, but it was different with Grant.

She said: "No. They left this morning. I don't even know where they went."

She dribbled Arbuckle's coffee into the pot and, filling it with water, set it on the front of the stove. She turned to him, thinking that this was one of the few times she had ever had a chance to talk to him alone. She was silent for a moment while he fired his cigarette, then she walked to the table and sat down across from him, her small hands fisted.

"Grant," she said in a low tone, "take me away from here."

He frowned at her, surprised. "Why?"

"I just can't stay here. That's why. You know what it's like. You know Red and Bugeye. I never get to go anywhere. I don't even have any decent clothes. I'd have left a long time ago if I had any place to go."

"Red wouldn't like it."

"Of course, he wouldn't," she cried. "Does that make any difference?"

He pulled at his cigarette, staring at her as if he didn't see her. He was not a man, she thought, who worried about things, but he was worried now. Irritation stirred in her. He acted as if he hadn't heard what she said.

"Grant, I told you I've got to get out of the valley. Red says that I've got to marry Bugeye. I'd kill myself first. I . . . I'd kill him if I had to!"

Still frowning, he said: "I thought you were supposed to be his sister."

She laughed. She was so surprised at the high, strained sound that was so unnatural, and then she was aware that her fingernails were biting into the palms of her hands. "I'm

46

not related to them. I'm just a maverick. I don't know who I am, but I do know there's a better way to live than this. There must be."

"Reckon there is," he agreed. "I never figured this deal out. Red always acted like there wasn't any other place he wanted to go."

"He's satisfied. Don't ask me why. Don't even ask me where they go when they ride away and leave me alone for two weeks at a time. When they get back, their horses are tired, and they're all in. They always have money until they play a game of poker with Gib Lane. Then he gets it."

She saw a sudden interest come into his eyes. "You're saying they knock a bank over? Or rob a stage?"

"That must be it. They're safe here. Steve Ollard never bothers them. Why would they stay in a place like this unless it was a hide-out where they'll be perfectly safe?"

"I've wondered about it." He tapped his fingers on the table, the frown still lining his forehead. "What would Red do if you left?"

"I don't think he'd do anything. He'd be awful mad, but he'd probably take it out on Bugeye. I'm just somebody to cook for them."

He rose and, walking to the stove, dropped his cigarette into it. He came back, moving slowly. "Rennie, I can't take you. Not now. We may have trouble the way things are stacking up, and, if I took you, we'd have it sure. Anyhow, it ain't none of my business."

"What kind of trouble are you looking for?"

"Linda aims to sell the Wagon Wheel. A gent named Cole Fenton is here to buy it. He thinks he wants High Valley if he makes the deal."

"There'd be hell to pay then," she said.

Grant nodded. "I know. That's why I came up. I wanted

to tell Red. I figured that if we could stall things for a while, Fenton might decide he didn't want to buy the Wagon Wheel."

"You don't want the ranch sold. That it?"

"That's it. Right now we need time. Linda might be satisfied if she could live in town. I don't know. Anyhow, I wanted to stave off trouble. Joe made the Wagon Wheel mean something in the basin. I'd like to keep it that way."

She understood how that was. Red had always liked Grant, but he wouldn't if he worked for this Fenton and Fenton tried to shove cattle into High Valley.

"There won't be any trouble this fall," she said. "Fenton wouldn't put cattle up here till next summer."

"I don't know. Something about this deal doesn't add up right. Anyhow, I can't do anything for you. That's between you and Red, but I'll talk to him when he comes in. Maybe I could give you a job on the Wagon Wheel."

"Anything!" she whispered eagerly. "I'd do anything to get out of High Valley."

He rose. "I'll be sloping along."

She jumped up and came around the table to him, suddenly panicky with the realization that Grant Talbot was the only one who could help her. She gripped his arms with frantic urgency.

"Take me with you tonight while they're gone! Please, Grant! You can talk to Red about it later."

"I told you I couldn't," he said roughly. "I'd just be kicking the lid off a pot of trouble, and that's the very thing I'm trying to keep from doing."

"Don't leave me here, Grant!" She was almost hysterical now. "Red doesn't care anything about me. He won't tell me who my folks were. Said the Indians killed them and he raised me."

48

"But he's taken care of you," Grant said. "No reason for you getting boogery now."

"Yes, there is. I told you he's going to make me marry Bugeye. I won't! I just won't!"

He pulled her arm down from his neck. He said softly: "Rennie, you're all worked up tonight. Nobody can make you marry a man you don't want to, not even in High Valley."

"You don't know Red. He's no good, Grant. None of them are. Bugeye and Gib Lane and all of them."

"Talbot!"

It was Bugeye standing in the doorway, a gangling man with a wide, flat nose and protruding green eyes that gave him his name. He stood with his long legs spread, one hand on his gun butt, his face ugly with jealous rage.

Rennie whirled from Grant and ran to the stove. "I'll get supper right away!" she cried, and took the biscuits out of the oven. She didn't know how long Bugeye had stood there or how much he had heard, but she knew he went crazy when any other man even glanced at her.

Bugeye acted as if he hadn't heard. He started walking toward Grant, each step slow and deliberate. He said: "I've been wondering why you came up here. It was Rennie all the time. Now I'm going to show you that sweet-talking to her don't pay. I'll fix your mug so you won't be so damned purty."

"I came up here to see Red," Grant said. "Where is he?"

"You're a damned liar!" Bugeye shouted. "You was sneaking around to see Rennie when we was gone."

"No, Bugeye," Rennie screamed. "Stop it! You hear?"

But there was no stopping Bugeye. He kept on, moving in that slow, deliberate way, his insane eyes fixed on Grant's face. Rennie grabbed the knife and jumped at Bugeye.

Grant shouted: "Look out!" Bugeye wheeled and ducked aside, cursing at her. She stumbled and fell, and Bugeye kicked her in the ribs.

"You damned little floozy," Bugeye said. "We leave you alone and this . . . !"

Grant was on him then, hitting him in the face with a swinging right that swiveled his head on his shoulders and sent him spinning half the width of the room. Bugeye had no chance to regain his balance.

Grant went after him, his face hard set with anger. He ducked a blow that Bugeye swung instinctively; he brought his right through again, a powerful, turning fist that caught young Johnson on the jaw and knocked him against the wall. Bugeye's feet went out from under him, and he sat down, his eyes glassy.

Rennie was up now, the knife in her hand. She screamed: "Kill him, Grant, kill him!"

Grant moved back and drew his gun. He said: "I don't like a yahoo who calls me a liar, and I like him a hell of a lot less when he kicks a woman. If you want real trouble, get up and pull your iron."

"I reckon there's no need for that," Red called from the doorway. "You handle your fists real well, Grant."

"He kicked me, Red!" Rennie cried. "Bugeye kicked me!"

"I didn't get here in time to see the beginning of the fracas," Red said, "but maybe Bugeye had reason to kick you. What are you doing with that knife?"

"He was going after Grant," Rennie cried, "and he didn't have any reason to kick me. I was trying to stop him. You don't want to make an enemy out of the only friend you've got in the basin, do you, Red?"

For a moment Red gave Rennie no answer. He stood

with a slack shoulder against the door jamb, a big, heavy-boned man, his pale eyes fixed speculatively on Grant. He rubbed a stubble-covered cheek, jaws moving rhythmically on his chew of tobacco.

"No, not if he is a friend," Red said finally. And to Bugeye: "Get up, kid. You ain't hurt."

Bugeye rose, feeling his jaw where Grant had hit him. He said in a low tone: "I'll kill you, Talbot. I'm going to kill you."

"Shut up," Red said. "You talk too much. Now what was this all about?"

"I came up here to see you," Grant said, "and this pup of yours got it into his head I came to see Rennie."

"He was honeying up to her!" Bugeye shouted. "I saw 'em. She had her arms around his neck. I saw 'em, I tell you!"

Red nodded at Rennie. "How about it?"

She lowered her eyes. "I was trying to get him to do something for me."

"Do what?"

Rennie raised her eyes and glared defiantly at Red. "I wanted him to take me away. I won't waste my time rotting up here in this damned old valley."

"He wouldn't do it?" When Rennie shook her head, Red added: "Well, now, maybe he is my friend. What'd you want to see me about, Grant?"

Grant told him about how Linda wanted to sell the Wagon Wheel and about how Fenton had said he'd run cattle in High Valley if he bought the outfit. Then he added: "I didn't want you going off half-cocked, Red. We've always got along, and I didn't see no reason for trouble over this."

"Well, sir," Red said, "you'll have trouble the minute I see a Wagon Wheel critter in the valley. You can tell Fenton that."

"He wants to see you. Maybe tomorrow. I came up to tell you first."

"That's real smart," Red said. "Real smart. All right, Grant. I'll be around in the morning. Fetch your man up here and I'll show him what he's up against."

For a moment Grant hesitated, looking at Rennie's pale face and then at Bugeye's sullen one. He brought his eyes back to Red.

"Mamie Dolan's making war talk. Can I figure on help from you, if I need it?"

"So the Wagon Wheel is going to need help from High Valley!" Red roared a laugh. "It's downright comical, you talking about needing help. When Joe was alive, the Wagon Wheel never asked for help from nobody."

"I ain't asking for it," Grant said angrily. "Not yet, but I'm getting a smell out of this deal I don't like. If Fenton does buy the Wagon Wheel, the basin'll be hotter'n hell. I'd like to discourage him."

"Fetch him around," Red said. "I'll discourage him."

"See you in the morning," Grant said and, stepping past Red, left the cabin.

For a moment Red didn't move. He was staring at Rennie with the cool detachment of one who had no strong feeling about her. He said finally: "So you want to leave the valley?"

She laid the knife back on the stove. "I am going to leave the valley, and I'm not going to marry Bugeye."

"You're half right," Red said. "You're leaving the valley, but you're marrying Bugeye. I've got plans for you, and I've waited a long time. I ain't passing it up now."

She glared at him, hating him, but at the same time she was fully aware of the strength of his will. He was lazy and indolent, and he seldom made an issue about anything, but when he did, there was nothing that could turn him from his purpose. In the end he would wear her down, if she stayed.

"There's biscuits, and I made coffee," she said in a low tone. "You fry the trout. I'm going to bed."

"Was I you," Red said, "I wouldn't try to get out of the valley. I'll beat hell out of you, if you do. On the other hand, you'll be in clover if you do what I tell you."

She walked to her lean-to room and shut and barred the door. She heard Red shout: "Let her alone, you fool! You've waited a long time. You can wait a few more days."

"Hell, I'm going to marry her, ain't I?"

"You bet you are, but you'll wait till you are married. Don't forget it."

She sat down on her bunk, her head in her hands. She did not light the lamp. She just sat there, the seconds ticking away as childhood memories crowded into her mind of gunfire and death and a long ride through the dark night, of being carried in the saddle by a man she had never seen before or since. She remembered whimpering, and the man threatening: "Shut that up or I'll whop you good." They had reached a mountain cabin at dawn, and Red had been there. It was the first time she had ever seen him.

"Get him?" Red had asked.

"He was gone," the man who had brought Rennie had said. "We got the horses and five thousand he had in his safe. Here's the brat, but I'm damned if I know what you're going to do with her."

"I know," Red had said.

Funny, she thought, how that one scene stood out so clearly in her mind that had been clouded by time and fear. She had no memory of her father or where she had lived. She remembered leaving the mountain cabin with Red and

Bugeye who had been just a kid then; she remembered drifting from one place to another. Red had been afraid to stay anywhere for more than a few years.

Then they had settled in High Valley. There had been no more drifting, although Red and Bugeye and most of the other valley men made long trips which they never explained. When she had asked Red about her folks, he had said blandly he didn't know, that she was his girl now.

She had to get out. She said it over and over in her mind. She considered trying to escape tonight. There was one small window that was big enough for her to slip through, but she knew one of them would be outside. They would not take any chances tonight.

She took off her clothes and put on a worn nightgown, but it was a long time before she could sleep. When she did, the nightmare came again, of gunfire and dead men and the smell of powder smoke. She was sitting up when she woke, her throat dry, and she realized she had been screaming as she always did when she had the nightmare.

Red was pounding on her door, shouting: "What the hell's the matter with you?"

"Go away!" she said. "I was just dreaming."

She heard Red walk away, and she lay back, cold sweat breaking through her skin.

VI

It was nearly midnight when Grant turned his buckskin into the corral. The darkness was relieved only by the faint glitter of the stars. There was a light in Linda's room. He hesitated, remembering how she had welcomed Fenton, insisting that he have his supper in the house with her. Grant wondered if Fenton was sleeping in the house. He found the thought distasteful, even though it was no real business of his.

Grant hesitated for a moment, knowing it would be difficult to see Linda alone tomorrow. He walked to the house, feeling that he had to talk to her, yet not sure that this was the right time. He never knew what Linda would do or say. He had no real hope he could change her mind about selling, but he had to try.

He opened the front door and stepped into the living room. A shaft of lamplight fell halfway across the room from Linda's bedroom, and he heard her call: "That you, Grant?"

"It's me. You in bed?"

"No. Come in, Grant."

He paused, eyes on the gilt-framed picture on the inside wall, the fringe of light touching it. It was of a young woman, an attractive one dressed in a wedding gown. Joe had never said who she was, but Grant had often seen him stand before it and stare at it, a pensive expression on his deeply lined face. Grant had often wondered about her, but Joe had made it plain that it was one thing he would not talk about.

"Break your leg, Grant?" Linda called.

He walked into her room and stopped. She was sitting in front of her mirror, brushing the hair that lay in a long red mass down her back. She gave him a quick smile and, looking into the mirror again, went on with her brushing. She was in her nightgown, a gossamer silk garment with fine white lace barely covering her round breasts.

"I didn't know . . . ," he began.

"Don't be bashful," she said tartly. "After all, you're one

of the family, aren't you?"

"Not exactly," he said.

He sat down in a rocking chair, stiff and uncomfortable. Looking at Linda, he was stirred as any man would have been, then he remembered what Mamie had said about her, and for the first time he half believed she was right.

As he had many times before, he wondered why Joe had married Linda. Yet the reason was not hard to find. She was attractive, and Joe had often talked about what a woman could do for the Wagon Wheel. But in that regard he had made a poor choice, for she had changed nothing. She had been too lazy even to paper the walls, and they had needed new paper for years.

There was no sound for a moment except the steady whisper of the brush, then she laid it down, and turned to him, asking: "How do you like Fenton, Grant?"

"I don't. I don't like anything about him."

She laughed softly. "You wouldn't like anybody who wanted to buy the Wagon Wheel, would you?"

"No, reckon I wouldn't."

"Well, you can quit worrying about losing your job. I made it clear that you went with the ranch, and he promised to keep you on as foreman."

She said it as if that made everything right. She was shallow, he thought, shallow and utterly selfish, and, if he talked the rest of the night, he could never make her understand how he felt.

"Thanks," he said.

"He wants to look at High Valley tomorrow," she said. "He says that the Wagon Wheel could run twice the number of cattle we have now, if we had the valley for summer range, and it would give the other basin men more grass in the Big Bears."

"I'll take him up in the morning," Grant said, "but it won't do any good."

"You underestimate Fenton," she said. "We had a long talk after supper. He said you were doubtful about his ability to pay for the ranch, so he promised to have the money deposited with Ira Connors before we close the deal."

Grant rolled a cigarette. "Linda, I had a couple of ideas today that you might like. I was hoping you'd like 'em well enough to keep the ranch."

"I doubt it, but I'm glad you're thinking about me."

"I figured you wanted to sell because you're lonesome. There ain't another woman within five miles of here except Mamie Dolan, so I thought I'd get a girl who'd do your housework and you'd have somebody to talk to. No reason why you shouldn't go to dances and have a good time. I mean . . . well, Joe's been dead for three months. No need for you to go on mourning for him."

"Would you take me?"

He fished a match from his vest pocket. "Sure. Or Bruce Mayer could. There's a passel of single men in the valley who'll come courting you soon as they find out you're of a mind for it."

"What girl are you thinking about?"

"I might be able to get Rennie Johnson."

"I thought so." She whirled back to the mirror and began brushing her hair again in short, angry motions. "I think I'll sell."

Anger stirring in him, Grant lit his cigarette. Linda had never seen Rennie. There was no reason for her to take that attitude. Rennie kept the Johnson cabin scrupulously clean, and she would work hard to please Linda, because she wouldn't want to go back to High Valley. But there was no use pressing the point.

57

"I had another idea," he said. "I talked to Marty Reem today. He has a nice little house in town, and he said we could rent it. I thought you'd like to live in Rocky Fork where you could talk to other women."

"That would be wonderful," she said sarcastically. "There are so many places in Rocky Fork to go. I'll sell, Grant, and I'll take my money and go back to Denver. It isn't women I'm interested in talking to."

He pulled on his cigarette, the anger growing in him. "Linda, this ain't a proposition of keeping my job. I can always make a living. Mamie offered me a job today."

Linda dropped her brush, making a loud clatter on the marble top of her bureau. She turned to look at him, her lips parted. "What kind of a job could she give you?"

"She says a big one. She's going to bust the Wagon Wheel. She'll have Seven Bar Seven cows all over this end of the basin. I don't know what she's got in her head, but she's crazy enough to try anything."

Linda shrugged. "Well, it'll be Fenton's worry."

"No, it's yours. Fenton won't buy the Wagon Wheel. Not for fifty thousand like you're counting on. Nobody but you would be fool enough to think he would."

She rose, her cheeks touched by the torch of anger. "So I'm crazy! All right, maybe I am. Maybe I'll take less than fifty thousand. I just want you to get it through your thick skull that I won't stay in this god-forsaken hole."

"You deal with Fenton," Grant said hotly, "and you'll leave here broke. He's a fake, if I ever saw one. I ought to run him off the ranch."

She stood, looking at him, the anger in her dying. Smiling, she said: "Grant, you're just a dreamer. I've had enough hard luck to be practical. This is the first chance I ever had to get money . . . real money, I mean. Saying I'm

58

crazy and calling Fenton a fake don't change anything."

He got up, shaking his head. "There's one thing I'd give a pretty to make you understand. When Joe was alive, I never really savvied how big he was. He never went around talking about it, but, when he was alive, the basin had peace because of him. He had a way of making men talk their troubles over and settling them. That's why the Wagon Wheel is different from the other ranches. If you stay and I run it, it can keep on being like it was."

"I see," she breathed. "You want to wear Joe's boots. You want people looking up to you. That it?"

That wasn't it at all. Perhaps no one, unless it was Marty Reem, could understand how Grant felt. Money had never been important to Joe. Integrity and self-respect had been. That was why the Wagon Wheel had been the ranch it was, but it was all part of a pattern that meant nothing to Linda.

"You can put it that way," he said grimly, "but that ain't the point. I know what'll happen if we don't get rid of Fenton."

"You said he wouldn't buy," she jeered.

"He will at his own price, and I'm thinking that's what Mamie's working for. I've got a hunch she's the one who had him write to you."

"Now you're the one who's crazy."

"Maybe so. Well, go ahead and sell. Men will die, and you can blame yourself for it."

"I'll be a long ways from here." Then she smiled and put her hands on his shoulders. "You're such a child, Grant. I've offered you the way to keep the ranch, but you don't like me well enough to take it that way."

She was close to him, so close that he could feel the pressure of her breasts. Her full, red lips were parted, waiting for his kiss. A sudden weakness was in him, and with it came the thought that maybe Joe would have wanted it this way.

"Maybe I do," he said.

Her arms went around his neck and brought his lips down to hers, and in that moment of heady passion he lost his certainty that this was not the thing he wanted. His arms went around her, hands pressed against the silky softness of her back, and her lips were sweet and filled with promise.

She drew back, laughing softly. "You are a child, Grant, but I'll make you grow up. I like size, and I like money. You can get them for me, and I can do so much for you."

"How?"

"Joe wouldn't listen to me, but it's simple. We'll go after High Valley. I've heard Bruce's ideas, and they're good. About winter feeding. We'll flood the meadow land along the creek and raise hay. We'll build a big house. We'll double the size of our herd. Big money, Grant. A vacation every year in Denver and all the clothes I want."

He looked at her, hating her and hating himself for his moment of weakness. He wanted her, and, if it had been another time and she had been another woman, he would have taken her, but she was Joe's widow, and Grant understood now more than he ever had that marriage to Joe had not changed her. She stood for everything that was opposite to what Joe had stood for as completely as Mamie Dolan and Cole Fenton did.

"No," he said bitterly. "It wouldn't work."

"Your damned conscience," she breathed. "You're not a man, Grant, not a real man who wants what other men want."

"I want it," he breathed, "but not your way."

"My way!" she cried. "You've got milk in your veins or you'd want it my. . . ."

He heard the rifle shot, the tinkle of glass falling to the floor, the snap of the bullet that missed him by a few inches and buried itself in the wall. He hit the floor, dragging Linda with him. She swore angrily, not understanding, but he held her there, an arm about her waist. Two more shots smashed more glass from the window.

"Stay down, damn it!" he said. "Flat on your belly."

He lunged out of the bedroom and crossed the front room. Outside the darkness seemed absolute as he stood with his back against the wall of the house, gun in hand. Again the rifle cracked from the willows along the creek. He fired at the flashes, and dropped flat as the rifleman emptied his Winchester, bullets ripping into the wall beside which he had stood.

Men spilled out of the bunkhouse. Bruce Mayer bawled: "What's going on?"

"Stay out of the light!" Grant called.

"Who the hell's doing the shooting?" Mayer shouted.

It was a crazy question, and Grant wondered why the man had asked it. Then he heard the receding drumbeats of a galloping horse, and Curly Tell shouted: "He's pulling out! Just busting up our sleep."

They came on to the house, Fenton with the crew. They had pulled their pants over their drawers, and they had their guns. Mayer said: "Let's go after him."

"No use," Grant said. "He'd be a mile away from here by the time we got saddled up."

Linda had put on her robe. She brought the lamp from the bedroom and stood in the door, the light falling across the yard. The men instinctively stepped away from it, and Grant said irritably: "Take the lamp back."

But she stood there, looking at Grant uncertainly. She asked: "Who do you think it was?"

Grant thought: *It was probably Ben Piper, or Bugeye Johnson.* But he could not prove anything against either of them, and he saw no reason to tell Linda whom he suspected.

"Hard to tell," he said.

Bruce Mayer swaggered up, his chin thrust defiantly at Grant. "So we've got ourselves a fight with somebody, but you don't know who it is. That right?"

"That's right."

"And chances are we'll have more of it when we start the drive. Somebody don't want us to get that herd to Placerville. Ira Connors maybe. That right?"

"Don't know about that."

"Looks that way to me," Mayer said. "What I want to know is are we getting fighting wages from now on."

Grant could not see the expressions on the faces of the others, Curly Tell and Dick Sharples and the rest, men who had ridden for the Wagon Wheel for years. Grant asked them: "You boys expecting fighting wages?"

"Hell, no," Sharples said.

"There's your answer, Bruce," Grant said.

"Then I don't want no part of it," Mayer bawled. "I'm quitting."

"Suits me," Grant said. "You can draw your time in the morning."

"Hell, I'm pulling out now." Mayer swung to Fenton. "You can see what you're buying. Well, you ain't buying me with it."

Mayer wheeled and disappeared into the darkness. Fenton moved up, and in the lamplight Grant saw that he was trembling, but whether his fear was real or pretended was a question in Grant's mind.

"You must have some ideas about this, Talbot," Fenton said.

62

"Not much. There's always somebody trying to pull the top dog down. We'll handle it." Grant nodded at Tell. "You'd better stay up, Curly."

"Sure," Tell said.

They drifted away into the darkness. Linda went back into the living room and set the lamp on the table. When Grant followed her, she said: "I wouldn't put it past you to arrange this so Fenton would be scared out of buying."

"It would've been a good idea, if I'd've thought of it," he said, "but, if I had, I'd have fixed it so that first bullet wouldn't have come as close as it did."

She considered that a moment, her face taut with fear. She said in a low voice: "You can forget about kissing me. You're right. It wouldn't work. I've been chasing the wrong man ever since Joe died."

"Yeah, the wrong man," he said. "I'll have Curly fix your window in the morning. Go to bed."

She picked up the lamp and walked into her bedroom. For a moment Grant lingered, eyes moving to the picture on the wall, and again he wondered who she was. Then he thought about Joe Dexter and his sense of loyalty to Joe's memory and to Wagon Wheel. Anyone else would have considered it foolish, but it was a part of him, something that had developed through the years of working and living and riding with Joe Dexter. He could no more free himself from it than he could do without his right arm.

He went out, closing the front door, and crossed the yard to the bunkhouse. Perhaps Mamie Dolan had been right in saying he was in love with a ranch. In that respect he was exactly like Joe when the old man had been alive. All of his dreams and hopes were tied up with the Wagon Wheel and Rainbow Basin.

VII

Mamie Dolan was still awake when Ben Piper rode in and put up his horse. She fumbled for a match, found one, and lighted the lamp on the stand at the head of her bed. She pulled herself upright and slipped a pillow behind her back. When Piper came into the house, she called: "Ben!"

He appeared in the doorway, his battered face as raw as a piece of beefsteak. Mamie shook her head as she looked at him. She said: "Talbot's the best fighting man in the basin. I didn't figure he'd listen to me today, but he can't help hating the Dexter woman. I thought it was worth a try."

Piper dropped onto a rawhide-bottom chair, his Winchester across his lap. "He's damn' near a corpse. I sure had a bead on him, but I missed."

"You fool!" Mamie shouted. "I didn't want you to kill him. I just said to stir things up so the Dexter woman would be willing to sell."

"I figure I done that. Talbot rode in late. 'Bout midnight. Don't know where he'd been. Linda was in her bedroom, and Talbot went in to talk to her. Looked like they was arguing, then he kissed her."

"You're lying!" Mamie cried.

Piper shrugged. "All right, I'm a liar. You want to hear this or not?"

She picked up a cigar from the stand. "Go ahead."

He scowled at her. "You ain't purty smoking a cigar. I don't know why you think you are."

"I'm not purty without one, neither. Get on with your yarn."

"Like I said, they was close together, and I took a crack at him. I missed, and they hit the floor. I shot a couple more times, then he comes out on the porch and throws some lead at me. I threw some back, but it was dark as hell outside the house, so don't reckon I got him."

"You are a fool," she said again angrily. "We've got one killing to our credit. A second one would stir up a hornet's nest."

He shrugged. "Reckon it would if Steve Ollard knew Joe was killed. Anyhow, I've got a hunch there'd be damned few tears wasted on Talbot. A lot of men want Wagon Wheel range. If he was out of the way, they'd try for it."

Mamie Dolan was silent a moment, rolling the cigar between her fingers. Piper was right. Grant Talbot shared Joe Dexter's talent for leadership. As long as he was alive and rodding the Wagon Wheel, he would retain the respect that Dexter had held.

"I don't want him killed," she said finally. "Not yet. We're taking that range ourselves, and we don't want to buck every other outfit in the basin to get it."

"All right, all right," Piper grunted. "But I say you were loco for calling him in and showing him your hand."

"I tell you it was worth trying. Nobody's going to worry about us. Not yet anyhow."

He rose. "Well, I'm going to bed."

"Ben, that fight was your idea. Now get it out of your head that you have to drill Talbot because he licked you."

"It was Fenton's notion. He figured Talbot could be run out of the country if he got a good licking. Then I pulled a knife, and Fenton tripped me, damn him."

"Cole's got more brains in his little finger than you have

65

in your head," she said coldly. "You wouldn't be any good to us in jail. You got a licking and you won't be happy till you beef Talbot. Wait till the sign's right, Ben. You hear?"

He glowered at her, gently feeling of his face with his left hand, his Winchester in his right. She knew that he was proud, that he was a man who could never forget an injury, but the years had established the habit of obedience in him, and she had no doubt that he would continue to obey.

"You're fighting Dexter's ghost," he said complainingly, "and his ghost is in Talbot. I tell you we can't win till he's kicked the bucket."

"Damn it," she shouted, "I've waited a long time for this! I won't have you busting my chances by beefing Talbot before I'm ready for it."

"Why?"

"For one thing I don't want Ollard on our necks."

He laughed scornfully. "Who's afraid of Ollard?" he asked, and left the room.

She fired her cigar, finding some satisfaction in it. She had never understood the complexities of her own nature. She only knew that as far back as she could remember she had cursed the luck that had caused her to be born a woman. It was a man's world, and she had to live the way the men did, require obedience and get it, be looked up to in the way Joe Dexter had been. That was why she had challenged him ten years ago, but she had been too young. She had made a bad gamble and lost.

The fact that Joe Dexter had let her stay in the basin had not made her think any better of him. If anything, it had made her hate him more than ever, the kind of hatred that had seared her soul. But she had learned to wait, to be patient, until she had the strength to win. She had that strength now. Dexter's killing, carefully done so that it would look like an accident, had been the first step in her plan.

She could count on Piper, for he had the kind of dog-like devotion that would remain constant as long as he was alive. She could count on Bruce Mayer as long as she could pay him. She could count on Cole Fenton. He was her brother, and in her family blood ties were strong.

It had taken her a long time to persuade him that this was a good plan, that the money he had made in mining camps could be doubled in Rainbow Basin. She knew that he had long wanted to go into the cattle business, and she had convinced him that this was the time and the place, that he could start off with her as a partner, owning a big spread without nursing a small outfit as she had done.

She possessed a sharp and calculating mind, and the capacity to weigh every aspect of the situation with cold logic. The men in town formed the one imponderable, but she was convinced that their respect for Joe Dexter had been based on fear as much as anything, that Ira Connors would have no scruples about closing out the Wagon Wheel if he had the chance, now that Dexter was dead.

For ten years she had nursed her hatred for Joe Dexter, saving every cent she could with miserly persistence, even against Piper's judgment. He had insisted that an investment in a good bull would more than pay dividends.

She had succeeded in buying Mayer, but it was not until Dexter had married Linda and brought her home from Denver that Mamie had worked out the details of her plan. Mayer had told her that Linda was cheap and shallow and unprincipled. She had correctly gauged Linda's willingness to sell if Dexter were out of the way. Now it was a simple matter. Linda could be frightened until she was willing to take Cole's offer.

She had finished her cigar, when she heard a horse coming up the trail from the creek. She called: "Ben!" She could hear him snoring in the other bedroom, and she called once again, suddenly frantic: "Ben, somebody's coming!"

He grunted sleepily, and she screamed: "Damn it, Ben, get up and see who it is!"

The bed squeaked as he swung his feet to the floor. "All right, all right," he said sleepily, and she heard him pat to the front door. He opened it, calling: "Who is it?"

"Mayer."

Mamie swore. She could hire a man and give him orders, but she couldn't give him brains. He had no business coming here. Talbot might have followed, and once Talbot understood what Mayer was doing his usefulness would be ended.

A moment later Mayer came into the house. She heard the hum of low talk between him and Piper, and she shouted: "Get in here, both of you! Don't stand out there, gabbing to each other."

They came in, Piper in his underclothes, his Winchester in his right hand. Mayer was tired and cranky, and for a moment panic touched her. Something was wrong.

"Ben was currying me down," Mayer said truculently. "I don't like it. I done what I thought was best."

"You done what?"

"I quit."

"Why, damn you . . . !" She stopped, warned by the dark and barren quality of his face. "What happened?"

"After the shooting, everybody was boogered," Mayer answered. "I put up a holler for fighting wages, figuring that would break the widow, and, if she didn't give in, some of the boys would pull out with me."

"Did they?"

"No. After it boiled up, I had to get out."

She nodded, thinking he should have known that Dick Sharples and Curly Tell and the others who had worked for the Wagon Wheel for years would not follow him. Actually it didn't make much difference whether Mayer stayed on the Wagon Wheel or not. The showdown was close.

"All right," she said. "It was a good play, if it had worked."

He stood there, scowling, and it struck her that Piper had been right when he'd said they were fighting Joe Dexter's ghost and the ghost was in Talbot. It was in Sharples and Tell and all of them as long as Talbot was alive and heading the outfit.

For a moment she was tempted to tell Piper to go ahead and dry-gulch him, then she pushed the thought from her. Talbot had to suffer. She wanted to mock him with her triumph.

"You see Fenton?" Piper asked.

"He's there," Mayer said. "Ate supper in the house with Linda, and they had a palaver. I didn't get no chance to see him alone, but he slept in the bunkhouse and he did some talking about keeping the crew on when he bought the spread. He's going to High Valley in the morning."

"With Talbot?" Mamie asked.

"He didn't say, but I reckon he will."

"You can't stay here," Mamie said. "Sleep in the timber. Tomorrow after Cole and Talbot get back into the basin, you go see Red Johnson. Offer him five hundred dollars to hit the Wagon Wheel when the crew's gone. Burn the buildings, but don't have them hurt Linda. After Cole talks to him, Johnson will be ready to listen to you."

"How'll you get the crew away from the Wagon Wheel?"

"It'll be done. You just get them to do the job."

Mayer took off his Stetson and rubbed his bald head. He shifted uneasily, glancing at Piper, then bringing his gaze back to Mamie. He said: "I don't cotton to that idea, ma'am. Like as not them High Valley *hombres* will fill my hide with lead."

"Not if you tell 'em you're working for me."

"Send Piper."

"No!" Mamie cried. "I can't take my chances on being left alone."

"It's risky," Mayer muttered, "and I ain't getting enough. . . ."

"You're getting paid damned good!" Mamie shouted angrily. "You ain't done a hell of a lot to earn your *dinero* so far."

"I cracked Joe on the head and tossed him over the cliff, didn't I?" Mayer demanded. "That's worth all you've paid me."

She laughed, a taunting sound that stirred the sullen anger in Mayer. She saw now how she could hold him as long as she needed him. Fear was a stronger force to Mayer than his greed.

"That's exactly what you did, Bruce," she said. "Now remember one thing. I sit on my front porch every day. I watch the Wagon Wheel, and with the glasses I've got I can recognize every pair of pants the Dexter woman puts on the line. I can spot a fly walking up the trail to High Valley. Suppose Steve Ollard gets to wondering what made Dexter fall off that trail? Suppose I tell him I just happened to be watching the trail that day?"

"You'd be in trouble, Bruce," Piper said. "Yes, sir, you might even get your neck stretched."

"And suppose I tell Ollard what I know?" Mayer demanded bitterly. "Me spying on Dexter and Linda and you paying me to beef the old man?"

"Can you prove that?" Mamie asked, and, when Mayer lowered his gaze, she added: "If you're as smart as I think you are, Bruce, you'll keep on playing with us and you'll wind up a rich man."

Mayer stared at her, the tip of his tongue running over dry lips. "All right, I'll tell 'em."

Wheeling, Mayer left the house. Piper stood motionless until they heard his horse leave, then he said: "You got a mighty weak link in your chain, betting your pile on that *hombre*."

"No, he'll be all right," she said. "He's afraid to pull out now."

"Maybe," Piper said, and quickly left the room.

Mamie drew the lamp toward her and blew it out. She slid onto her back and slipped a pillow under her head. She closed her eyes, but she could not sleep. She wondered why she was not like other women, feeling the need of a man, wanting nice clothes and a home and children.

But she was the way she was; she would never be any different, and she must use men to achieve her purpose. They were like wild animals in the forest, she thought, she and Grant Talbot and Ira Connors and her brother Cole and the Dexter woman. All of them. She must devour the others or be devoured, and she could not bring herself to consider the possibility of a second defeat. She preferred death to that.

VIII

Breakfast was eaten by lamplight. Grant ate with the crew. No one mentioned Bruce Mayer, yet Grant sensed the men were thinking about him. In all the time Bruce had been here, he had never quite fitted, but he was a top hand and that was the reason Joe had kept him.

After Joe's death, Linda had insisted that Mayer remain, probably because he was the only man on the ranch who frankly courted her. Now Grant was glad the man was gone. He could count on the others.

Fenton came in as the crew rose from the table. Grant said: "I'll saddle a horse for you. Linda says you want to go to High Valley."

"That's right," Fenton said.

Grant left the bunkhouse with the crew. He saddled his buckskin and caught and saddled a bay mare for Fenton. Dick Sharples said slowly: "He wants to be a cowman. Why don't you let him ride Thunder?"

Thunder was a roan gelding, a mean horse possessing a deceptive air that took in the unwary. Curly Tell laughed shortly. "Good idea, Grant. With a little luck Thunder might break that ornery son-of-a-bitch's neck."

"That'd suit me," Grant said, "but I ain't giving Linda any excuse to fire me if I can help it. She might get Mayer back to rod the outfit."

Sharples swore. "She might at that."

"Curly, you fix Linda's window before you ride out. There's some glass in the storeroom."

Grant looked at grizzled old Dick Sharples, who had ridden into the basin with Joe Dexter when he had brought the first Wagon Wheel herd across the Big Bears, and on around the half circle of riders to young Kit Bellew. He knew they were thinking the same thing he was, that time was short and Ira Connors would not give Linda an hour he didn't have to.

Everything, or so it seemed to Grant, was playing into Cole Fenton's hands. Funny how Joe had regarded money. It just hadn't been important. He could always borrow from Connors when he needed to and owing the banker had never given him a moment's worry. Now his indifference to being in debt was putting a burden upon all of them.

"We'll make it, boy," Sharples said. "You go play nursemaid to the greenhorn."

"Keep your eyes peeled," Grant said. "If I'm reading the sign right, the business last night was just a beginning."

They nodded and rode away, and Grant led his buckskin and the bay mare to the bunkhouse. Fenton came out, firing a cigar as he stepped through the door. He cast a wary glance at the mare and cleared his throat.

"I ain't much of a horseman," he said. "It's something I'll have to learn. I know cowboys like their fun, but if that mare bucks me off, I ain't going to call it fun."

"You're sure you want to get in the cattle business?" Grant asked.

Fenton gave him a thin smile. "I want in it all right, but I don't aim to entertain you while I'm getting in. I'll learn the business just like I learned how to handle mining claims, but it won't be overnight."

"Climb on," Grant said testily. "Sadie here wouldn't pile a buttercup."

"Well, I ain't a buttercup," Fenton said, and swung awkwardly into the saddle.

As they passed the house, Linda stepped out on the porch and waved to them. She was wearing a robe over her nightgown, her red hair reaching far down her back. On her rich, full lips was a smile for Cole Fenton.

"When will you be back, Grant?" she called.

"About noon," he said shortly.

"I'll have dinner for you, Mister Fenton," she said. "I hope you like peach pie."

He touched his derby, smiling genially. "I love it, Missus Dexter."

They rode on, angling northeast across the gently sloping floor of the basin to the wall. When the house was half a mile behind them, Fenton said: "She's mighty attractive, Talbot. It's surprising you haven't married her."

"Joe's been dead just three months," Grant said curtly.

"Why, that's time enough to get engaged. It would seem the natural move for both of you."

"My business."

"Of course," Fenton said smoothly. "No offense, Talbot. Missus Dexter is a charming woman and an excellent cook. I'm interested in her myself. The only reason I'm bringing this up is because I don't want to step on your toes."

"You won't get nowhere. Not after last night. Linda wants to go to Denver."

Fenton chewed on his cigar a moment. "Well, I've known women to change their minds."

They were silent until they reached the base of the north wall. Fenton, staring up at the ribbon-like trail, shook his head. He asked: "This mare sure-footed?"

"Like a goat," Grant said, and started the climb.

Fenton followed, one hand gripping the saddle horn.

When they reached the first switchback, they stopped to blow their horses. Grant, glancing at Fenton, saw that the man's face was gray and pinched, and that he carefully avoided looking below him at the basin floor.

"You couldn't drive cattle up here, could you?" Fenton asked in a low voice.

"I wouldn't."

"Must be some other way into High Valley."

"Yeah, there's another trail in from the east. It's the long way around, but the best way to take cattle in."

They went on, their mounts laboring under them. The sun was well up now, driving the last of the night shadows from the basin and taking the chill from the air. It would be warm, contrasting sharply with the cold, windy morning of the day before.

Half an hour later they reached the top, making the last sharp climb through a break in the slick, red rock rim, and again Grant stopped to blow their horses. Color returned to Fenton's face. Piñons crowded the trail, the cliff fifty feet to the south. Grant knew how it was with Fenton. Panic had momentarily left the man, for at this point he was far enough from the edge to have the feeling of security that comes from being on level ground again.

"Scared?" Grant asked contemptuously.

Fenton gave him a wry grin. "I'm not enough of a hypocrite to deny that I was when we were coming up. I've always been scared of steep places, so I feel some satisfaction in being able to make a ride like this."

Grant rolled a smoke, remembering that Fenton had appeared frightened last night after the shooting. Grant had had the feeling he was play-acting then, but he wasn't acting now. Sweat made a bright shine across his face, and the corners of his mouth were still trembling.

"You'll never pay fifty thousand for the Wagon Wheel," Grant said. "Who are you trying to fool?"

Fenton shrugged. "Myself, perhaps. What I pay will depend on what I find in High Valley. I'm a man who looks ahead to the potential, Talbot, not at what Dexter did in the past."

Fenton stared at the basin, a great yawning hole before him, its tawny, grass-covered floor sweeping out before them to the east until it was lost in a jumbled land of foothills and mesas. On beyond were the San Juan Mountains, granite teeth raking the sky.

Watching him, Grant wondered what was in his mind and what had actually brought him here. He wondered, too, whether it was Mamie Dolan or Fenton who had lied about them not knowing each other. The more he thought about Mamie, the more he was puzzled by her, but he was convinced she had made an honest effort to hire him.

"Last night Missus Dexter said that this fellow Mayer had talked about flooding the meadow along the creek," Fenton said thoughtfully. "She believed it was practical and that it would be smart to put up hay and winter feed."

Grant said nothing. From where he sat his saddle he could see the Wagon Wheel and Seven Bar Seven buildings and several other ranches to the east. In the distance the town of Rocky Fork was visible, cut down to toy size by the miles. Bell Creek made a meandering green streak across the floor of the basin.

A few dirt dams would do exactly what Bruce Mayer had said, and in time someone would build them. Joe Dexter had been satisfied to go on the way he had always gone, and Grant had not known until last night that there had ever been any discussion between Joe and Linda about the way he had run the Wagon Wheel.

"Well?" Fenton demanded. "It is practical, isn't it?"

"Sure, but it would take money."

"Hell, Dexter was the biggest cowman in the basin, wasn't he?"

Grant nodded. "Which same didn't mean he had much cash. He always owed money to the bank. Being a good cowman didn't make Joe a good businessman."

Reining his horse around, Grant started down the slope into High Valley. They were in the pines at once, hoofs dropping softly into the thick mat of needles that had slowly piled up through the centuries. Fenton, riding behind Grant, called: "Good grass here. Any water?"

Grant pointed downslope. "There's a good creek yonder. Never goes dry."

"Well, sir, I'll be damned if I can see why Dexter would pass this up."

"You will when we get to Johnson's place," Grant said.

The trail angled down a steep pitch and twisted through close-growing aspens, a bright orange island in a sea of pine. Presently they reached the creek, with the Johnson cabin directly ahead of them. Grant saw at once that Red had done his job well.

There were a dozen men in front of the cabin. All of them were armed, as tough a crew as Grant had ever seen, and he thought of what Rennie had said about them. If they were outlaws who made High Valley their hide-out, the sheriff was satisfied to remain ignorant of it.

As Grant rode up, he saw that Rennie was standing in the doorway, dark brown eyes pinned questioningly on him, her fine-featured face filled with worry. She was wearing men's clothes, as she always did, but they did not disguise the fact that she was very much of a woman, although Grant judged she was unaware that she possessed a face and figure that would honestly attract the attention of any man who saw her.

Grant reined up, nodded at Red Johnson who stood a pace ahead of the others, his jaws working steadily on a chew of tobacco. Grant said: "Howdy, gents."

Red kept on chewing, a big man who looked smaller than he was because he seldom stood erect. Bugeye was at his right and somewhat behind his father, protruding eyes filled with a baleful wickedness as he stared at Grant.

It struck Grant that for years he had got along with everybody. Now, in less than twenty-four hours, he had succeeded in making enemies of Bugeye and Ben Piper, both dangerous because they were the kind who would have no scruples about dry-gulching a man.

Gib Lane, bearded and dirty, threw out a hand toward Fenton. "Where'd you pick that up, Talbot?"

"Shut your mug, Gib," Red said without turning. "What's on your mind, Talbot?"

Bugeye snickered. "He can't have something on what he ain't got."

Red gave him a clout on the back of his head. "Damn you, shut up! I'll do the gabbing."

"This is Cole Fenton," Grant said. "He's fixing to buy the Wagon Wheel."

Red scratched a stubble-covered jaw, grinning. "First time I ever see a feller who wore a derby that was aiming to be a rancher."

IX

Cole Fenton was leaning forward over the saddle horn, making a cool study of the men before him. Grant, glancing at him, could detect no fear in him. He was surprised, for there was danger here, so evident that it was an invisible force laid against them. He could not believe that Fenton was unaware of it. It did not make sense that he would be afraid of high places, yet would not fear men like these who would kill both of them if Red gave a sign.

"I figure that what a man wears on his head is his own business," Fenton said to Red Johnson. "I asked Talbot to bring me here for two reasons, but there's one thing that bothers me. I didn't expect to find all of you together."

"I sent for 'em," Red said. "I got a smell that persuaded me a man-sized polecat was around. Now you said something about reasons."

"Two of them. But about that smell. Sure it wasn't a whiff of yourself you got?"

Gib Lane guffawed. "What'd I tell you, Red? You ain't had your bath this year."

Red wheeled on him, a great fist swinging to Lane's jaw and knocking him flat on his back. "If I hear any more smart aleck talk from any of you, I'll gun whip the man." He turned back to Fenton. "Get on with your talk."

"If I buy the Wagon Wheel," Fenton said easily, "I'll need this valley for summer range. The way I understand it, you boys run only a few head of stock. Now I said I came here for two reasons. One was to have a look at the grass.

The other was to tell you that next spring I'm aiming to drive a herd into this valley."

"You won't do no such of a thing!" Red shouted. "We've been here a long time, and we like the valley the way it is. We don't cotton to the notion of having a passel of strangers messing it up."

"I'll pay you anything within reason," Fenton went on. "No hurry about it now, but come spring I'll want to know your price. Stay, if you want to, but my crew and my herd will be here."

Red leaned forward and spat, the brown stream stirring the dust at his feet. Then he wiped his mouth with the back of his hand, a boldly contemptuous gesture. "Come ahead, mister, and I'll kill you."

"Hell . . . what are we waiting till spring for?" Bugeye bawled, and went for his gun.

It was unprovoked and surprising, and Grant was caught flat-footed. As he reached for his own gun, he knew he was too slow, that Bugeye could kill both of them. But the boy's gun was never fired, for Rennie let go with the Winchester, firing from her hip, the slug kicking up dust between Bugeye's feet.

"Drop your iron," she screamed, "or I'll raise my sights!"

Bugeye let his gun go and made a slow turn to face Rennie. Fenton jerked a short-barreled gun out from a shoulder holster. Grant said: "Put it back."

Fenton obeyed, nodding as if he understood. Red laid a hand on Bugeye's shoulder. He said: "Go to the barn. You ain't too big to whip."

Bugeye hesitated, staring at Rennie, then he turned and shambled across the dusty, hoof-trodden yard to the log barn.

Red jabbed a finger at Fenton. "I'm giving you fifteen

minutes to get out of High Valley. Otherwise I'll put a window in your skull. Don't never come back."

"You've had your chance for a fair deal," Fenton said coldly. "You throwed it away, so I'll take the High Valley for nothing when the time comes."

Reining his mare around, Fenton rode back up the creek. Grant hesitated, his eyes on Red. He said: "This wasn't my idea."

"Sure, son," Red said, "but, if you ride for that hairpin, it might just as well have been your notion."

Wheeling his buckskin, Grant caught up to Fenton. They were silent until they reached the rim, then Grant said with deep bitterness: "Joe went out of his way to get along with that bunch. Now you've spoiled it in five minutes, and for nothing."

"The more I hear of Joe Dexter," Fenton said carelessly, "the more I'm convinced he was the most overrated man in Colorado. This bunch will be out of High Valley by spring, and I'll move in without trouble."

They started down the trail to the basin, Grant musing: *He knows better. He never figured on taking High Valley.*

When they were halfway to the bottom, Grant saw that Fenton was gripping the saddle horn, his shoulders hunched forward, his face turned so that he could see only the cliff side of the trail. *Courage runs in strange patterns,* Grant thought. At this moment Fenton was as close to panic as a man could get without giving way to it, yet only a few minutes before he had faced a dozen men, any of them capable of killing him, and he had not shown the slightest sign of fear.

Fenton let his mare take her own pace down the trail, and he was far behind when Grant reached the bottom. Grant waited, rolling a cigarette, his mind on the drive to

Placerville. It was nearly noon now, and the morning had turned hot. There had been no rain for weeks, and he wondered if the water holes on the way to Placerville had dried up. The steers would be all right once they reached the San Miguel, but there were long, dry miles between Rainbow Basin and the river.

Fenton came alongside him, his shoulders back, the hand that had gripped the saddle horn now swinging at his side. He gave Grant the thin grip of one who knows he has permitted another man to see the naked fear that had knifed into his belly and made a weakling out of him.

"If I never take this ride again," Fenton said, "I'll be just as happy."

"I figured that," Grant said dryly, and turned his buckskin toward the Wagon Wheel.

"I've been wondering about Dexter's death." Fenton reined in beside Grant. "I can see how a greenhorn like me might get boogery and do something foolish, but Dexter must have ridden up that trail dozens of times. How come he got killed?"

"I think somebody did it for him," Grant said. "Some day I'll find out, but right now there ain't no proof."

"That why you're hanging around here?" Fenton asked. "From all I hear, you thought a lot of the old man."

"I did, but that ain't the reason I'm hanging on."

"Then why haven't you pulled out? It's pretty damned plain you don't like me and you wouldn't work for me if I bought the Wagon Wheel."

"No, I wouldn't."

"Then why?" Fenton asked doggedly.

Grant was silent for a long moment, his eyes on the ranch buildings and the big cottonwood in front that shaded the house. It was a question he had never answered to anyone, and he knew that Fenton, like Linda, would not understand if he tried to put it into words. He wondered if Dick Sharples or Curly Tell could have put their tongues to the right words, or even if Joe Dexter could have expressed his feelings if he had been alive. Probably not, Grant thought, for Joe's attitudes had been instinctive.

"I can't tell you so you'd savvy," Grant said finally, and Fenton let it drop at that.

Grant rode with his head down, strange thoughts crowding his mind. He could not even tell Fenton what the ranch was for him, that it was far more than buildings and corrals and grass and cattle, the things a man could buy. Some outfits were nothing more, but not the Wagon Wheel. Joe Dexter had built his spread on the basis of integrity and fair dealing with his neighbors; he had loved it with the sort of passion that a man might love something which was alive. Grant had come to share that passion. Sweat and blood and broken bones, hopes and dreams and ideals — those were the things that had gone into the making of this ranch. Somehow the entire way of life in Rainbow Basin had been built around the Wagon Wheel.

Grant glanced at Fenton who had been coolly watching him. Suddenly stirred by the violence of his thoughts, Grant said harshly: "Fenton, I think I'll kill you before I'll let you buy the Wagon Wheel."

Fenton smiled. "That's tough talk. Why?"

"What you did this morning in High Valley proves a hunch I had from the minute I laid eyes on you in Rocky Fork. You don't believe in anything that Joe did."

"I'm a businessman," Fenton said. "I'll make this outfit pay, if I buy it. That wrong?"

"It is the way you mean it. Maybe Joe wasn't no great shakes as a businessman, but he was honest and he lived in peace, and he had a way of making everybody else live that way."

"You figure that as long as Missus Dexter owns it and you run it, you'll go on like Dexter did?"

"That's right," Grant said. "I told you I couldn't make you savvy."

"I don't," Fenton said. "I don't for a fact."

They had reached the cottonwood. Linda, standing on the front porch, called: "Dinner's almost ready. Come in and wash up."

She was wearing a calico house dress, white with bold red flowers, the bodice cut so that it made a neat fit across the round swell of her breasts. Her hair was done up in a crown on her head; her ripe lips held that warm, inviting smile she could put on for a man as easily as she wore a garment.

"I'll be right in." Fenton eased out of the saddle and wryly rubbed his seat. "I'll be eating off a high shelf for a few days, Talbot. Don't reckon I'll take that look at the cattle for a few days. Coming in?"

"No. I'll get something to eat in the cook shack and give the boys a hand this afternoon."

He rode on toward the corrals, leading the bay mare, and he thought with a vitriolic burst of bitterness: *If he doesn't buy the Wagon Wheel, he'll make Linda a lot of promises, and he'll marry her and get it for nothing.*

X

After Grant and Fenton had ridden away, Rennie Johnson did not move from the doorway for a long time, the Winchester held on the ready. She watched Red and Gib Lane and the others until the riders had disappeared up the creek. Then Red swung to face his neighbors, his great shoulders held erect in a way that was unusual for him, his stubble-covered chin thrust defiantly at them.

"You boys never made a mistake taking my orders," he said ominously. "We've made *dinero* when we wanted it . . . we've had a safe place to live, and we've had the kind of fun we like. Now if any of you ain't satisfied, start your tongue to wagging."

Gib Lane, his clothes still covered with the red dust of the yard, rubbed his face where Red had hit him. He said wickedly: "I ain't satisfied. Not by a hell of a lot. If you figure you can knock me around like you do your own boy. . . ."

"I figure I can," Red broke in. "I let you rake in my *dinero* over your table when I ain't always sure you're dealing square, but when it comes to deciding things, I do it."

"But hell," Lane bawled, "Bugeye was right! No reason why we couldn't have plugged both of 'em."

"Plenty of reason!" Red shouted back. "If you had a brain instead of a custard pudding between your ears, you'd savvy. Linda Dexter knows where the huckleberries went. If they didn't show up, she'd get Steve Ollard in here *pronto*."

"We could have hid their carcasses so they'd never have

85

been found," Lane said truculently.

"But we'd have Ollard on our necks," Red said. "That's something we don't want. There'll be time to do something if Fenton buys the Wagon Wheel, which maybe he won't. This is one place where we can sleep without holding one eye open. I aim to keep it that way."

"Sure," one of the men said, "sure," and, wheeling, walked to his horse and mounted.

The rest followed, all but Lane who stood there, facing Red and hating him with the virulence of his kind. When the sound of hoofs died, Red said: "If you're hankering to make a try, get at it."

"Not today," Lane said. "I'm thinking about the girl. I've mentioned it before. I'll buy her."

"You ain't got enough *dinero*," Red said. "She belongs to Bugeye."

"She needs a man, not a kid. I want a woman. . . ."

"Go get one. Now vamoose."

Lane made a slow turn, pausing for a moment to stare hungrily at Rennie, an expression in his eyes that sent prickles down her spine. Then he moved to his horse in the strange, slinking way he had. Rennie watched him, the barrel of the Winchester pointed at him until he lifted himself into leather.

He was a keg of a man on short legs, a keg filled with evil, and she was afraid of him in a way she had never been afraid of Bugeye. She could handle Bugeye, for he was still more boy than man, but she knew she could not handle Gib Lane if he ever surprised her when she was alone.

Red remained motionless until Lane had gone, then Rennie walked toward him. She said tonelessly: "That's why I can't stay here, Red. It's why I wanted Grant to get me out of here."

"Gib won't bother you," Red said. "I'll kill him, if he does, and he knows it."

"That wouldn't help me!" she cried.

"I tell you he won't never lay a hand on you," Red said. "Now, go get dinner. I've got business with Bugeye."

She went into the cabin, not wanting to see the licking Red would give Bugeye. She wondered how long the boy would take the beatings his father gave him. Bugeye had the feelings and pride of a man, and he was as tall as Red if not as thick of body. There would come a day when he would use a gun rather than submit, and, if he killed Red, the only protection she had would be gone.

She built a fire in the coal stove and sliced venison; she made biscuits and set the coffee pot on the front of the stove and started the meat frying, hearing the sound of fists on flesh, the grunts and curses of violently angry men. When she looked out, she saw that Bugeye was down and Red was kicking him in the ribs.

"Any pup I raise toes the mark!" Red shouted with the white-hot anger he always showed when he licked the boy. "If you ever get to be man enough to handle me, you can clear out. Until you are, you'll mind. Hear me?"

Rennie turned back to the stove, sickened. She could not understand Red. The way he had raised her proved that he had a streak of decency in him, decency that controlled him even when he was drunk. In all other ways he was like the rest of the High Valley men. He took great pride in rodding the tough bunch that lived in the valley, but he could be king only as long as he maintained his position with his fists and his gun. She had seen him kill a man who had defied him. It would have taken little to have made him kill Gib Lane this morning, and she was sure Lane knew it.

Red came in, his shirt wet with sweat, and there was a

dark bruise under one eye. Bugeye had hit him once. It was the first time that had happened.

"The kid ain't hungry," Red said as he sat down at the table. "We won't wait for him."

Rennie placed food on the table and sat down across from him. She forced herself to eat, knowing that Red would ask what was the matter with her if she didn't. When he was done, he sat back contentedly, and gnawed off a chew of tobacco from a frayed plug.

She leaned forward. "Red, what would happen to me if you got killed?"

He scratched an ear, frowning. "Hell, that ain't going to happen. I like living."

"But if it did?"

"I reckon I ain't going to live forever," he said as if the thought was new to him. "Well, I guess you'd have to light out for the Wagon Wheel. Grant Talbot would look out for you."

"I want to go today," she breathed.

"I ain't dead yet," he snapped. "What's got into you?"

"You talk about me marrying Bugeye," she cried, "but I'd kill him first. You know that, don't you?"

He laughed. "I believe you'd try." He sobered, his face showing a bitterness that was unusual in him. "Funny thing. I raised my own pup who turned out to be a sniveling lap dog instead of a wolf, and I raised you who ain't no kin to me and you turned out to be a wildcat."

"Let me go, Red."

"You're marrying Bugeye," he said roughly. "I've waited a long time for it. Well, you're eighteen next week, old enough to get married."

He rose and stalked out, leaving her staring after him. She resolved: *I'll go tonight.*

She got up and cleared the table, expecting to hear Red ride away, but there was no sound of horses, and, when she glanced out, she saw that he was hunkered in the yard, repairing a bridle. Bugeye sat with his back to the log wall of the barn, whittling on a piece of pine.

Rennie washed and dried the dishes and was hanging up the dishcloth when she heard a horse coming down the creek. Her first thought was that it might be Grant, and she took the Winchester down from the antlers on the wall. When she stepped to the door, she saw that the visitor was Bruce Mayer.

She had seen Mayer once when he had come with Joe Dexter and Grant, and she knew that he had killed Dexter. Bugeye had seen it from the rim. She had wanted to tell Grant, but the only chance she'd had was the night before when she had been alone with him, and she had not thought about it then.

Both Red and Bugeye were on their feet, and Red had his gun out. He said: "Get out of here, Mayer. I'd rather have a sidewinder around than a double-crosser like you."

Mayer reined up, surprised. "I never double-crossed nobody. What're are you driving at?"

"You beefed Dexter," Red said. "If Steve Ollard was worth a damn, he'd have hung you before now."

"I didn't."

"No use lying. Just get out of here."

Mayer shifted in his saddle. "I ain't riding for the Wagon Wheel. I've got something to say you'd better listen to."

" 'Bout time you quit riding for the Wagon Wheel," Red said contemptuously. "I figured old Joe's ghost would have run you out of the basin a long time ago."

Mayer took off his Stetson and wiped his bald head. He was in his middle thirties, Rennie judged, but now with his hat off he looked years older. He seemed to shrink in size under Red's scornful stare, yet he continued doggedly to work at the job he had come here to do.

"I signed on with Mamie Dolan," he said, "but before I left the Wagon Wheel, I heard what Fenton aims to do. He's gonna clean High Valley out."

"Big talk for a greenhorn . . . ," Bugeye began.

Red wheeled on him. "Ain't I learned you nothing this morning? Shut up."

Bugeye stepped back, his battered face filled with a cold and bitter rage. He put a hand on his gun butt, trying hard to meet Red's eyes, but in the end he failed and lowered his gaze.

"It ain't big talk," Mayer went on. "It's a proposition of wiping out the Wagon Wheel, or come spring the Wagon Wheel will run every damned one of you over the hill."

Red brought his eyes back to Mayer. "So Mamie wants us to go down into the basin and raid the Wagon Wheel. She wants us to do what she ain't big enough to do. That it?"

"She's going to be big," Mayer said, "but that ain't the point. She allows you're both on the same side, so it's just smart to work together. She'll pay you five hundred dollars to hit the Wagon Wheel. She'll fix it so the crew's gone. She wants the buildings burned. It'll bust the Dexter woman, owing as much *dinero* to Ira Connors as she does."

"Five hundred dollars." Red threw back his head and laughed. "She takes us for a bunch of chowder-headed fools for sure. Tell her to do her own dirty work. We'll handle Fenton when the sign's right."

"Then you'll do it alone," Mayer said. "Seems to me it's smarter to hit the other fellow a lick before he hits you. Me 'n' Piper will ride with you, if you want to take Mamie's proposition."

"I wouldn't ride to hell with you!" Red shouted. "Go on . . . get out of here! I've got a good notion to slope into town and tell Ollard you beefed Dexter. I always allowed I was purty ornery. Alongside you I'm a saint."

Mayer slapped his hat on his head and, wheeling his horse, rode back up the trail. Then Red, turning, saw that Bugeye had saddled his sorrel and had mounted.

"Where you going?" Red demanded.

"Riding," the kid said sullenly. He had his hand on his gun butt again, and he was staring at his father with a violence that Rennie had never seen in his face before. "You ain't never gonna lay a hand on me again. I'm pulling out."

"You'll come back, when you get hungry," Red said.

"I ain't figuring on getting hungry. You've made your living off other folks. I aim to do the same, and, while I'm at it, I'll fill Talbot's guts full of lead."

Concern was in Red's face then. He said in a softer voice than he usually used with the boy: "I've had plans for you, and I never gave you a licking that wasn't for your own good. I'm wanted by the law in three states, but you ain't. Don't spoil what I've done for you."

"I'm aiming to spoil a lot of things!" Bugeye shouted. "You've kicked me around like a hound pup as long as I can remember. I tell you, you've done it for the last time."

Cracking steel to his horse, Bugeye whirled the animal upstream and rode after Mayer, the animal laboring up the grade.

Red yelled after him: "Slow up, you damned fool! I've taught you how to handle a horse, if I never taught you nothing else."

But Bugeye didn't stop or look back. Red went back to his bridle. He worked on it a moment, then slammed it down in a fit of temper. He caught his black gelding and

91

saddled him. Rennie still stood in the doorway, the Winchester in her hands. As Red mounted and turned toward the house, she slipped back into the kitchen, replaced the rifle on the antlers, and ran into the pantry.

When Red came in, she was sifting flour into a pan.

Red took a whiskey bottle down from a shelf back of the stove, calling: "Rennie!"

She stepped out of the pantry, the flour sifter still in her hand. "What do you want?"

Red took a long pull from the bottle. He wiped his mouth and set the bottle back on the shelf. He stared at Rennie a moment as if trying to gauge her temper, and for the first time in her life she sensed that he was worried. He had never been a man to be concerned about the future. With him every day was to be lived when it came, confident that he could handle anything it brought to him, but now she realized he was worried about Bugeye, his only son.

"I've been more'n fair with you," Red said as if his own thoughts had put him on the defensive. "I've raised you like you was my own kin, and you ain't no relation to me at all."

"I've earned my keep," she shot back with a righteous anger.

He glowered at her, thumbs hooked inside his belt. "Soon as Bugeye gets back, we're riding into town, and you're marrying him so everything will be fit and proper. You and him won't have no trouble dodging the law like I have. You'll live in the basin, and Bugeye will make you a good husband, or I'll beat hell out of him."

"You're done beating him," she said. "I heard him tell you so."

"Kid talk," Red said loudly, too loudly. "I tell you I've got it planned."

She came toward him, the flour sifter still clutched in her

hand. "Who were my folks, Red? I've got a right to know."

"I reckon you have," he said. "I'll tell you on your wedding night."

He stalked out and mounted. Moving over to the doorway, Rennie watched Red until he disappeared, riding downstream toward Gib Lane's place. She went back into the pantry and set the flour sifter on the counter. There was no sense in baking a cake. She'd just be leaving it for them to eat.

She remembered the broken axe handle that Bugeye had dropped behind the stove a day or two before. She picked it up, knowing that Red would not be back for hours, but she wasn't sure about Bugeye. He might return, when he cooled off. Then she thought with a sudden flare of anger that she would probably never know who her folks were, not if Red was going to tell her the night she married Bugeye.

She went into the lean-to room and stood staring at her bunk, at the clothes she would never wear again, man clothes that she hated. There was no horse in the corral, and it was a long walk to the Wagon Wheel. She would have to take the Winchester. It would be a burden, but she could not afford to be unarmed. If Bugeye returned and found her gone, he would guess where she had gone and catch her before she got to the Wagon Wheel.

Kneeling beside her bunk, she reached under it and brought out a small cardboard box. She opened it, fingering the few childhood treasures she had collected through the years — a rag doll, a whistle, some colored stones she had found along the creek, and a locket with a fine gold chain.

She opened the locket and looked at the picture of a young woman. It was her mother, she thought, although Red had never said so. The locket was the only thing she had that went back to her childhood. She must have been wearing it when the man had taken her to Red that night.

Closing the locket, she put the chain around her neck, fumbling with it a moment before she could fasten it. She seldom looked at it because it reminded her of those nightmarish hours of the fighting and the gunfire and the sight of dead men on the floor of the ranch house, then the long ride.

She closed her eyes, fighting against the panic that threatened to sweep through her. It was always this way when she let herself remember it, but now it was worse because she was leaving the only security she had ever known, and she told herself she was foolish to count on Grant Talbot when he had already told her he couldn't help her. Foolish or not, it was the only thing to do.

Rennie had never seen Linda Dexter, but she had heard about her. Nothing good, but Red and Bugeye might be wrong. They were never able to see anything good in a decent woman, and Linda must be decent, or Joe Dexter wouldn't have married her.

She heard the jingle of spurs, then Bugeye's strident voice.

"Rennie!"

She grabbed the axe handle and jumped up, holding it behind her. There was no chance to reach the Winchester in the kitchen. She struggled for breath. Her stomach seemed to be pressing against her lungs. Sweat broke through her skin. She stood motionless, trembling, hoping that Bugeye would go away and knowing he wouldn't. He must have seen that her door was open. He came across the kitchen and stood, looking at her, grinning with the one good side of his mouth that had not been bruised by Red's fist.

"Hiding, were you?" Bugeye asked. "Well, it won't do you no good."

She knew what he meant to do, what he had wanted to do for a long time. She whispered: "Leave me alone. Red will kill you, if you touch me."

He laughed. "I'm thinking maybe I'll kill him first. It'd take a killing to get square for the rawhidings he's given me."

"Let me alone," she whispered again. "He said we were going into Rocky Fork and get married when you get back."

Bugeye snorted derisively. "Hell, I'm done waiting."

He took a step toward her, his protruding green eyes crazy with passion. She cried out: "Bugeye, who were my folks?"

He stopped, surprised that she would ask such a question at a time like this. He said: "Find out from Dad. He's spent half his life talking about plans he's never made stick." He laughed. "Yeah, big plans about you and me and the Wagon Wheel. To hell with 'em! I caught up with Mayer before he got out of the valley. I made a deal with him, and I reckon me 'n' Gib Lane can do the job. Maybe with Piper's and Mayer's help. But you ain't so smart, trying to get me off the track."

He came on, still walking slowly, the words flowing out of him.

"You've hit me too many times, and Dad always kept me from doing anything back. I wasn't no son to him. Just somebody to kick around. That's all I ever have been."

Bugeye was a step from her then, big hands reaching for her. She stepped quickly to one side, and he swore and lunged at her. She swung the axe handle, hitting him on the head with all the strength that was in her body. He raised a hand to ward off the blow, but he was too late. The club made a sharp crack, when it hit him, and he spilled forward, his mouth gaping open. She had to jump aside to avoid being caught under him as he fell. She thought: *He was crazy or he'd have guessed why I had my hands behind me.*

For a moment she stood, staring at his body. She dug a toe into his ribs, but there was no movement. Stooping, she jerked his gun from its holster and ran out of the room. She slipped the Colt under her waistband and fled from the house. Bugeye's sorrel was not more than a dozen paces from the kitchen door, the reins on the ground.

She grabbed the reins and swung into the saddle. She kicked the horse in his sides, wanting only to get away before Bugeye came to. Then the thought struck her that she might have killed him. She couldn't go back to see. She brought the sorrel into a run, up the trail that Bugeye had followed when he had ridden after Mayer. This was the moment she had thought about for a long time, but she had not foreseen it would be like this. She wished she knew whether Bugeye was alive.

Presently she realized that this was foolish, and pulled the sorrel down to a slower pace. He was already gummed with lather from the ride Bugeye had taken. Rennie looked back once, but the trail had turned toward the rim, and the timber blotted out the view of the cabin. She did not know why she had looked back. She never wanted to see the cabin again.

She reached the rim and drew up to let the sorrel blow. She sat her saddle, listening, but heard nothing except the faint sound of the wind in the pines behind her. For a moment she sat with her eyes closed, trying to shut out the picture of Bugeye, lying on the floor of her room, and the thought crowded into her mind that she was doomed to trouble all of her life. She could never expect peace and decency and the kind of life that other women had.

The afternoon sun beat down upon her. She opened her eyes and shook her head, and thought of Grant Talbot. She would know how it was the first minute she saw him and told him what had happened. Then it occurred to her that she had information to offer him about Mayer's visit and what Bugeye aimed to do.

He would help her. He'd have to now. She clung to that hope as she rode down the narrow, twisting trail to the floor of the basin.

XI

The sun was a scarlet arc behind the Big Bears, when Grant and the crew rode into the Wagon Wheel yard, their long shadows moving before them. The heat of the day was gone; the night would be clear and cold enough to produce a film of ice on the horse troughs.

What the weather would be tomorrow was anyone's guess, but Grant didn't worry about it. With luck the gather would be finished in two more days, and they could start the drive to Placerville. If their luck held, the steers would be delivered with time to spare.

Perhaps it was just getting back into the saddle and combing the aspens for a few reluctant mossyhorns that had a way of hiding out under a man's nose. Or perhaps it was being with the crew again and away from Cole Fenton, but, whatever the reason, Grant was more optimistic than he had been for days. Getting rid of Bruce Mayer had helped, too. The man's rawhiding had gotten under Grant's skin more than he had realized.

They dismounted, Dick Sharples saying: "I'm hungry enough to enjoy even Dutch's cooking."

And young Kit Bellew: "Me, too. Maybe his biscuits won't be so damned hard. Some ornery son put a rock on the plate last night, and I had it buttered before I figured out it wasn't a biscuit."

It was natural talk, easy and good. There hadn't been much of it since Joe had died, and suddenly it seemed to Grant that these three months had been an eternity, three months when nothing had been right. Mamie Dolan had called it, when she'd said that Joe's death had produced a vacuum, a vacuum of uncertainty that had been hard on all of them.

Then the good feeling was gone from Grant, for Dick Sharples asked: "Where'd that sorrel in the corral come from?"

Grant wheeled to look at the animal. It was Bugeye's horse. For a moment Grant stood motionless, trying to make some sense out of this. Bugeye wasn't in sight. He might be in the barn, watching, holding a gun on Grant. No, that was crazy. He wouldn't be here alone. Or if he had come to square accounts with Grant, he wouldn't have pulled the gear off his horse and turned him into the corral.

"He's Bugeye Johnson's sorrel," Grant said in a low voice, handing the reins of his buckskin to Sharples. "I'd better have a look around."

"Grant."

It was Rennie, standing with her slim back pressed against the trunk of the big cottonwood. Grant had not noticed her before. She must have been on the other side of the tree, or in the house.

"It's the Johnson girl," Grant said, relieved. "Reckon she rode down on Bugeye's horse."

Sharples stared at Rennie, his eyes bulging in the way of a man who is seeing something come alive out of his past. He breathed: "Who did you say she was?"

"Rennie Johnson," Grant said. "Red's girl. I'll see what she wants."

He strode toward the cottonwood, knowing what she wanted and wondering what he could do about it. Linda wouldn't stand for the girl's staying. With her it was simply a case of not wanting another woman around. It was typical of Linda, Grant thought. Well, Rennie would have to stay the night. Tomorrow would be time enough to decide what to do with her.

When Grant came up to Rennie, he saw that she was frightened. He wanted to tell her that she had no business coming here, not after what he had told her, but he didn't say it. He couldn't. Something had happened, something that had forced her to come to him because she had no one else to turn to.

Rennie's Stetson was dangling down her back from the chin strap, the last of the sunlight on her tanned face. She did not move from where she stood against the tree trunk. She just looked at him, anxiety squeezing her chest so that breathing was an effort for her.

"What is it, Rennie?" he asked.

"I had to come." She touched dry lips with her tongue. "I . . . I didn't have any other place to go." Then she fainted.

He caught her before she fell. He had not realized how small she was until she was in his arms. She was like a child, he thought, homeless and scared, and, as he carried her into the house, he realized that Red and Bugeye would come after her, and the trouble he had been striving to avert would be at hand.

Linda came into the living room, when she heard Grant. Fenton was a step behind her. Grant laid Rennie on the leather couch, saying over his shoulder: "She'll be all right in a minute. Just fainted."

Tight-lipped, Linda said: "I won't have her here."

Turning, Grant looked at her, sensing the anger that was in her. She had, he thought, the smallest soul of anyone he had ever known. He said: "You'll have her."

"No, I won't," Linda snapped. "She came here this afternoon, asking for you. I told her you weren't here, and I wouldn't let her in the house. She waited outside. That's where she belongs. Now get her out of here."

There was a satisfied smirk on Fenton's face. "She's right, Talbot. We have no room in Rainbow Basin for High Valley trash."

Steadily Grant kept his eyes on Linda. He said to her: "Joe made one mistake, when he married you. He made a hell of a bigger one when he left the Wagon Wheel to you. I've taken your orders, figuring that Joe would have wanted it that way. Now I know better."

"You'll go on taking my orders," Linda flared, "or I'll fire you."

"No," Grant said. "I've been afraid you would. That's what's been the whole damned trouble. I ain't afraid now because I'm going to start giving you orders. If Joe knew you'd kept Rennie outside all afternoon, he'd come out of his grave a-kicking. He never turned anybody away from his house, and you ain't starting now."

Fenton reared back, his chin jutting forward defiantly. "You're getting out of line, Talbot."

"You're damned right I am. Now shut up."

"Grant." Rennie was tugging at his arm. "Grant, where am I?"

"Wagon Wheel," he said without turning. "You're all right, Rennie."

Rennie was sitting up, her eyes wide as she stared around the room. "I've been here before, Grant, but I don't remember when. This couch and that table. The picture up there on the wall." She put a hand to her head as if trying to think. "I've seen them before. I just can't remember when it was."

"Get her out of here!" Linda screamed.

"Shut up, or I'll put you across my knee," Grant said. "And I ain't stuttering when I tell you. I'll pound some sense into you, if that's where your brain is."

Linda's face was ugly. He had never seen her like this before. He wondered how many times Joe had, and he understood then what she had done to the old man. But Joe had never been one to let others share his unhappiness or help him bear the weight of his mistakes.

"You'd be better off without Talbot," Fenton said. "I know how much you've depended on him, Missus Dexter, but when a hired hand starts giving orders to his. . . ."

"Fenton, I told you once to keep your mug shut," Grant said in a low voice. "You open it once more, and I'll throw you out of here."

"You're fired!" Linda cried.

"Fire me, and you'll walk out of here without anything but the clothes on your back. You want some *dinero* for the Wagon Wheel. All right. Leave me alone and I'll get it for you."

Rennie was on her feet now, a hand gripping Grant's arm. She said: "It doesn't make any difference where I saw these things. I've got something to tell you. It's the reason I came."

Still watching Fenton, Grant asked: "What is it?"

"After you and Fenton left the valley, Bruce Mayer showed up. He said Mamie would give Red and the others five hundred dollars if they'd raid the Wagon Wheel and burn the buildings. Mayer's working for Mamie. He and Piper were going to ride with them."

"That's the craziest thing I ever heard!" Fenton burst out. "This girl is making it up."

A suspicion that had been nothing more than a nagging thought in the back of Grant's mind now began taking shape. He asked softly: "What did Red say?"

"He didn't want any part of it, but Bugeye rode after Mayer and talked to him. Bugeye came back, after Red left. He said he'd taken the job, and Gib Lane would be with him. He said the four of them would be enough."

There was a strained look in Fenton's face, the look of a man who is seeing something break up in front of him, something he had counted on. He shouted: "Missus Dexter, I was in High Valley this morning. Those men are riffraff! Cowards, hiding out up there. They don't have enough sand in their craw to try anything like that. I don't know why this girl is saying what she has said, but she must have her own reasons."

"Of course, she has," Linda said harshly. "She wants you, Grant. All right, take her and get out."

"If I do, the crew will go with me," Grant said, "and you'll be left up the creek with nothing but a leaky paddle. Can't you see that's what Fenton and Mamie want?"

"Hogwash," Fenton snorted.

Grant pulled Rennie's hand away from his arm and moved toward Fenton. "This whole business has looked funny to me from the start. Now it makes sense. Mamie sent for you to talk Linda into selling. You went up to High Valley and talked tough to Red so his bunch would be mad enough to listen to Mayer. Then, when our buildings were burned and the herd scattered to hell an' gone, Linda would be so scared she'd take any penny ante offer you made."

"The girl just said Johnson wouldn't listen," Fenton shouted.

"But Bugeye did. You're finished, Fenton. Get out."

Linda jumped at Grant, slapping him across the face, her left hand grabbing his gun arm. He shoved her aside. Then Rennie was on Linda, biting and gouging and yanking at her hair. If it had not been for her interference, Grant would have been a dead man. Fenton had yanked out his gun, his face livid with fury.

Grant grabbed Fenton's right wrist as the gun swung out of the man's shoulder holster. He twisted until the gun fell to the floor, then he hit Fenton on the jaw, and knocked him flat on his back.

Grant heard Linda swearing at him, but he didn't look at her. Rennie would keep her out of it. Fenton had been dazed by the blow. He started to get up, shaking his head, but before he could struggle to his feet, Grant had him by the coat collar and the seat of his pants. He carried Fenton, kicking and squirming and cursing, to the door and heaved him into the yard. Fenton fell on his belly and scooted like a sled, his face in the deep red dust of the yard.

"Dick!" Grant called.

Sharples came out of the cook shack on the run, Curly Tell and Kit Bellew and the others behind him.

Grant said: "Fenton's pulling his freight. Get him a horse and start him out. If he makes a kick, slap hell out of him."

Sharples grinned. "It's a chore I'll plumb enjoy. I sure will."

"There's something up," Grant said. "Curly, you and Kit

103

finish your supper and get back to the herd. If you need help, start shooting. We can't let anybody scatter them steers now, or we're licked."

Nodding, Tell swung back to the cook shack with Kit Bellew. Grant wheeled into the house. Linda was sitting on the floor, whimpering. Her face was streaked with scratches; her hair was a tangled mess. She stared up at Grant and began to swear.

"There's one lady in the house," Grant said, "and it ain't you. Shut up."

He pulled Linda to her feet and pushed her down on the couch.

Rennie said apologetically: "I'm sorry, Missus Dexter, but Fenton would have killed Grant if I hadn't got you off his arm."

"I wish to hell he had!" Linda screamed.

Grant stood in front of her, looking at her and thinking of the night before when he had kissed her. He could not understand why he had done it, and he never would. He must, he thought, have known how utterly worthless she was, that every thought and desire she'd ever had centered on herself.

"You're right about one thing," Grant said. "You don't belong here. I'll buy you out, and you can get the hell off this range, and we'll both be satisfied."

"Where would you get fifty thousand?" Linda demanded.

"It won't be fifty thousand," Grant answered. "You'll take my note for what I can't raise, but you'll get something. That's more'n you'd get if I'd let this go the way you wanted to."

She began to cry, the violence of her anger spent.

Rennie said: "There's something else, Grant. Bruce Mayer killed Joe."

He turned on her, taking a moment to understand the

104

full implication of what she had said. He asked: "How do you know?"

"Bugeye saw it from the rim. Joe had been in High Valley and was on his way down. Mayer was halfway up, blocking the trail. Joe got off his horse, and they had a fight. Bugeye was too far away to hear what they said, but he saw Mayer throw Joe over the edge."

"Why didn't Red tell me?" Grant demanded. "Or go to Steve Ollard?"

"You know why. Red didn't want to get tangled up with the law, but he threatened to today when Mayer was talking about this deal with Mamie."

Grant sat down, his head pounding, weariness bringing a slackness to his muscles. This was something he had guessed, that Joe had not died accidentally, but he had not suspected that Mayer was the killer. Now, knowing that the man worked for Mamie, he could understand how it had been.

There was this moment of silence, the only sound in the room that of Linda's sobbing. Then the drum of a galloping horse came to them. Grant said more to himself than to the women: "Fenton will go to Mamie now. We'll have hell to pay before morning."

Sharples came in. "He's on his way, Grant." He walked to where Rennie stood at the end of the couch and gave her a long, studying stare. He asked: "You Red Johnson's daughter?"

"No," Rennie answered. "He raised me. That's all. I don't know who my folks were."

Sharples scratched his cheek. "You're the spittin' image of someone I used to know. Don't make sense, though. Got anything from where you came from, or do you remember where it was?"

"I was too little to remember anything. I think my

mother died when I was a baby. I know there was a fight and some men were killed and I was carried off. They took me to Red, and he kept me."

Sharples shook his head as if there was something in his mind he could not believe. "It just don't make sense. I must be getting old and foolish."

"What's biting you?" Grant asked.

"No use getting everybody worked up on account of a crazy notion I've got." He glanced up at the picture on the wall. "I'll go see Red. He's the only one who'd know."

There was no use pressing Sharples. The old man would not talk until he was ready.

Grant said: "I'm riding into town tonight. Dick, you stay with Linda. Don't let her get away, and keep your eyes open for trouble. It might bust open before I get back."

"You'd better keep me here," Linda said bitterly. "When I get to the sheriff, I'll have you and this little slut in jail, and I'll keep you there till you rot! You hear?"

"I ain't deaf." Grant nodded at Sharples. "Think you can handle her?"

"I may have to hog-tie her," Sharples said, "but I'll handle her all right."

Grant moved to the door. He paused, looking back at Rennie. "Did you come down just to tell me about Mayer and what they had cooked up?"

"No. I had to get out. Red was taking me to town to marry Bugeye, but Bugeye came back when Red was gone. I hit him. Maybe I killed him. I don't know."

Grant understood then. He had been about to ask her to go to town with him, but she had been through too much. She was better off here. He said: "Thanks, Rennie."

"I didn't aim to stir up so much trouble," Rennie said, "but I thought it was a fair trade, you giving me a place to stay for telling you."

"More'n fair," Grant said. "Take care of Rennie, too, Dick. I'll get back as soon as I can."

He went out into the dusk. He caught and saddled a leggy roan, leaving his buckskin in the corral, and took the road to town.

XII

It was nearly ten when Grant reached Rocky Fork. Main Street was quiet, the only lights being in the hotel lobby and the Silver Dollar. Grant had hoped to catch Marty Reem before he left the store. Ordinarily Reem closed at eight, but he often spent several hours working on his books or stocking the shelves. He had no help now, so he tended to chores like that in the evenings after he closed. But there was no light in the back of the store. Grant rode on to the end of the block and turned right, along a side street to Reem's house.

Again Grant felt the rub of irritation. The house was dark. If Reem was asleep, he might not be in any mood to listen, but Grant had no choice. Dismounting, he went up the path and knocked at the door. When there was no answer, he knocked again, hammering the door this time, and a moment later a light came to life in the bedroom.

Reem poked his bald head through an open window, saying in a sleep-thick voice: "The store's closed, and it stays closed till morning."

"Sorry to wake you up, Marty," Grant said, "but I've got to talk to you."

It took a moment for Reem's sleep-fogged mind to recognize Grant's voice. Then he asked worriedly: "What's wrong, Grant?"

"Trouble. A hell of a lot of it, and I'm counting on you to help."

Reem pulled his head in and quickly opened the front door, the lamp in his hand. He said: "Come in, boy. I don't usually go to bed this early, but I was up most of last night talking to Ira and Steve."

Reem stepped aside for Grant to come in. He had nothing on but his underclothes, a comical-appearing, pudgy man, his belly making a round little ball beneath his undershirt. Grant sat down on the horsehair sofa and glanced around the tidy room, thinking as he always did when he was here that Marty Reem was a better house-keeper than most women. He lived alone and he had no kin, so the wreath on the wall always struck Grant as being ridic-ulous. Inside the wreath were the words: **God Bless Our Home.**

Reem dropped into a rocking chair. "Let's have it, Grant."

"What was the palaver with Steve and Ira about?"

Reem scowled. "It's a damned nasty world, Grant. Sometimes I'm ashamed of being a man, and I get to won-dering if God ain't ashamed of Himself for having created us. He must get mighty disgusted when He looks down at the world and considers the ornery things we do."

Grant rolled a smoke, sensing the corroding bitterness that was in the little storekeeper. He said: "You ain't an-swered my question."

"I'm getting to it. What I'm saying is that everybody is so damned selfish we can't see straight." He paused, frowning. "Well, I don't mean everybody. That's what strikes me as being funny about the whole thing. When Joe was alive, this basin was a right pleasant place to live in. He kept it that way without even trying because he wasn't selfish. Or maybe he was. Maybe he got his pleasure out of life just by living that way."

It was a long speech for Marty Reem who ordinarily was no philosopher at all. Grant, not knowing what to say, was silent. He fished a match out of his vest pocket, fired his cigarette, and waited for the storekeeper to go on.

"I keep thinking about what you said yesterday," Reem said. "There's a lot of sense in your notion about keeping the Wagon Wheel like it was. It would be, with you running it. In time you'd be elected president of the cattlemen's association, and you'd be wearing Joe's boots without ever remembering when you'd pulled 'em on. There's a lot of Joe in you."

"You said we were all selfish," Grant murmured. "I reckon you're right. The Wagon Wheel means a home and a job to me. I don't want to lose either one."

Reem nodded. "The point is it'd be better for all of us if you didn't lose 'em. I mean, looking at it from the selfish point of view. I had the notion me and Ira and Steve would form a company and put up the money it'd take to buy the Wagon Wheel. We'd keep you and the crew on, but we'd sure get rid of Linda. I still think it was a good notion."

"They couldn't see it?"

"Hell, no. Steve wants to go along without no trouble, and Ira figures he'll get the Wagon Wheel without it costing him anything. Wouldn't surprise me if he hired some men to scatter your herd so you couldn't get to Placerville and pay him off."

"I'll cut the old buzzard's heart out, if he does it," Grant growled.

"Then Steve will hang you on the first limb he finds."

Reem rose and, walking to the table, filled his pipe from a can of tobacco. He lighted it, eyeing Grant through the clouds of blue smoke. "Well, what fetched you here?"

Grant told him what had happened and about Mayer having killed Joe. Reem rocked steadily, head tipped forward. When Grant finished, Reem said: "It ain't surprising, none of it. We've underestimated Mamie right along, but we shouldn't have, knowing she's been sitting on her front porch, living on hate for years."

"What do we do?"

"You've got a man-sized job of fighting to take care of first."

"Sure," said Grant impatiently. "After we do the fighting, we've still got Linda on our hands, and we'll wind up in the same place we started from."

"You've got an idea or you wouldn't be here," Reem said.

Grant had finished his cigarette. Now he rolled and lit another, taking his time because he was reluctant to put his idea into words. "I've got a few hundred dollars in the bank," he said, then, slowly. "The crew could raise some more, but it won't add up to anything like enough. I don't know what we could make Linda settle for, but I was hoping you'd put up the rest, whatever it'd be."

Reem rose and knocked out his pipe. "I've got three thousand dollars in cash. It wouldn't be enough."

"Ira would loan you the rest."

"By putting up my store and house," Reem said with a touch of anger. "You expect me to do that?"

"Yeah," Grant said. "That's what I expect."

Reem filled his pipe again and began to pace restlessly around the room. He said: "I'm not young, Grant. It's different with you. Hell, you could get a good job on half a dozen spreads I could name right here in the basin. I'm too

110

old to start over. The store's all I've got."

"Marty, suppose you lost your house and store to Ira." Grant leaned forward. "You'd still have the Wagon Wheel. I'll guarantee that me and the boys would stick with you."

"I ain't a rancher. I'm a storekeeper." Reem pulled hard on his pipe, torn between what he wanted to do and what he was afraid to try. "And if your herd did get scattered and you didn't get to Placerville in time to sell the cows, Ira would pull in the pot."

"There's that chance," Grant agreed. "Me and the crew ain't got nothing much to lose but our lives. There's a good chance some of us will before this is done."

"All right," Reem said reluctantly. "Get back to the Wagon Wheel. I'll roll Ira out of bed, and I'll see what I can raise. I'll be out there by sunup."

Grant rose. "I'll have it out with Linda. If Fenton hadn't given her his gab about fifty thousand, I could make her listen to reason, but I don't know how it'll be now."

"You ought to stop at Mamie's," Reem said. "She might pull in her horns, if she knows what we're fixing to do."

"Won't hurt to tell her," Grant said, "but I've got a hunch she'll play her hand out now that it's gone this far. What about Ollard? Think he'd arrest Mayer?"

"Not on hearsay evidence," Reem answered. "You'd have to get Bugeye to swear to what he saw."

Grant walked to the door. He paused and grinned at Reem. "It isn't such a damned nasty world, Marty. Not with you in it."

"Go on," Reem said hoarsely. "Get, before I start thinking about what a fool I'm making out of myself. If I wind up with nothing but the Wagon Wheel, I'll work the tail off of you."

Grant left, still grinning. Mounting, he left town at a

111

brisk pace. The sky was clear and star-filled, the air sharp and biting. It would freeze tonight, Grant thought absently. He considered the possibility of Mamie's sending Piper and Mayer to stampede the herd tonight. It was her natural move, and it would leave the Wagon Wheel wide open for days while the steers were gathered again.

But luck was not all on Mamie's side. Grant had foreseen the danger, and he thought he could depend on Curly Tell and Kit Bellew, holding the steers in the pasture at the upper end of the basin.

As Grant rode, he considered Reem's suggestion that he see Mamie tonight. It would not take him far out of his way, and it would mean only a few minutes wasted. He weighed those minutes against the chance that he could make Mamie change her mind, and decided it was worth a try. Mamie was a hard-headed gambler. It was quite possible she would size up the situation realistically and try to save what she could. It was wishful thinking, and Grant was fully aware of that. More than that, he might run into a slug if Piper, Fenton, and Mayer were with her, but he doubted that they would be.

When Grant reached the fork in the road, he saw that there was a light in Mamie's house. He reined up, listening, but he could hear nothing except the coyote chorus from the rim above her place. He rode on up the steep slope, one hand on his gun butt, eyes on the trail.

In spite of himself a faint prickle of uneasiness ran down his spine. He fought the temptation to turn back, telling himself that he was allowing imaginary fears to get the best of him. Logic told him that only Fenton would be here, that Piper and Mayer would be gone, either to stampede the Wagon Wheel herd or to join Bugeye and Gib Lane in their raid on the ranch.

He stepped down in front of the Seven Bar Seven house and paused, eyes probing the shadows. Still he could not see or hear anything that seemed out of the way. Mamie's shades were up. He could see the lighted lamp on the table in the living room, but apparently no one was in the room. Mamie might have gone to bed, or possibly she was in her wheelchair, hidden from his sight by some angle of the wall.

Carefully he walked up the path, his gun riding loosely in leather. He stepped across the porch, boards squeaking weirdly under his boots, and knocked on the door. It swung open at once, and Mamie stood in front of him.

"Come in," Mamie said cordially. "I had a hunch you'd change your mind about working for me."

He stood motionless, staring at her, shocked by this thing that seemed nothing less than miraculous. He said hoarsely: "I thought you couldn't get out of your chair."

She smiled. "I wanted folks to think that. I'm hard to lick, Grant, even by Joe Dexter. It's taken me a long time, but I'm walking a little now, and it won't be long until I'll be riding." She motioned to him. "Come in."

"I didn't change my mind, Mamie. I stopped to tell you that you're licked. I know about Mayer and how Joe was killed. You did it."

"It was long overdue," she said easily. "Well, come in and tell me how you found out."

XIII

One step took Grant through the door. He caught the movement of a down-swinging gun barrel and threw up a hand. He was too late. He went down on his knees, exploding stars rolling across his vision, then he toppled forward. He was not entirely unconscious, but he could not move.

From what seemed like a great distance he heard Mamie shout: "Get his gun, Ben!"

Someone yanked his gun from its holster. Piper said: "I'll kill him with his own iron, damn him."

"The hell you will!" Mamie screamed. "Let me have it. Now drift, both of you. Get them steers scattered from here to hell and gone."

Grant heard the jingle of spurs as men walked out of the house. He lay there for a moment, fighting the aching pain, then he raised himself on his arms. Mamie was in her wheelchair, his gun lined on him, her face filled with malicious triumph. Fenton was standing beside her. It must have been Mayer and Piper who had left.

"You made a mistake when you turned my offer down," Mamie said with cold venom. "I could have used you."

"You're making a mistake, leaving him alive," Fenton said hoarsely. "He knocked me around and threw me out of the house. I ain't going to overlook it, if you do."

"I haven't made a mistake yet, Cole," Mamie said. "I ain't making one now."

"You're making a hell of a big one," Fenton shouted. "He's dangerous as long as he's alive."

114

"He won't be alive, if he makes a wrong move," Mamie said. "I aim for him to see the fire from my porch. Hear that, Grant? . . . from my porch where I've sat for years, watching you and Joe and that red-headed floozy he fetched to the basin. It'll be a nice fire, the house and the barn and every damned building on the Wagon Wheel."

Strength went out of Grant's arms and his face hit the floor, pain rocketing through him, and with it was the feeling of utter hopelessness.

Grant realized, afterward, that he must have passed out then. Because later, when he tried to remember everything that had happened, there was this blank spot that he could not fill. What he did recall was that he was aware first of the hammering ache in his head, then of the flow of talk, and presently the words became intelligible to him. Still he did not move. He would be overlooked as long as they thought he was out cold.

He had guessed right in thinking that Mamie would try to scatter the herd tonight. Probably it had been part of the agreement with Bugeye. The one thing that would pull the crew away from the Wagon Wheel was a stampede.

Now, with his head feeling as if someone was pounding it with a club at regular intervals, he found it hard to think. He could not be sure what Dick Sharples would do. If he tried to save the herd, there would be only the two women left at the Wagon Wheel ranch house. Linda would be no good, and Grant could not bring himself to consider what would happen to Rennie if she was taken back to High Valley.

Then Mamie's words focused Grant's mind on the immediate problem of getting out of here. She was saying to Fenton: "You'd better start. Know what you're going to tell the Dexter woman?"

115

"Sure," Fenton answered irritably. "Sometimes you talk like you think I'm a fool."

"Sometimes I think you are. Let me hear what you're going to say."

"If I'm a fool, it's because I let you drag me into this crazy scheme of yours," Fenton said bitterly. "Or maybe I'm a fool because I ever thought I wanted to be in the cattle business. My seat's so sore I can't sit a saddle."

"Don't get weak in the britches, not when you're ready to haul in the pot," she said caustically. "What are you going to tell her?"

"I still want to buy Wagon Wheel," he said, parrot-like. "I don't want to lose the cattle, and I overheard Mayer and Piper talking about stampeding the herd."

"Maybe Sharples won't leave," Mamie said uncertainly.

"He'll go, if Linda tells him to," he said. "I'll offer to stay with the women. Besides, Sharples will figure on Talbot showing up any minute."

"All right," Mamie said commandingly. "Get moving."

Grant heard Fenton take two steps, then he stopped, and from the sound of their voices he knew that Mamie was still directly in front of him, that Fenton had moved toward the door so that Grant lay between them.

"I tell you it's bad business, leaving this *hombre* behind," Fenton said. "It's like what you said Piper told you. Talbot's got the ghost of old man Dexter in him, and you can't win with him still alive."

"I'll plug him," Mamie said coolly, "soon as he sees the fire. I've been promising myself a look at his face, and I ain't going to lose my fun. I just wish it was Dexter."

Slowly Grant brought himself up to his knees, the room spinning before him. There was one chance, he thought, a crazy, wild chance, but it was the best he could think of. He had to stop Fenton before he left.

"I'll plug him now if . . . ," Fenton began.

"Cole, if you don't make tracks, I'll shoot your ears off."

"Where am I?" Grant asked.

The room had stopped spinning. Grant looked at Mamie who was sitting with the gun on her lap, a cigar in her right hand. She was staring at him curiously.

"He's out of his head," she said. "I hope to hell he comes out of it in time."

"Let me tie him up," Fenton urged.

"No fun hunting a bear after you get a rope on him," Mamie said. "You think I'm helpless?"

Grant came to his feet, a hand raised to his head, eyes on Mamie as if he could not see her clearly. "Linda," he whispered. "Are you Linda?"

He could not see Fenton, but he thought the man was still standing behind him. This had to be done slowly, and it had to be done right, and he was fully aware that he was running the risk of having Fenton shoot him in the back.

"No, I ain't Linda," Mamie said. "You're all balled up, Talbot. You won't see Linda again. You can count on that, just like you can count on us getting the Wagon Wheel for ten per cent of what it's worth. By sunup she'll be so scared she'll sell for anything Cole offers her." She motioned to Fenton with her left hand. "I won't tell you again, Cole. Get over to the Wagon Wheel."

Grant started toward Mamie, lurching crazily. "You *are* Linda. You ain't fooling me."

He was close to her, eyes wide and staring. Frightened now, Mamie screamed: "Hit him on the head again!"

Grant toppled forward and sprawled across her, knocking the wheelchair over. He rolled onto the floor. He heard the roar of Fenton's gun, but he had not been hit. He scooped up his Colt that Mamie had dropped and lunged away from her as Fenton fired again, the bullet slapping into the floor inches from his hand. It took an instant to turn so that he faced Fenton, a precious instant that gave the man time to fire again, but Fenton was rattled and his shot went wild.

Grant pulled trigger and came up onto his feet. He shot again, then a third time, the room filled with the hammering explosions. Fenton fell to his knees, then to the floor. Grant did not shoot again. He stood there, watching Fenton crawl across the room to Mamie, leaving a bloody trail behind him.

Slowly Grant stepped back, holding his gun on Fenton. Mamie was a motionless, grotesque heap on the floor. Then Grant realized what had happened. Fenton's first bullet had killed her.

Fenton reached her and took her hand. He said: "I killed my sister." Turning, he looked at Grant, his long hair disheveled, some of it stringing down over his stricken, gray face. "I loved her. She could always make me do what she wanted me to. I . . . I didn't mean. . . ." The last of his strength fled. His head dropped to the floor, and he died that way, still gripping Mamie's hand.

The Wagon Wheel foreman walked out of the house, out of the room with its smell of death and powder smoke. He took a deep breath and, removing the empties, thumbed new loads into the cylinder of his gun. So Cole Fenton was Mamie Dolan's brother. These last few minutes had made a good many things clear.

Grant dropped his gun into his holster and ran to his horse. He was remembering about Bugeye and Gib Lane, about Piper and Mayer, and time was running out.

He swung into saddle and put his horse down the trail to

the creek. He had no idea of time, for he could not tell how long he had been unconscious. He splashed across the creek, seeing the pinpoint of light that marked the Wagon Wheel ranch house. For some reason he found reassurance in that light. Nothing had happened yet. There was still time. Perhaps it was not as late as he thought.

A call came to him from his right, a man's voice shouting for help, a note of urgency in it that could not be denied. For a moment Grant fought his indecision. It might be Curly Tell or young Kit Bellew, wounded by Piper or Mayer. The need to get to the Wagon Wheel was not great enough to make him go on without finding out who it was.

As he reined his buckskin off the road, he heard the call again. He found a man, lying in the grass not far above the creek. Stepping down, he knelt at the fellow's side and struck a match. It was Red Johnson. He was alive, but his face was pale, and his eyes were filled with the knowledge that death was at hand. He had been hit in the chest, the front of his shirt dark with a patch of dried blood.

"Grant," Red breathed. "I'm glad it's you. I heard a horse, and I was afraid you'd go on by."

Grant knew he couldn't stay. There was nothing he could do, but Red had his hand, gripping it tightly with the frantic desperation of one who knows he has only minutes left.

"Listen to me," Red whispered. "I never gave no thought to dying before, but I'm thinking now, and I've got to do one decent thing before I die. Rennie is. . . . You listening, Grant?"

"I'm listening."

"Rennie is Joe Dexter's daughter. You hear me?"

For a moment Grant was too shocked to answer. It was incredible; it was unbelievable, but a dying man would not lie.

Red's grip tightened on his hand. "Hear me, Grant?"

"I hear. Can you prove it?"

The grip relaxed. "She's got a birthmark between her shoulder blades. Always had it. Sharples will remember. She's got a locket with her mother's picture, too. Show it to Sharples." Red took a labored breath. "Bugeye shot me. He went to Lane's cabin and talked him into playing Mamie Dolan's game. Rennie was gone, he said. Where is she?"

"Wagon Wheel."

Red struggled for his breath again. "That's where she belongs. Funny how it goes. I kept Bugeye out of trouble so he could get the Wagon Wheel, when he married Rennie and settled down. Figured we'd move in when Rennie was eighteen, but I didn't figure on Joe getting married again. Didn't know what to do after that, but the Wagon Wheel still ought to go to Rennie. Bugeye turned out bad. Didn't give me a chance. Plugged me to get even for the lickings I gave him. Rennie's the one who's good. Funny, ain't it, Grant?"

"Yeah," Grant said. "Funny. Joe didn't know about her?"

"He had his suspicions, on account of Rennie looking so much like her mother, but he didn't have any way of knowing. He'd quiz me, and I'd laugh in his face. You see Rennie gets the Wagon Wheel, Grant!"

"I'll see to it."

XIV

Red was so silent for a minute that Grant thought he was gone. He struck another match. Red's eyes were open, and he was smiling as if an inner peace had come to him.

"Yeah, it's funny," he mumbled. "Bugeye's ma died. I was in love with Rennie's mother. Asked her to marry me. She said yes, then she ups and marries Joe. It was in Idaho. Joe didn't know. I was an outlaw. He was a big rancher. I hated him. Blamed him for me losing Rennie's mother. She ran away with another man after Rennie was born, but I still hated Joe."

Grant knew then why Joe had never wanted to talk about the woman whose picture was on the wall. He asked: "How'd you get Rennie?"

"Stole her. Hired some fellers on account of I was hiding out. Joe and Sharples was gone, when my men hit Joe's ranch. They killed some of the crew and got Joe's horses. Took five thousand, but I made 'em give it back to me. I've still got it. In the cabin under the floor. Get it for Rennie, Grant."

"I'll get it."

"We drifted around some. Then I got wind of Joe's leaving Idaho and settling here in the basin. When you're riding the owlhoot, you hear the leaves whisper. I brought my bunch in, and we settled in High Valley. We'd knock a bank over or a stage and high-tail back to the valley. We was safe long as Ollard let us alone. Got a lot of fun watching Joe ride up there just to look at Rennie, but he never said nothing to her about who she looked like, and I wouldn't tell him."

Red was silent again. Grant asked: "They're hitting the Wagon Wheel tonight?"

" 'Bout dawn," Red whispered. "Be more'n Bugeye and Lane. Five or six. Bugeye wants to drill you for licking him the other night. Aims to take Rennie back. You take care of her, Grant. She likes you. Make you a good wife." Red was panting now. "Saint Peter's going to have one good mark to

121

put in the book . . . for . . . me."

The sound of his breathing ceased. When Grant struck another match, he saw that Red was gone. He rose and moved to his horse. He stepped into the saddle with the first gray hint of dawn showing in the east. And it struck him that fate had had a strange way of bringing justice to the man who had stolen Joe Dexter's infant daughter.

Grant heard the thunder of hoofs coming in from the north, and he put his horse into a run. It came to him, then, with the cold wind needling his face, that Mamie had been wrong when she had told him he was in love with a ranch. Linda had been wrong, too, in saying he was not a man who wanted what other men wanted. He was in love with Rennie Johnson. No, Rennie Dexter.

When Grant had been a boy, he'd had a nightmare he had never forgotten. He was trapped in a room; there was no escape, and the walls were falling in on him. Now it came back to him as he heard gunfire to the west, somewhere between him and the pasture where the steers were being held. The High Valley bunch was ahead of him. He could not beat them to the Wagon Wheel, and the terrible, helpless feeling that had possessed him when he'd had the nightmare was in him again.

The light in the ranch house went out. Grant heard Bugeye's shout.

"Come out of there, Rennie! Fetch the Dexter woman with you. We're going to burn every damn' building."

A rifle cracked from the living room. Grant saw the twinkling ribbon of flame. Rennie screamed defiantly: "Come and get us!"

In the pale light Grant could make out the milling horses in front of the house. The gunfire from the west was closer now. Bugeye and Lane and the others dismounted and ran toward the front door. A Winchester cracked, and the high screech of a man, mortally hit, rode the wind.

Someone yelled: "It's Talbot!"

Grant pulled up and swung down, knowing he would shoot straighter on his feet than on a horse that might be boogered by gunfire. Colt in hand, he raced toward the cluster of men.

Bugeye yelled: "He's my meat!"

Grant held his fire. He saw the burst of powder flame from Bugeye's gun as the others pounded at the barred door. Inside, someone was firing a rifle. Grant came on as Bugeye let go with another shot, the slug burning along Grant's ribs like the passage of a white-hot poker.

Riders were coming in from the west. Grant did not look to see who they were. They might be more of the High Valley bunch, or they might be Piper and Mayer. In either case, Grant would be caught in a crossfire. He was close enough now to make his shots count. The door had been slashed open, and again a man screamed. The Winchester inside was still working.

Grant fired from the hip as Bugeye threw a third shot that missed by inches. Bugeye toppled back against the wall, and his feet went out from under him like a clumsy pup's on a sheet of ice. Grant let go again, and Bugeye spilled over sideward and lay still.

Gib Lane lay flat on his belly on the porch, his gun less than an inch from an outstretched hand. When Bugeye dropped, the rest of them broke for their horses. Dick Sharples's voice bawled: "Throw down your guns!"

One of the High Valley men wheeled and pitched a shot at Grant, and Grant knocked him off his feet with a slug in the chest. The two who were left had had enough. They threw up their hands as the Wagon Wheel crew pulled up in a whirling cloud of red dust, young Kit Bellew yelling: "We got Mayer and Piper, Grant. They tried to stampede the steers, but we held 'em off till Dick and the boys got there."

Grant stood motionless, his gun at his side, smoke twisting from the barrel. He felt a dull ache where Bugeye's bullet had hammered against a rib. He knew that blood was trickling down his side, but it didn't matter. The nightmare was over, and the walls had not fallen in on him.

Rennie was there, an arm around him. She cried: "Grant, Grant, are you all right?"

"Just lost some hide along my ribs." He looked down at her pale, anxious face, and he wondered why it had taken him so long to realize how he felt about her. "You ain't hurt?"

"Not a bit."

He swung to Sharples and the others who had ridden up. "Why didn't you stay here, Dick?"

"I didn't figure on so many riding in," Sharples answered. "We heard the shooting, and I knew damned well somebody was trying to get them steers to running." He looked at Rennie, grinning a little. "Anyhow, that there girl is worth ten ordinary men."

Then Grant noticed Rennie was wearing a red-flowered dress, one of Linda's that was too big for her. He said stupidly: "You've got a dress on."

"That's right," she said. "I have."

Sharples said: "Somebody else coming. Now who the hell could that be?"

"Don't make me no never mind," Kit Bellew bragged. "Hell, we licked this bunch. We can lick anybody."

"That'll be Marty Reem," Grant said. "Don't know who the other *hombre* is, but they ain't here for trouble."

They waited, facing the east that was aflame now with

the sunrise, and presently Reem and Sheriff Steve Ollard rode in. Looking at Ollard, a wild hatred for him rose in Grant. If the lawman had done his job, most of this trouble could have been averted.

"We've got a couple of prisoners, Steve," Grant said in a tough, flat voice. "Likewise some carcasses for you to take to the undertaker. You'll find two more in the Seven Bar Seven house, and you'll find Red Johnson's body on this side of the creek. You're too damned late as usual."

"Red," Rennie breathed. "He . . . he's dead?"

"Bugeye shot him," Grant said. "I don't know how he was able to ride as far as he did, but he wanted to tell me who you were. You're Joe's girl."

"I know," she whispered. "Sharples looked at the picture in my locket. It's just like the picture on the wall. He said it was my mother. And he knew about the birthmark on my back."

"Linda know?"

Rennie nodded. "She knows."

Ollard shifted uncomfortably in his saddle. "You don't need to lay the blame on me."

Grant turned from Rennie, and he laid his tongue on the sheriff like a whip. "You've been riding along mighty easy, Steve, on account of what Joe done, but you're lazy, and you're no good. Now are you turning your star in, or do I take it away from you?"

Outraged, Ollard bawled: "Who do you think you are? Joe Dexter?"

"Maybe," Grant said. "I told you in town that the thing to do was to make the Wagon Wheel stand for everything Joe made it stand for. That's what I aim to do."

"Take your prisoners, Steve," Marty Reem said. "I think the boy means what he says."

"I ain't turning my star in," Ollard snapped. "I'm going to High Valley, and I'll clean it out."

"You're a little slow again," Grant said, "but you might still find some men the law wants. Come spring, the Wagon Wheel will be using High Valley for summer range. You can spread the word around." He motioned to Sharples. "Hitch up the wagon and tote these carcasses into town. Come in, Marty."

Turning, Grant walked into the house, his right hand holding Rennie's. He asked: "Where's Linda?"

"Under her bed." Rennie laughed. "I never saw anybody as scared as she is."

The light inside the house was thin. Grant lighted a lamp and turned to Marty. "How did you make out?"

The storekeeper grinned. "Fine. I borrowed ten thousand from Ira. That enough?"

"Plenty. We won't need much of it, except what it takes to get Linda off our necks, and we'll pay that back *pronto*."

Picking up the lamp, he went into Linda's bedroom. He got down on his knees and looked under the bed. He said: "Come out of there."

"I can't," Linda whispered. "I can't move."

"You'll move," he said. Taking her by the arm, he pulled her out from the under the bed and yanked her to her feet. "Fenton's dead. Mamie was his sister. They were figuring on scaring you into taking a small price for the Wagon Wheel. They didn't know about Rennie."

Linda swayed uncertainly, and for a moment Grant thought she was going to faint. She sat down on the bed, looking at Rennie and Marty Reem, and she said with a burst of defiance: "The Wagon Wheel is still mine."

"You done anything to deserve it," Grant demanded, "crawling under a bed when the shooting started?"

"It's still mine," Linda said.

"If we went to law, you wouldn't have anything," Grant said, "but we don't want to take all that time. You'll take what we give you, or we'll throw you out of here, and you won't get anything."

"I don't want to be . . . ," Rennie began.

Grant motioned for her to be silent. "You're going into town with Marty," he said to Linda, "and he'll get a lawyer. When you sign everything over, Marty will give you five thousand, and then you be sure you're on the next stage out of the basin."

Linda lowered her eyes, the defiance flowing out of her. "All right, Grant."

Grant turned to Rennie. "I'm bleeding a little. Want to patch me up?"

"Of course," Rennie answered.

She followed him out of Linda's bedroom. When he reached the kitchen door, he looked back and saw that she had stopped to look at the picture on the wall. She asked: "Did Red say anything about my mother?"

He hesitated, not wanting her to know what Red had said. He asked: "Dick know anything about her?"

"He thinks she's dead."

"Yeah, she's dead," Grant said, relieved, and went on into the kitchen.

He waited until Rennie came in, wondering how he would say the one more thing that must be said. He took her hands, looking down at her fine-featured face. He said: "I'm sorry Joe didn't know about you. He'd have been proud of you, and he'd want you to stay here. The Wagon Wheel is yours. Me and the crew go with it. Mamie said I was in love with a ranch, but I'm in love with you. I didn't know until tonight. I mean, I've been thinking about the

Wagon Wheel and worrying about it. . . ."

"Grant, Grant!" she said. "You know I couldn't stay here without you."

"That's what I wanted to hear," he said. "It's all mixed up, you and me and the crew. Well, it's just that we all go together."

She looked at him for a moment, her dark eyes bright and expectant. She said: "You know, Grant, I've always been in love with you, but I didn't say it. I should have, because when I wanted to think of something nice, I thought about you."

He took her into his arms and kissed her. For that moment he forgot how tired he was; he forgot the steady, nagging ache in his side. Her lips were sweet and clinging under his; her arms were tight around him, and she was all fire and passion.

Red had been right. She would make a good wife.

Chumley's Gold

Prologue

Bill Chumley had never dreamed of helping rob a Durango bank until the evening his brothers rode in. He needed money, all right, but he had things going his way. His father had died a year ago and had willed the Circle C to him because he'd stayed home and worked while the older boys were raising hell all over the country. It wasn't much of a spread, the way it was tucked into a little valley above the old mining camp of Calamity, but it was his along with a few head of cattle and half a dozen horses. That was the important thing. They were his.

Just one fact was a burr under his saddle. He had a girl in Durango he wanted to marry so badly he could taste it, but he didn't have a decent house for her. Just a cabin with a dirt floor and no money to fix it up or add to it. He could barely scratch a living from the little spread, so when it came to raising money to make improvements, well, it was impossible unless he sold his cattle and that was no solution whatever.

Bill had considered riding down to Calamity and jumping Samuel Gerard, the banker, for a loan, but that meant slapping a mortgage on his outfit, and he couldn't take that risk. He had reached the point of being so boogery, worrying his problem around, that he was about out of his mind.

That's the way it was one evening in late June when his brothers showed up. He hadn't seen or heard of them for two years, and he didn't really give a damn about them one way or the other. They'd never been much on work; they'd abused him when he was little; and they'd given their pa trouble as long as he could remember. So when they rode off to see the world seven years ago, it was good riddance as far as Bill and his father were concerned. They'd been back a few times, but they were always bored after a few days and rode off again. That was all right with Bill and his pa, too.

When Bill saw them riding across the meadow between the house and the creek, he sat down on the end of the log trough beside the corrals and cursed. They were friendly enough, big, bearded men who carried rifles in the boots and .45s on their hips. They dismounted, shook hands, and asked about their pa. They didn't seem much surprised, when Bill told them he'd died a year before.

Rip, the oldest, asked: "You making out all right, kid?"

Bill was a week short of being twenty-one and, having done a man's work since he was twelve, didn't consider himself a kid. He held his resentment down as he said: "Tolerable." He didn't want them horning in on his plans and claiming part of the estate which didn't amount to much, anyhow.

The older Chumleys stripped gear off their horses, put them into the corral, and crossed the yard to where Bill sat on the trough. Ed said: "We've got a business deal to talk over with you, and then we'll be riding south to Mexico."

"We don't aim to ever come back," Rip said, "and you're sure as hell welcome to this hard-scrabble spread."

Bill was relieved to hear that, but at the same time he was wary of any deal his brothers had to offer. He couldn't remember a time when they had given him anything without getting more in return than they gave.

"I'm listening," said Bill.

"We've been hanging around Durango, looking the bank over," Rip said. "We never talked about it when Pa was alive, but we've knocked over a dozen banks, so we know what we're doing. Well, there's this little bank on a side street. Don't have nobody in it but the banker and one teller. We figger to hit it in broad daylight and be out of town before anybody knows what's happening."

"The sheriff's an old man," Ed added. "He couldn't get a posse together in an hour. We'll be on our way to hell and gone before that. He'll never get within ten miles of us. We figger there's about twenty thousand dollars in the safe. We've never spotted an easier layout."

"The truth is, we need your help," Rip said. "We've had the experience, but we're willing to split the *dinero* three ways because we need a third man for it to work right. We had a partner, but he got . . . he ain't with us no more."

Probably caught a slug in the brisket, Bill thought. He shook his head. "Not me. I've got a different notion about what I want my life to be than you fellows have."

Rip looked around the yard, out across the meadow at the grass that was getting a good start, at the cabin and the shed with its sagging roof. He said: "You've sure got a sorry spread, son. Get smart. You'd make six, seven thousand dollars for a couple of days' work. You could use it to fix this place up and buy some good stock. Pa could never fix it up, and it looks like you can't, either."

Bill shook his head again. "I've got a girl I'm gonna marry, and I sure don't figger on her having a jail bird for a husband. I'll get along."

They glared at him for a moment, looking as if they wanted to beat him into going along with their plans, but finally they looked away. They walked around for a time, built and lit cigarettes as if trying to think of something that would change Bill's mind, then Rip dug out an envelope from his back pocket.

"We stopped in town and asked for your mail," Rip said. "This is all there was."

When he looked at the handwriting, his heart took an unexpected leap. It was from Ann Larsen. He couldn't mistake her beautiful, Spencerian handwriting.

He tore it open and scanned the note quickly. She told him how much she loved him, how much she missed him, and then his heart pounded harder than ever. She wrote:

We can't put our marriage off any longer, darling. I'll be having your baby in about six months. I can live in your cabin. We can't wait for the improvements you want to make. Please come and get me right away.

He crumpled the sheet of paper and stuffed it into his pocket. He asked: "What do you want me to do?"

"I'll be damned," Rip said, surprised. "That letter must have been filled with giant powder."

"We'd better take him up on it before he changes his mind," Ed said. "There's two things we need you for. You'll hold the horses while we're in the bank. The other thing is we've got to have fresh horses. We'll leave ours in a corral on top of Morgan Pass. We spotted one up there that ain't being used. We'll split the money as soon as we get back to Morgan Pass. You go on home, and Rip and me'll head for Mexico."

It sounded good, too good, but Bill knew he'd have to watch his back. They were being mighty considerate and polite right now, but once they were in the clear, they'd shoot him in the back and take all the money. He had known them too well and too long ever to doubt their intentions. Being brothers had nothing to do with it.

He nodded, and said: "It'll work."

"Like taking candy from a baby," Ed said. "How about something to eat?"

"Sure," said Bill, and led the way into the cabin.

They rose before dawn, ate a quick breakfast, and headed out before the sun was anything more than a faint promise in the east. They led two of Bill's horses, and, when they reached Morgan Pass shortly before noon, the older Chumley brothers moved their saddles to the horses they had been leading and turned the other two into the corral.

They clattered across the bridge that spanned Las Animas, turned up a side street that paralleled Main Street, then rounded a corner that brought them directly in front of the bank that was their target.

Dismounting, they pulled masks over the lower part of their faces and pulled down their hats. Rip said: "Just hang onto the reins till we come out. Won't take us long. If anything goes wrong, start shooting." They entered the bank.

Even though the afternoon was a cool one, sweat broke through Bill's skin as he took the reins. He hadn't pictured how it would be, but now he was here, and he was scared clear down to his boot heels. It would be a hell of a note, if he wound up in the state pen while Ann had their baby. How would she make out? She had no parents and had been making her own way since she was fourteen by working in people's homes or doing washing.

The minutes dragged. It seemed to Bill that his brothers were taking a hell of a long time in the bank. He was having trouble breathing, and the sweat was pouring down his face when he glanced toward Main Street where people had been moving back and forth. At that moment the whole deal went sour. A man stopped dead still in the middle of the intersection and stared.

The man was Fred Murray from Calamity. Bill had known Fred since the time he could walk. He didn't move or yell. Not then. Fred couldn't see worth a damn, and with his Stetson pulled low and his neckerchief pulled up over his chin, Bill figured he wouldn't be recognized at this distance.

Nor would Bill have turned a hand, if Fred hadn't caught on to what was happening and yelled: "The bank's being robbed!" Bill lost his head the instant he heard the man's yell. He pulled his gun and started shooting at the man, but Fred started running out of the intersection and had reached the corner of a building before Bill got off his shot.

The next second Rip and Ed ran out of the building, each holding a gunnysack. Ed never made it. Standing in the doorway, the banker cut loose with a shotgun and blew off the top of Ed's head. Rip wheeled and killed the banker with one shot, grabbed the gunnysack out of Ed's slack fingers, and climbed aboard his horse, yelling: "Move."

For an instant Bill froze, then he came out of it and swung into the saddle as the second man in the bank stepped into the doorway and fired. Rip turned in his saddle and gunned the teller down, then dug in the steel, and roared into the street they had used to enter town, Bill three jumps behind him.

There was no pursuit, just as Rip and Ed had said there wouldn't be. At least none that they were aware of, and they kept glancing back to see if there was a posse on their tails. Bill thought it was going to be all right, that Fred Murray hadn't recognized him and by now the posse would be milling around and not have any notion where they had gone.

For the first time Bill started taking good, deep breaths.

He did not realize that Rip had been hit until they were almost to the corral where they had left the horses. He was riding ahead, not thinking about why Rip had slowed down until he heard his brother groan. When he looked back, Rip was on the ground.

Bill reined up and dismounted. The front of Rip's shirt was soaked with blood. He lay there, his face ashen, the gunnysacks in the dirt beside him. He breathed: "The son-of-a-bitch got me. We should have plugged both of 'em before we left the bank." He closed his eyes, and Bill, kneeling beside him, thought he was dead. A moment later Rip opened his eyes and whispered: "Fix the old place up, kid. It's all yours." Then he was gone. Bill picked up his wrist and felt for a pulse, but there wasn't the slightest flicker of life.

For a moment Bill couldn't think straight, a crazy picture of bars and locks and cells forming in his mind, then he rose, knowing he had to get out of there. He picked up both sacks and tied them behind his saddle. They were heavy, and, although he had never held more than a few dollars in his hand at any one time, he knew the sacks held a lot of money. He stripped Rip's horse of the saddle, then opened the corral gate, and chased the two animals out of the enclosure.

For a moment he stared at his brother's body, thinking it should be buried, but he also thought there was a chance the posse would ride over the hill to the east and be right on him. He couldn't take the risk. It wasn't likely that anybody in the posse would identify Rip as a Chumley. He had been out of the country too long.

He mounted and rode on toward Calamity, more worried than he wanted to admit to himself. He cursed his brothers for bringing him into the robbery. He'd been happy. He would have brought Ann to his cabin, and they would have made out. He'd never been one to try for easy money the way his brothers had. He'd liked to work, and he had never been impatient with his life until he had met Ann, or maybe even until he knew she was pregnant.

For a time as he rode, he let himself think back to the times he had been with the girl, the happiest days of his life. He had never been around girls, mostly because there weren't any in Calamity who had interested him. He'd gone to last summer's Fourth of July celebration in Durango and had met Ann at a dance. Life had never been the same after that.

He'd gone to see Ann as often as he could get away from the Circle C. He would never forget the last time he had been there, and Ann had taken the initiative and led him to her bed. He had his standards, and he had lived by them. One of them was to stay out of whorehouses, but that had nothing to do with what had happened in Ann's little house. What she had offered was an act of love, and he had taken it in that spirit.

They both wanted to get married, but Bill had kept putting it off, hoping that something would turn up and he could find the money to make the cabin comfortable for Ann. He had never given the possibility of having a baby a thought, but now that she was having one, they'd get married right away, if he survived today's business. He'd write her a short letter as he went through Calamity, so she'd know he was coming to get her in a few days.

He had slipped a stamped envelope, a piece of paper, and a stub of a pencil into his pocket before he'd left home. When he reached Calamity, fully dark by that time, he stepped into the post office long enough to scribble a note. Mailing it, he was glad that no one was around to see him who might answer the sheriff's questions, if a posse showed up here later on.

When he reached his cabin, he dropped the gunnysacks

on the table, took care of his horse, then stepped into the shed and picked up his shovel. He had thought about how he'd hide the money all the way down from Morgan Pass. He'd decided on a plan and as a part of it he had told Ann in the note where he planned to hide the money, just in case the posse did trail him here and he was caught or killed.

He lifted the heavy hearthstone from in front of the fireplace and started to dig. Anyone looking for the gold would probably think about burying it under the hearthstone, but he'd figured out a scheme that would fox them. He dug into the dirt for a good five feet until he struck several big rocks, poured most of the money into a Dutch oven, set the lid into place, then lowered the oven into the hole. The money was largely gold, but there was a good deal of silver and a number of large bills. The money he had left in the sack was silver dollars along with a few pieces of gold.

He had lifted several rocks to the cabin floor. Now he dropped the rocks on top of the oven — so anyone digging there would think he had stopped when he hit the rocks — then filled dirt in around the rocks. He packed this down as hard as he could, and, when he had it so hard that anyone would think this was the way it was originally, he laid the two gunnysacks on top of the packed dirt, and finally shoveled the rest of the dirt into the hole and leveled it off.

He replaced the hearthstone, remembering he hadn't eaten since early morning, but he was dog-tired and decided he needed sleep more than food. He took the shovel back to the shed, then returned, and carefully swept up all the loose dirt that was around the hearthstone. He barred the door and sprawled across the bed. He was asleep the instant he hit the mattress.

Hot morning sunshine was streaming through the

window, when he woke. For a time he lay motionless, so tired and stiff he didn't think he could move. He thought about the previous day and night, and worry began gnawing at him. That damned Fred Murray! If he hadn't been in Durango . . . ! But he had been, and, if he had recognized Bill, the posse would have been here before now.

Bill doubted the old man could have recognized him, given his bad eyesight. Probably no one would have recognized his brothers, either. Besides, he had a good reputation in Calamity. No one would believe he'd get involved in anything like a bank robbery. Yes, he was going to be all right. He'd ride to Durango in a day or two, marry Ann, and fetch her back to the cabin. They'd live this way for a while, then he'd begin to use the money slowly to make the cabin fit for Ann. By the time she had the baby, he'd have everything livable for her.

He was tempted to go back to sleep, but he was ravenously hungry, and the need to relieve himself was pressing. He rose, grimacing from the pain that shot through him as he walked to the window. He'd be a day or two getting over this, he thought.

At first, he glanced out of the window cautiously, then boldly as he studied the meadow in the front of the cabin, the willows along the north fork of Calamity Creek, and finally the timber that made a dark circle around the meadow. Nothing was stirring. It was all right, he told himself. A posse wouldn't hide. The men would have been hammering on his door the minute they got here and would have started questioning him a long time ago.

He opened the door and stepped out into the bright sunlight. The next second gunfire exploded from the corral, but Bill Chumley never heard it. He was killed instantly.

The deputy who led the posse — young Matt Clay — cursed like a wild man as they crossed to the cabin. "You

140

god-damned, killing bastards!" he raged. "I told you to hold your fire until we had a chance to talk."

"We know he done it," one of the men said defensively. "If we tried talking, he'd have gone back inside, and we'd have had to root him out. Some of us would have got killed."

"A bank robber and murderer don't deserve nothing better'n a slug," Fred Murray said virtuously, "and that's just what he got."

"If he'd had a trial," another added, "he'd probably have got clean off."

They reached the cabin, and Clay checked the body. "He's dead," he said. "If I was the sheriff, I'd arrest the bunch of you for murder."

"But you sure as hell won't," a man said, "knowing damned well the old man won't back you up."

One of the posse members had gone to the shed, found the shovel, and he came back, grinning. "From the looks of the shovel he's been doing some digging. I reckon we'll find the *dinero* around here somewhere."

"Maybe in the cabin," Murray said.

"Or the shed," another added.

They went into the cabin, looking around as the man with the shovel said: "Chances are it's under the hearth-stone. He'd think that was a safe place."

They lifted the big rock and in a matter of minutes had dug deep enough to find the two gunnysacks. They heard the clink of coins as the man with the shovel said: "I told you it'd be here."

They passed the sacks around, each looking inside, one of them saying: "That ain't worth five men getting killed for."

"Looks to me," another said, "that old man Rose was operating with mighty little cash."

"I'm glad I never put any of my money in his bank," one said. "I'd heard too much about his poker playing."

"Let's ride," Clay said in disgust.

They took Bill Chumley's body to Calamity where it was buried two days later. If it hadn't been for the money that had been found in Bill's cabin, no one in Calamity would have believed he was guilty.

I

Dan Larsen was saddling up with the rest of the Anchor crew when a deputy rode in on a lathered horse. Everyone stood motionless and expectant as the lawman reined up beside Dan. He said: "The sheriff wants to see you *pronto*."

"Now just hold on," the foreman interrupted angrily. "We're moving a bunch of beef and I need. . . ."

"Nothing to hold up on," the deputy said. "The sheriff's your boss, ain't he? Anchor belongs to him, don't it? You gonna send me back to town telling him you wouldn't obey his order?"

"Oh, hell," the foreman said. "I reckon he don't know we're short-handed, with Stub laid up for a week." He scratched his head. "I tell you what. You take Dan's place, and I'll let him go. Not that you can take his place, but you might be of some help."

The deputy swore, glared at the foreman, then said: "Dan, tell Matt he's got an ornery, mossy-back, bull-headed son for a ramrod, but I'll do it just to keep him quiet. You best bust the breeze getting to town."

"What happened?"

"Matt can tell you," the deputy answered. "Now, get moving."

Dan swung into the saddle and pointed his horse west. This wasn't like Matt Clay. Dan had worked for the sheriff since he'd been a button, first helping the cook, then doing general chores around the ranch, and finally for several years he'd been cowboying and was considered a top hand. No, Matt wasn't inclined to give him a holiday just for the sake of a holiday.

Maybe something had happened to his mother, Dan thought, but that didn't seem likely. He'd been home Sunday, and she'd been in good spirits. She was a comparatively young woman, not yet forty, but she had worked hard all her life. That could be it. Matt would know, if anything had gone wrong. He'd been more than a friend to her as long as Dan could remember. He was a good man, maybe a little overbearing at times but he had a tender side. That was probably it, Dan decided. She'd taken sick and wanted to see him.

An hour later he tied in front of the courthouse and strode along the boardwalk and on into the building. He found Matt sitting at his desk, his head in his hands, and that, Dan thought, was even more ominous than being sent for in the middle of the week.

Matt Clay wasn't aware that Dan had come in until he said: "I'm here, Matt."

The sheriff straightened up and sat back in his chair. He said: "Sit down, Dan."

Then Dan knew the worst had happened. Clay had been crying. Dan didn't think the sheriff would ever cry at anything or for anybody, but if he did, it would be over Ann Larsen.

"Your mother died last night, Dan." Clay pulled a ban-

143

danna out of his pocket and wiped his eyes, then blew his nose. "By God, Dan, it just don't seem possible she's gone. She was young. It just ain't right. My bitch of a wife has been sick since our wedding night and never lets me forget it, but she'll outlive me. Now Ann, who was still young and pretty and with half a lifetime in front of her, is gone."

Dan discovered he was sitting in a chair in front of Clay's desk. He didn't know how he got there. He did not remember when he had sat down. In that dull, sickening moment he didn't know anything except the one terrible fact that his mother was no longer living. He had never given a thought to her dying. Dying was for old people.

"Doc says she had a heart attack," Clay went on. "She got sick about midnight. Terrible chest pains. She got over to Miz Caller's house and woke her up, and Miz Caller put her to bed and got the doctor. Ann asked for you, but they sent for me. I wanted to be there with her, and I didn't see no use to get you up in the middle of the night. She was unconscious when I got there, but I sat beside her and held her hand. We never wanted folks to know about us, though I reckon some like Miz Caller did. I knew your mother was dying, and I didn't give a damn who knew."

Clay rose and shoved the bandanna back into his pocket. "She's down at Marcy's Funeral Home, if you want to see her."

"No," Dan said. "Not now."

Clay nodded. "I savvy that. Well, you'd best go home and go through your mother's things. I don't know what you aim to do. I don't figger there's any market for her clothes and personal things that you won't want to keep, but if you want to sell the house and furniture, I'll buy 'em from you. I can use the house for a rental. You can decide that later. I just thought you wouldn't want to live here in town by yourself."

144

Dan couldn't think straight, but he did know he didn't want to live in Durango. He'd wanted to leave before this, but he knew how much his mother had depended on him, so he hadn't done anything more than dream about how the rest of the world looked.

He got to his feet and suddenly found the room spinning around and around in front of him. He gripped the back of the chair until the dizzy spell was over. It was the first time in his life that anything had happened that was truly terrible, and this was.

"No," Dan heard himself say in a voice that did not sound like his, "I don't want to live here."

"I've got some things to say that maybe I should have said a long time ago," Clay told him. "I don't want to say 'em here because somebody might walk in on us, so I'll come over later to your place."

Clay walked around the desk and put an arm across Dan's shoulders, the first time in Dan's memory that he had ever made an affectionate gesture. "By God, son, this is the worst thing that could have happened to either one of us."

Dan nodded and, turning, walked out of the sheriff's office. His mother had never worn a wedding ring. He had never known who his father was, but he had always suspected it was Matt Clay. When he'd asked his mother about his father, she would say vaguely: "He's been gone a long time. He never lived around here, and he wasn't anybody you'd know. The only thing I can tell you is that he was a brave and good man."

He rode the five blocks to his home, wondering if his mother had lied about his father, that it might very well have been Matt Clay and she had not wanted him to know. He had not raised the question for a long time, knowing she did not want to tell him anything more than she had, and,

145

now that he was twenty-one, he had been mature enough to respect her feelings. In any case, Matt Clay had been as near a father as a man could be who had carefully kept his relationship with Ann Larsen a secret in his community.

Dan put his horse in the shed back of the house and off-saddled. He walked up the path to the back door, past the garden his mother had carefully tended, past the lilac bush whose blossoms had come and gone, and opened the screen door. He paused a moment, looking at the tub and copper boiler and the old washing machine that he'd operated for what had seemed hours at a time when he was not in school.

His mother had made their living doing washing or house cleaning for people who could afford those services, and he remembered with regret that too often he had been sullen about helping when he had wanted to go outside to play ball or go fishing.

He opened the back door and went into the house. It looked exactly as it had last Sunday, everything in order and everything clean. She had always been a good housekeeper, a good mother, and she would have made a hell of a good wife for Matt Clay.

He walked slowly through the living room and into the bedroom that had been his when he'd been home. His mother had always slept on a cot in the living room, but once he was out of school and working on Matt Clay's spread, she had taken the bedroom.

The bed had been made up by someone, probably Mrs. Caller who lived next door and had been a good neighbor as long as Dan could remember. For a moment he stood staring at the bed, wishing his mother could have died here instead of in Mrs. Caller's house.

Suddenly the waves of emotion that were washing

146

through him were too much, and he sprawled across the bed. He began to cry, the first time since he'd been a small boy. He had no control; the sobs were body-shaking, and he knew he was making a strange noise that did not sound like any noise he had ever made. It lasted a long time, but he was over it when Matt came. He rose and went into the front room, when he heard the front screen door bang shut.

Matt looked at him gravely and nodded. He said: "I'm glad you could cry. I would have exploded, if I hadn't, and, all the time I was doing it, I wondered what the voters of La Plata County would have thought if they had seen their tough old son-of-a-bitch of a sheriff crying like a two-year-old."

Dan would have smiled at any other time, but today he went into the kitchen, grim-faced and sick of heart. Filling a basin with water, he washed his face. He dried it with the towel that hung on the wall and returned to the front room. Matt was sitting in a rocker near the open front door. Dan dropped down onto the ancient leather couch.

"What do you want to say, Matt?" Dan asked. "I can't go through her things. I just don't feel like it."

"No hurry," Clay said. "There's a little silver box in your mother's bureau that has a letter in it for you. She told me sometime back, so I could tell you if anything happened to her. I guess she had a notion that this might hit her. Maybe you'd better read it first. I'll come back later this afternoon."

Dan nodded. "What about the funeral? I don't know anything about things like that."

"I'll take care of everything," Clay said.

"How soon can we have it?"

"This is Wednesday," Clay said. "I guess about Friday."

"Good," Dan said. "I don't know if you'll understand,

Matt, but I want to get out of here."

"I savvy, all right," Clay said, "but it will take a little time. You don't want to leave with any strings dangling."

"No," Dan agreed. "I sure as hell don't. It's not that I haven't been happy here, and I appreciate all you've done for me and Mom, but I hear there's a big world out there. I just want to see what it looks like."

"I felt the same way, when I was your age," Clay said, and left the house.

Dan returned to the bedroom and pulled open the top drawer. It was filled with neatly folded clothes, but the second drawer held the box along with an assortment of toys that Dan had used as a boy: a sack of marbles, a badly scuffed baseball, a top, a number of colored picture books, and other odds and ends. He'd no idea she had kept these things.

He set the silver box on top of the bureau and opened it. She had stored a few keepsakes here: a pressed violet, a Valentine that said **with love from Bill,** and a lace handkerchief with a yellowed piece of paper pinned to one corner that said **from Bill for Christmas**. He frowned, trying to think who Bill might be, and failed. It had to be someone she had known before he was born, or at least when he was very small.

The letter Clay had mentioned was folded in the bottom of the box. He opened it and saw that another sheet of paper was folded inside the first. The letter from his mother was written in ink on a piece of the stationery he had given her three years before for Christmas; the other letter was written with pencil on a sheet of cheap paper torn from a schoolboy's tablet. The paper was yellow and brittle with age and cracked in several places, as he unfolded it.

He picked up his mother's letter first, knowing she would want it read in that order.

Dear Dan,

I have often wanted to tell you who your father was, but I never found the right moment, or perhaps I never found the courage. I hope you will not think I am a bad woman as some people in this town do. I make no apologies for my sin, if that's what it was, and I know it would have been considered a sin in the days of THE SCARLET LETTER, but I thought people might be more forgiving. Perhaps they are. At least, almost everyone has forgotten by now.

Your father's name was Bill Chumley. You were conceived in an act of love because it seemed impossible to be married right then. When I found you were on the way, I wrote to Bill about it. He was going to come right away and marry me, but he was killed before he could.

Please do not hold it against him that he helped hold up a bank. What he did was wrong, but I know he did it because he wanted to make his little ranch more comfortable for me to come to. God forgive both of us for our mistakes, and I hope you will, too.

I love you very much, and I'm proud of you. You have grown up into a fine man. The doctor told me my heart might go. I didn't want to worry you or Matt, so I haven't told either one of you, but I am writing this letter so you will know about your father if I die suddenly.

Mom

Bill Chumley! Dan stared at the letter a long time. He had heard of the man, but he couldn't remember much about him except that he had helped rob a bank here in

Durango years ago, but he had always wondered how much was fact, and how much was legend. Matt would know. He'd ask him, when he returned.

Dan picked up the second sheet of paper very carefully because it threatened to fall apart in his hands. It was hard to read. Some of the words were smudged, and the handwriting was a scrawl that was hard to decipher, but he finally made it out.

Dear an

i am coming to marry you right away i got the money to fix the place i had nothing to do with killing the men in the bank. my brother rip done that i will berry the money in my cabin real deep under the big rock in the fireplace i want you to have it if i get killed or caught

Bill

Dan laid the letter on the bureau and sat down on the edge of the bed. So Bill Chumley, a bank robber, was his father, a man who had never married his mother, and yet she said he was a good and brave man. He wondered how she arrived at that judgment, but he could not find in himself a sense of condemnation for either of them. He might have done the same thing, if he had been in either of their places.

One thing he did know. His mother had been a fine and good woman who had always loved him, and, if there was any fault, it was on the part of the people who condemned her. He wasn't that sure about Bill Chumley. If he remembered right, Chumley had lived in Calamity, a booming mining camp at one time, but it was close to a ghost town now. He would find out, if he could, just what kind of a man Bill Chumley had been.

II

On the morning after the funeral, Dan walked from his house to Judge Philip Wren's office on Main Street to meet Matt Clay. He was tired. He had slept very little since he had been told of his mother's death. He had not asked anyone about Bill Chumley, but the young bank robber had been on his mind ever since he'd read the two letters that his mother had left for him to read. He had to find out all he could about the man who had been his father, and Calamity would be the place to go.

Matt Clay had come to Dan's house several times, but the sheriff had never talked to him as he had said he was going to. Dan sensed that Clay felt much the way he did, that time was standing still, that the bottom had dropped out of his life, but one thing was different with the sheriff. He had to stay here whether there was any meaning to his life or not, but Dan knew he could not get a hold on himself or his destiny until he was on his way out of Durango.

Clay was waiting in the judge's office when Dan arrived. The judge rose and shook hands with Dan and motioned to a chair as Dan nodded at Clay. Judge Wren was an old man, one of the first settlers in Durango, and for a short time had actually served as judge, but the title by which he was generally known was given more as a compliment than something he had earned. Wren looked and carried himself like a judge; he was big, white-haired, dignified, and majestic.

"I want to extend my sympathy, Dan, for the loss of your mother," Wren said. "I knew her quite well. I had done some legal work for her, and she often worked in our house. She was, in every way, a fine woman."

Dan nodded, knowing very well that these compliments had seldom been given his mother during her lifetime, that Mrs. Wren was one of the worst gossips in Durango and had been one of many who had branded Ann Larsen as a loose woman, and still she had hired her because his mother had been honest and worked hard. But all of that could rest as far as Dan was concerned.

"Now, then," Wren said, "Matt tells me you are selling your mother's house to him for five hundred dollars. That correct?" Dan nodded, and the judge went on. "Also that there is a small amount of money in a savings account in the First National that will go to you inasmuch as you are the only heir."

"I found the bank book in my mother's things," Dan said. "It's a little over nine hundred dollars."

"Quite so," the judge nodded. "Also the sheriff tells me you will be leaving the country soon. I hate to see that, Dan. You are the kind of young man who could help shape our town and county in the right direction."

"I've got to go, Judge," Dan said.

"I understand," the judge nodded. "I would not under any circumstances try to change your mind. However, I venture to say that if you travel and work all over the West, you will return after you've looked other places over."

"Maybe," Dan said, and let it go at that. At least, the judge was telling him he would have a place here even if everyone knew he was bastard. Still, folks did know it, some talked about it, and he would be aware of it. Although it had never been a real problem to him, he had often sensed that it was a topic of conversation behind his back.

The judge cleared his throat, then said: "Of course, you

152

want the estate settled and the money that is coming to you. However, it will take time, and you will have to send me your address when you situate somewhere. I will communicate with you, and, as soon as the estate is settled, I will forward the money you have coming after I subtract my fee which will not be exorbitant. I will mail the papers you have to sign, and you will have to get them notarized wherever you are. That, of course, should be no problem. Now, is there anything else?"

Dan hesitated, not wanting them to have any reason to suspect there had been anything between Bill Chumley and his mother, but he doubted that either of them knew about that relationship. He had never even heard the Chumley name mentioned by his mother or Clay, and, since Bill Chumley had never lived in Durango, probably no one had ever seen them together.

"I'm curious about a bank robbery that happened here years ago," Dan said. "I don't remember hearing much about it, but I found some old newspapers in our house, and one of them mentioned a robbery by the Chumley gang."

Wren laughed softly. "I remember it, all right. So does Matt. There really wasn't a Chumley gang, just two brothers who were small-time crooks and a younger brother who had been a decent, law-abiding citizen. How he ever got involved is more than I know. Anyhow, they killed the owner of the bank and his teller, but two of them were killed. The youngest one got away with the bank's money, then he was killed by the posse. Matt was there. He can tell you about it."

"What I wanted to know was what happened to the money," Dan said. "If it was buried on the Chumley property, and I guessed it might be, I thought I'd try to find it."

"Oh, hell." The judge dismissed it with a wave of his hand as if it were ridiculous. "The posse recovered the money. It was in gunny sacks under the hearthstone of the Chumley cabin. There wasn't much . . . three, four thousand dollars . . . and some folks tried to say there had to be more, that the posse didn't find all of it, but I think that's all there was. You see, I knew old Simon Wells who owned the bank. He was a poker player. I've seen him lose several hundred dollars in one night. I'm convinced he was running that bank with mighty little cash on hand. He'd gambled most of it away. If it hadn't been for the robbery, he'd have gone under in a little while."

"Suppose more was found?" Dan asked. "Who would it go to?"

The judge shrugged. "Finders keepers, I guess. The money that was found was returned to the depositors, about ten cents on the dollar, if I remember right. The bank burned not long after the robbery, and all the records went up in smoke." The judge spread his hands. "We don't have the slightest idea who the depositors were or how much each had in the bank. But then, if I was to find it, I'd keep my mouth shut just to avoid a potful of trouble. A thousand people would come running with their hands out, and I wouldn't believe any of them."

"Thanks, Judge. I was curious. If I find it, I won't open my mouth." Dan rose. "You busy, Matt?"

"Not very," Clay said. "I'll walk to your house with you and get the keys. I guess you've got 'em."

"Hanging on the wall by the back door," Dan said. "Mom never used them."

"I'll lock the house up until I rent it," Clay said. "There's always some son-of-a-bitch in town who knows about a death and tries to steal what he can."

Dan walked to the door of the office. Just as he reached it, the judge asked: "Dan, why were you interested in the Chumley robbery?"

"I didn't want to get too far from here until Mom's estate was settled," Dan answered. "Matt already told me it would take some time. Treasure hunting has always interested me. I thought I'd ride up to Calamity and nose around."

"Pretty country up there," Wren said. "You'll get more out of the scenery than you will treasure."

"Then maybe I'll go fishing," Dan said. "I guess I just don't want to take a job for a while."

Wren nodded approvingly. "Now that is a good idea. I've heard the fishing is real good up there." As Dan opened the door and stepped into the hall, the judge added: "You'll be hearing from me."

"I'll expect to," Dan said, and walked out into the hall, Clay right behind him.

As they turned toward Dan's house, Clay said: "About that robbery. I was a young deputy then, working under an old man who was fat and lazy and didn't want to do anything but draw the sheriff's salary. I was out of town, when the robbery took place. The sheriff couldn't seem to get a posse together. By the time I did, two of the Chumleys . . . young Bill and his brother Rip . . . were away to hell and gone. The third one was lying dead in front of the bank.

"We wouldn't have known who done it if it hadn't been for a Calamity man who had come to Durango to get his teeth fixed. There wasn't no dentist in Calamity. He saw what was happening and gave the alarm. He recognized the Chumley horses, so he joined the posse, and we lit out for the Chumley ranch, figuring that young Bill would head for home.

155

"We figured right. We got there before daylight and saw that his horse was in the corral, so we waited for him to show his face. I'd told the posse to hold their fire, but they didn't, damn 'em. I'll never forgive myself for what happened, but I was new to the job and didn't expect them to start shooting the instant the boy poked his head out of the cabin, but that's what they done. I never had a chance to question him. The part that's hard for me to savvy is that, when we took the body to Calamity to be buried, nobody could believe he'd had a part in a bank robbery. He was that well thought of in Calamity."

"He must have been a purty decent gent," Dan said.

"Yeah, I reckon so," Clay agreed. "His pa was, too. He'd been dead for a year or so, but folks in Calamity spoke well of him and Bill, and said the older boys were just no damn' good. I reckon they talked Bill into trying for some quick money, but how they did it only Bill in heaven knows."

Dan was silent the rest of the way to his house, but he was thinking that Clay was wrong about what he'd just said. Ann Larsen knew, and she was in heaven no matter where Bill had gone. When they reached the house, Dan led the way into the front room, saying: "Sit down, Matt. I'll get the keys."

He was back a moment later and handed two keys to Clay.

"I guess the house is yours now."

Clay shook his head. "Not till you've stayed as long as you want to stay. Actually it belongs to you until the estate is settled. When you have the house in your name and sign the papers that Wren will send you, then I'll mail you a check for the five hundred dollars."

"Meanwhile, it's up to you to look after it," Dan said. "I'm leaving sometime today. I'll sack up some grub and camp somewhere between here and Calamity. Anything that's here is yours, but I want you to get rid of Mom's things before you rent it."

Clay nodded. "I'll gather up her dresses and such and give 'em to the preacher. He always knows people who don't have the clothes they need, and your mom dressed well for a woman who didn't have much money. She always bought good material and was a fine seamstress."

He cleared his throat. "Dan, I've kept putting off saying what I've been wanting to say ever since your ma died. I have always felt guilty because I didn't do more for her. She meant everything to me, but I couldn't marry her as much as I wanted to because I couldn't divorce my wife.

"I'm not sure if you can savvy that or not, but I would have been run out of Durango if I had. You know, divorcing a sick and helpless woman who couldn't afford to take care of herself . . . ? Ann understood, and she also understood that I couldn't support two houses on my salary. She kept on working, and I'd give her what money I could, and I reckon most of it went to buy clothes for you."

He wiped a hand across his face as if somehow he could find forgiveness for not taking better care of Ann Larsen. "I knew your mother first when she worked for us. She was pregnant then, but we didn't know it. When she began to show, my wife got very virtuous and fired her. I realized I loved her by the time she left, and I've never stopped. I saw to it that she had a good doctor and enough to eat during the time before you were born and afterwards until she was able to go back to work. Miz Caller was real good to look after her, and she kept you during the day when Ann was working. In all those years before you started making money, she never complained. Not one word."

Suddenly Clay got up and walked to a window, giving his back to Dan. For a few seconds his body shook with sobs.

He wiped his eyes with his bandanna and turned to face Dan. "I'm sorry, son. Sometimes when I think of what's ahead for me, trying to live with my bitch of a wife, and without your mother's love, I just don't think I can make it."

"You will," Dan said. "So will I."

"I reckon," Clay said, "though right now I don't see how."

For a moment he stood looking at Dan, then he extended a hand. "God, son, I'm going to miss you."

"I'll miss you, too," Dan said. As Clay walked to the door, Dan motioned for him to wait. "Before you go, I wanted to ask about the Chumley Ranch. I'd like to buy it, if it's cheap enough. How much land did he own?"

"A quarter section several miles up the creek from town," Clay answered. "It's gone back to the county. Nobody wants it. They'll be so glad to have somebody paying taxes on it that you can buy it for a song and sing it yourself. You got cash on hand?"

"A little," Dan said. "I'll stop in at the courthouse and see what I can do before I leave."

"I'll advance you the five hundred dollars, or any part of it that you need, if you find you don't have enough," Clay said. "One thing about that Calamity country that will make it tough for you. Old man Apple owned Wineglass, the biggest spread in Calamity Basin. You remember him?"

Dan nodded, remembering the red-headed, feisty little man who had been a good friend of Clay's and had often spent time on Clay's Anchor when he came to town.

"He sold it about a year ago to a man named Dutch Dorfman. He is a genuine, old-fashioned son-of-a-bitch, the kind of man who don't think our laws have anything to do with him. He would have done fine years ago, when the country was being settled, but he's a problem now. I'm purty sure he's a horse thief, but I can't prove it. Your trouble will come if you try to work the Chumley place which you probably won't because there ain't nothing there no more. Dorfman claims all of the country west of town as his range, so he'll raise hell with you when he finds out you bought it."

Dan grinned. At that moment a good fight might be just the tonic he needed. He said: "Then I'll raise a little hell right back at him."

"Trouble is, you're alone and he's got a hardcase crew," Clay said. "He's just about the law in Calamity Basin. You want a deputy's badge?"

"Hell, no," Dan said. "That's the last thing I want."

"Well, keep an eye on him," Clay said.

"I'll do that," Dan said.

Clay hesitated, his gaze on Dan, then he wheeled and walked rapidly away. Dan, standing in the doorway, stared at his back until he turned the corner and disappeared. A strange and uncertain feeling took possession of Dan. He had seen his mother buried yesterday, and now Matt Clay was walking out of his life, the old life that was gone forever. His future would be different, and he wondered what it would be.

III

Dan struck out directly to the west, then swung to the north, riding at a leisurely pace because he was in no hurry to reach Calamity. He wanted a day or two of peace, to find again the serenity of spirit he had felt most of his life until that shocking moment that had set his world upside down, the shocking moment when Matt Clay had told him his mother was dead. Almost as bad was the moment when he read his mother's and Bill Chumley's letters and had discovered that his father had been a bank robber.

He had not been a mamma's boy. Ann Larsen had never held a tight rein on him as he had grown up; he'd been in his share of brawls and had done all of the foolhardy antics a normal boy does, but, as he had matured, he had gradually realized that his mother was having a hard time making a living for the two of them. He had always given her part of his wages, and he had come home as often as he could get away from Anchor.

Now, because of the suddenness of his mother's death, he felt as if he were adrift on a swift and dangerous river. He wanted some time by himself, to be alone and think, and perhaps discover the direction he wanted to go.

Finding the Chumley gold was not important, but it did seem important to see where his father had lived, to know more about the kind of man Bill Chumley had been. Anyone, he thought, could be forgiven for one mistake. Maybe holding up the bank had been the only serious mistake Bill Chumley had ever made.

Dan stopped in early evening beside a clear stream and staked his horse out in the tall grass, then gathered wood and built a fire. He dug a few worms and baited a hook and threw it into the stream. Within a matter of minutes he had caught three pan-size cutthroats. He cleaned the fish and fried them, made coffee, and with a few biscuits he had found in his mother's kitchen had a satisfying supper.

For a time he lay on his saddle blanket under a pine tree, his eyes on the starry sky, and let his mind drift back to his growing-up years. Most of all he thought about Matt Clay

160

and his relationship with his mother, a relationship he had not understood when he was small. He wasn't sure he understood it even now.

He used to wonder why Clay always came to see them after it was dark, why his mother would put him to bed early on those nights, and how, when he was older, he had realized what was happening and kept to himself when Clay and his mother were in the bedroom. Now he was glad that Clay had talked to him about his relationship with his mother. He did not doubt the big man's love for her.

Going back in his mind over those years, he was glad he had not been critical of his mother or Clay, glad that Clay had befriended him and given him a job. Although he had not been aware that Clay had given his mother money, he had often wondered how she had been able to buy his school clothes and to pay the taxes on the house. A good many things made sense now that he looked back on them, but that his father had been a bank robber was something he wished he hadn't learned. The opinions he had heard about Bill Chumley didn't help much. He had to know more about him. If he could find a job in or around Calamity, he'd stay a while, he'd find out more about what people thought of Chumley, and he might even take time to hunt for the gold.

It was not until he was in the saddle the following morning that he remembered what Matt Clay had said about Dutch Dorfman. He couldn't remember ever hearing Clay talk about a man in quite the intemperate way he had talked about Dorfman. The sheriff had always been hard on law-breakers, but he understood them and had never been a man to condemn them in the way he had condemned Dorfman. But his feelings about Dorfman convinced Dan that either he was a thoroughly evil man in every sense of the word, or Clay had some personal reason for feeling the way he did. If he was as evil as Clay claimed, what influence would he have on a small town like Calamity, or, more importantly, on the entire basin?

Dan did not follow a road, but angled in, around, and sometimes over mountains, through patches of aspens and pine, and across open meadows, often sending deer plunging away through the trees. Once he surprised a black bear that reared up and watched him with suspicious eyes before he ambled off down the slope toward a small stream.

By evening he reached the south rim of Calamity Basin. He had never been here before, but he had heard Clay and others talk about it, particularly of the early days when Calamity had been a roaring mining camp with the usual riffraff and whores and con men who always seemed to gather around a boom town as Calamity had been in those days.

Still, Dan was not prepared for what he saw — the prettiest park he had ever looked at. It was an emerald gem in a setting of tall, saw-toothed mountains, many of them still holding large patches of dirty snow that had survived from the winter storms. Dark fingers of spruce and pine ran down the lower slopes to the floor of the basin, here and there broken by the light green of aspens.

The grass looked as good as any he had seen in a mountain park, particularly this early in the year, and occasionally he could make out a small collection of buildings and corrals that marked a ranch. He could count a dozen or more scattered along the edge of the timber, probably located below a spring or stream. The ones he could see were on the east side of the basin, or below him on the south side. He could not make out any on the north side, probably because they were too far away.

What caught his attention more than anything else was a set of sprawling ranch buildings on the west side. It was by itself in the grass some distance from the closest timber and miles from the nearest neighbor. That, he told himself, would be Wineglass that Dutch Dorfman had bought from old man Apple.

He tried to remember what he had heard about Wineglass, but he couldn't come up with anything except that old man Apple had squatted here in the early days not long after the Utes had been driven to Utah or placed on two small reservations near the New Mexico line. Apple apparently had no first name. He was always just "old man Apple," and he had been old as long as Dan had known him. He must have reached the point where he had been unable to operate the ranch, so he had sold out to Dorfman and moved to Durango.

Dan considered riding on down to the floor of the basin, but it would take two or three hours to reach the bottom, and it would be dark before that. Again he found a camping spot in a meadow near a creek that tumbled over the rim about fifty yards from where he camped. He caught three trout, not as large as the ones he had caught the previous night, but large enough for a meal.

He built his fire up after he had eaten and sat beside it, smoking and wondering what the next few weeks and months would bring him. Time, at least, would dull the pain of his mother's death, but he knew he would miss working with the Anchor crew, men he had learned to like. For a moment he wondered if he had been crazy simply to ride away as he had, leaving his personal things in the bunkhouse, but Matt Clay would see that nothing was thrown away. He would return sometime, perhaps soon, but he knew his leaving had been right.

Twilight was settling in, when he heard a rifle shot from somewhere to the west, then another. He tossed his cigarette stub into the fire and rose, his head cocked as he listened. The shots might have been fired by hunters, but he had a hunch that wasn't the case. He stood motionless for a minute or more, then heard the sound of a running horse moving toward him. He stepped back from the fire and waited in the shadows of the timber.

The horse was close now. Dan drew his gun, having no idea why a man would ride that hard in a country like this unless a crime had been committed and a posse was on a hot trail. A moment later a man broke out of the timber to the west and pulled up beside the fire.

"Show yourself," the man called. "I mean you no harm."

Dan stepped out of the shadows, his gun still in his hand. The rider was older than Dan, thirty or more, very tall and very thin, smooth-shaven with a prominent nose and a sharp chin. He wore a red bandanna around his neck so that it came in tightly under his chin and covered his throat. He carried a .45 on his hip and a Winchester in the boot.

"You fire those shots?" Dan asked.

"No," the man answered. "They were shooting at me, but hell, Dorfman's men are notorious for their bad shooting." He leaned forward, dark eyes raking Dan. "Who are you?"

"The name's Dan Larsen, if that means anything to you. Who are you?"

"I'm called Angel," the man said. "By most folks, that is, but Dorfman's outfit has got another for me. You heard of him?"

"I've heard," Dan said.

"Then you know enough to stay away from him and Wineglass. You riding through?"

"To Calamity," Dan said.

"Looking for a job?"

"That's right."

"Don't. Keep riding. You'll find nothing but trouble in

164

this country." The man paused, listening. The sound of pursuing horses was distinct. "I've been teasing 'em to show 'em how stupid they are, but reckon I'd better slope out of here. I was setting too far ahead of 'em. I was afraid they'd lose the trail and then the fun would be over."

He nodded in farewell, a hint of a smile on his thin lips, and rode on across the meadow into the timber on the east side. Dan stared after him until he was swallowed up by the pines to the east. The twilight was deepening, and it would soon be too dark to ride at the hell-for-leather pace he had been.

Dan was puzzled. It was plain that he wanted to be chased, but why? What pleasure was there in being pursued by a posse, or whoever they were? Dorfman's men were bad shots, he'd said, so his pursuers must be part of the Wineglass crew. He'd also said that Dan would find nothing but trouble in this country.

Maybe a little trouble was just what he needed, Dan thought. His life had been dull, plenty of hard work but with nothing more exciting than breaking a broncho or riding on fall roundup. One thing was sure. He wasn't riding on through Calamity on the say so of a man who rode past his camp and warned him about what he'd find if he stayed, a man who called himself Angel and got his fun by teasing a band of riders into chasing him.

Dan was still thinking about it, when the pursuers broke out of the timber to the west, saw his fire, and swung toward it. They reined up, when they reached it, their horses blowing hard. There were three of them, big, bearded men who were heavily armed and carried themselves with an overbearing arrogance.

"A man ride through here just now?" one of them demanded.

Dan didn't answer. He had moved back from the fire again and still held his gun. He was offended by the man's tone. The light was so thin he couldn't make out the men's faces clearly, but there was no doubt in his mind about them being hardcases, the kind he'd seen ride into Anchor late in the afternoon, eat two meals, and be on their way the following morning without doing a lick of work or saying thank you.

"Well, damn it," the one who had spoken said. "You gonna answer my question or am I gonna have to get down and beat it out of you?"

"Try it," Dan said, and cocked his gun.

The spokesman cuffed back his Stetson. "Well, now, boys, we've caught ourselves a purty cocky rooster. Maybe we'd better take some of that cockiness out of him."

"You're loco, Reno," a second man said. "He's got us sitting here like three ducks in a shooting gallery. Let's head back. It's too dark to keep after that bastard anyhow."

For a moment Reno hesitated, the urge to give Dan a beating a throbbing hunger in him. He started to swing down until Dan said: "I'll drill the first man who puts his boot on the ground. I ain't standing still for you sons-of-bitches to beat me to death."

Reno shrugged and settled back in his saddle. "All right, Ace, I reckon you're right. We'll find Angel another day, and next time we'll hang him right." He hesitated, glaring at Dan. "Bucko, if you've got a brain in your skull, you'll keep riding."

He swung his horse and rode back across the meadow, the others following. Dan built up his fire again and retreated farther into the timber. It would be like Reno and his friends to pretend to ride away, then sneak back and catch him off guard. He had no illusions about what they

166

would do to him, if they had the chance.

One thing seemed sure. Angel had been right about his finding trouble in Calamity Basin. He'd already found it without even trying. Dorfman's men wanted to hang Angel, but why? It wasn't Dan's fight, but he was in it whether he wanted to be or not, so he'd better learn why the Wineglass men were on Angel's trail. Dan might find himself riding with Angel, and a partner had not been in his plans.

IV

When Dan studied the south slope that lifted directly above the basin floor for more than one thousand feet, broken only occasionally by narrow gullies, he decided he'd better look for the road. He kicked out his breakfast fire, saddled up, and headed west, knowing the road was somewhere in that direction.

He found the road in less than an hour, wide and well-traveled, the only way in and out of the basin as far as he knew. It was used by the freighters and the stagecoach that ran between Durango and Calamity. When he tipped over the rim and started his descent, he discovered that the road narrowed and wound back and forth in a series of switchbacks before it reached the bottom. It would, he thought, be a tough job bringing a loaded freight wagon down the grade.

It was mid-morning by the time he reached the basin floor. The sky was completely clear of clouds, and the day was very hot for this altitude and for so early in the year. He stopped at the first ranch he reached, a hard-scrabble place about a quarter of a mile off the road.

A woman was hanging up clothes, two small, dirty-faced children playing beside her. The buildings were made of logs, the corrals of poles, the yard a dust patch, and the hay field beyond the barn was covered by a scrawny growth of grass that was not going to yield much of a hay crop. Granted, the spring had been dry, but the creek that Dan had camped beside flowed a few feet west of the house. It was big enough to irrigate a field ten times the size of this one, but there was no sign of a ditch system.

Dan reined up beside the woman and touched the brim of his Stetson. He said: "Morning, ma'am. It's a fine day, ain't it?"

She shook out a square of cloth and glanced at him warily as if she wasn't sure whether she should run or stay. She nodded and jammed a clothespin over a corner of the cloth, turning to glance behind the house where a man was hoeing. The children, a girl and a boy, rose from where they had been playing and scurried to their mother where they cowered behind her skirt.

"I'd like a drink," Dan said. "It's a little on the warm side today."

The woman stopped, picked up another cloth square, and nodded at the creek. "That's all the water we have, mister," she said in a low voice as if she didn't want to frighten herself by speaking in a louder tone.

"Thanks," Dan said, and stepped to the ground.

He bellied down beside the creek and drank, then rose and watered his horse, wondering why the children and the woman were so frightened. He led his horse back to where the woman stood and asked: "Where's Wineglass from here?"

She jumped, and her face, darkened by wind and sun

168

and more deeply lined than it should have been for her age, turned pale. She picked up the clothes basket that was still not empty and ran to the house without a word, the children pounding behind her as fast as their skinny legs could take them.

Dan, staring after them, whistled softly then muttered: "I'll be damned." She was, he thought, a badly scared woman for no reason. Sure, it was a lonely place with no close neighbors, but the road was reasonably near, so she must see people move along it from time to time. It wasn't as if she lived in a cabin in the mountains where she never saw anyone but her own family.

Dan stepped into the saddle just as the man who had been hoeing came around the corner of the house, a shotgun in his hands. He said brusquely as if demonstrating his courage: "What do you want, mister?"

"I stopped for a drink." Dan said. "I thought you might have a well."

"Creek water's good enough for us," the man said defensively. "What'd you say that scared Mary Beth?"

"Not a damn' thing," Dan said. "I asked where Wineglass was from here."

"That's enough to scare her," the man said in a relieved tone. "She's kind of foolish that way. She probably thought you was a Wineglass man. You see, it's a big outfit and runs over the rest of us. Sooner or later one of their riders is gonna show up and tell us our place is part of their range and for us to get to hell off it. I guess Mary Beth thought you had been sent for to be an exterminator for 'em."

They were both sick, Dan thought, made sick by the constant cloud of this threat. He asked: "Wineglass need more range?"

"Hell, no," the man said. "They don't use all they have.

They don't even run no cattle no more. All horses, but they've chased several of our neighbors off their land . . . land they've proved up on and worked for years." He wiped a ragged sleeve across his sweaty forehead. "It's a hell of a fix we're in. Sometimes I figure I'd be better off to just walk off and leave our place."

He wouldn't be leaving much, Dan thought, but it was home, maybe the only home they'd had since they were married. "I still don't know where Wineglass is from here," Dan said, "and I don't know why I scared your missus just by asking. She didn't have any reason to think I was working for 'em."

"She's just scared of strangers," the rancher said. "She worries about losing our place more'n I do." He jerked his thumb in a northwesterly direction. "Get back on the road and keep riding. You'll come to a fence purty soon and a gate. There's a sign that says Wineglass. Another sign says no trespassing. They mean it, too."

"You never had this trouble when old man Apple owned Wineglass, did you?"

The man's eyes widened as he stared at Dan. "You ain't as new to this country as I figured."

"I've lived in and around Durango all my life," Dan said. "I've heard of Dutch Dorfman."

"All you've got to do is to hear of him." The man looked out across the basin floor. "No, you said it right. We didn't have no trouble when old man Apple ran Wineglass, but we've had plenty since Dorfman came. His range has the best grass in the basin. The soil's deeper. Holds the moisture better'n ours. Dorfman takes all the water from the creek. He don't need it, neither. We used to raise a purty good crop of hay, but not now."

"You ever tell this to the sheriff?" Dan asked.

170

"The sheriff?" The man's lips curled in distaste. "He don't even know Calamity Basin is in his bailiwick."

Dan thought about correcting the man, but decided the rancher wouldn't believe him. "What's the matter with Dorfman?" Dan asked. "It doesn't make sense for a man to grab what he doesn't need."

"Just greedy," the man said, "along with being a regular son-of-a-bitch by nature. Nobody knows why he does what he does, but he does it just the same." Suddenly the man stared hard at Dan. "I hope you ain't figuring to tell Dorfman what I've been saying."

"I'm no friend of Dorfman's," Dan said. "I'm not going to tell him anything."

The man seemed relieved, then worry flowed back across his thin face like a bright moment of sunshine that suddenly gives way to a shadow that follows a cloud covering the sun. "I've got to get back to work," he mumbled, and wheeled and strode back toward his garden.

Dan touched his horse with his spurs, thinking that Dorfman had succeeded in creating a reign of terror in the basin, a terror which was likely shared by all the small ranchers. But why?

Nothing about this made any sense to Dan, but maybe it would, if he knew all the factors that were involved. Dorfman might be mean and brutal and a law-breaker, but he wasn't stupid, so he must have his reasons.

He reached the road and swung north again. In less than an hour he reached the corner of a barbed-wire fence. Within another hour he came to a gate. A sign in large, black letters suspended above the gate between two tall poles read **Wineglass**. Another sign nailed part way up one of the posts announced **No Trespassing**.

Between the gate and the buildings were a number of tall

boulders, scattered in the grass like huge eggs deposited by some prehistoric monster. On beyond the buildings, perhaps three miles, the cliff rose as sheer and steep as the one Dan had just descended. He noticed that the grass was better here than it had been at the ranch where he had talked to the man and woman. He guessed that the man had been right in saying the soil was deeper here than it was on his place, that it held moisture better.

The south side of the basin was obviously hard-scrabble range, and this made Dorfman's greed even less understandable. It just wasn't worth the effort. Then the thought occurred to Dan that the rancher and his wife were scared for no good reason, that Dorfman really had no intention of driving them from their home.

A crazy idea took root in Dan's mind as he stared at the no trespassing sign. He wanted a look at Dorfman. A man as bad as he was reputed to be was worth seeing. Maybe he needed another rider. Besides, Dan thought, he might meet up with Reno and his two friends. He didn't seek a fight with all three of them, but he had a strong dislike for Reno and a hunger to cut him down to size. It would also be interesting, he told himself, to see just how much Dorfman meant by his no trespassing sign.

He opened the gate, rode through, and closed the gate behind him. Suddenly he laughed, the first time he had laughed since he'd heard of his mother's death. Here he was, trying to find some quiet time that would ease the pain of his loss, and now he was going out of his way to look for trouble. Chances were he'd find it, too. It could be disastrous, but on the other hand it might be just the right medicine for him.

He had not gone more than fifty yards when trouble came in a way he did not expect. A rifle cracked from the nearest boulder, the bullet kicking dust up beside him. Dan stopped and raised his hands as a man yelled: "Can't you read, you idiot?"

"I can read," Dan said, "but I didn't figure it meant me."

"It means you," the man yelled angrily. "By God, you are an idiot. In this country, if a man disappears on Wineglass range, nobody comes looking for him. Why in hell didn't you think it meant you?"

"Because I'm looking for a job," Dan said, "and Dutch Dorfman wouldn't know he had missed a good man unless he had a chance to see me."

The man laughed. "You're worse than an idiot to think that. I can tell you he don't need no more hands, and he don't want to see you." He stepped away from the boulder and moved toward Dan, eyeing him truculently, his rifle held on the ready. "Now you can turn around and mosey back through the gate and be damned sure you close it good."

"Can I put my hands down?"

"Sure, but if you make one move for your gun, you'll be seeing the pearly gates swinging open right before your eyes." The man came on another step, frowning, then asked: "Hey, ain't you the tough hairpin we ran into last night on the mountain?"

"I'm him," Dan said.

"Well," the man said, grinning, "old Reno would be plumb tickled to see you. I ought to let you go on in so Reno could clean your plow for you, but I've got strict orders. I'll tell you one thing. You hang around this country for a while, and he will meet up with you. Reno, he can't let no debt go unpaid."

"Neither do I," Dan said. "That's the real reason I wanted to get to your ranch. I figured I'd find Reno, and I'd

173

get a chance at him alone without having to tangle with three toughs."

The man started to say something, seemed to choke, and finally yelled: "Get to hell out of here before I waste a good chunk of lead on you."

Dan knew he had pushed as hard as he dared. The man had not relished being called a tough, and it might not take much more to make him lose his temper. He was probably right in saying that no one ever looked for a man who disappeared on Wineglass range. Matt Clay wouldn't even know where he had disappeared.

He turned his horse and rode back to the gate, opened it, and went through it. He hesitated, tempted to leave the gate open, then decided that he might be playing his hand for more than it was worth, so he closed the gate and turned toward Calamity.

The more he thought about Dorfman's way of operating, the less sense it made. Normally a man like Dorfman, good or bad, tried to get along with his neighbors simply because it was good business not to make enemies out of people who weren't by the nature of things his enemies. But Dorfman seemed to be trying to make enemies out of people who were neutral or might even be friends.

Sealing his spread off as he was doing and paying a man to stand guard to see it stayed sealed off seemed to Dan to be a useless expense as well as proving to his neighbors he didn't want to be neighborly. Dorfman was a schemer. He had to be. He couldn't be as stupid as he appeared.

Dan turned the situation over in his mind all the way into Calamity. He could come to only one conclusion. Dorfman was doing something on his ranch he didn't want an outsider to know about. Dan didn't have the slightest notion what it was, but he was curious enough to want to find out. That wouldn't sit well with Dutch Dorfman. Dan wasn't leaving the basin on account of Reno, either. Then he thought of Angel. He could probably get the whole story from him, if he could find the man, but he had a hunch that wouldn't be easy.

V

Dan found Calamity to be less of a town than he had expected, and he hadn't expected much. On beyond to the north the sides of the hills were pockmarked with prospect holes, with here and there a large dump that marked the successful mines, but little was left of the glory days here in the town. Most of the windows in the buildings that faced Main Street were boarded up. All were constructed of logs except the bank which was made of bricks. Whoever had been the banker in the boom days apparently realized that a brick building gave an impression of stability that a log building didn't.

The population couldn't be over thirty or forty people, Dan thought. The houses were scattered on both sides of the short business block, most of them one-room cabins. Besides the bank, there was a blacksmith shop, a sprawling building that was post office, general store, and saloon, and a two-story structure across the street that identified itself as **Ma's Boarding House**. In its day, Calamity must have had many more buildings, both business and residential, but they had been destroyed by fire or had been torn down for the logs, windows, and doors.

Dan rode through the town, feeling depressed because he had planned to stay here and wait for the money from his mother's estate, but there didn't seem much to do while waiting. He had hoped to find a job, but he wasn't a blacksmith, he had no knowledge of banking, and that left the store and the boarding house, neither of which appealed to him as a place to work.

At the end of the business block was a school with a log cabin behind it that was likely a teacherage. Beyond it was a church, a sizable log house beside it that would be a parsonage. He turned back and made a circle around the business block, following the side street that was on the south and returned on a parallel street to the north. One house had a sign in front that read: **Dr. Jasper Vance**. Probably an old man, he thought, who had retired from some larger town or a drunk who could no longer hold a practice anywhere else.

The biggest excitement that ever came to Calamity these days would be a dog fight, Dan thought sourly. Well, he could put up with a dull life for a while. He had enough money in his pocket to live at Ma's Boarding House for a while, if the food was edible, but the steak would probably be tough, the biscuits like lead, and the pie crust impossible to cut with a sharp knife. When Judge Wren sent him his money, he could build a cabin on the Chumley property which, he told himself, could then be referred to as the Larsen Ranch, and spend his time hunting for the gold. He laughed at the prospect of finding it as he reined back into Main Street and tied at the hitch rail in front of the bank.

His chance of finding the gold was zero, and there was no way in the world a man could make a living on a quarter section of mountain land even if he had the money to start a herd. He laughed again as he stepped up on the boardwalk, a humorless laugh as he considered riding back to Durango and asking Matt Clay for his old job.

The interior of the bank had not changed from the boom days, Dan thought as he stepped through the front door. There was a teller's cage, a safe set against the wall behind it, and a railing that ran from the teller's cage to the wall. Here in the opposite corner from the teller's cage was a rolltop desk, the banker sitting behind it.

For a moment Dan stood motionless, his gaze sweeping from one end of the room to the other, then fastening on the banker who stood up as he said: "Good day. Can I do anything for you?"

"Maybe," Dan said. "I take it you're the banker."

The banker nodded and smiled. He was not, in Dan's opinion, the typical banker. He visualized bankers as money-hungry, fat-as-toads old men who sat behind desks and squeezed every nickel they could from their customers.

"You take it right," the banker said, "though I'm not sure you can rightly call this a bank. At best it is a very small bank doing a very small amount of business. You see in me the teller, the cashier, the bookkeeper, the janitor, and the president of the institution." He pushed a gate back and stepped forward, his hand extended. "I'm Samuel Gerard."

"I'm Dan Larsen," Dan said as he gripped the man's hand. "I just rode in from Durango."

He instinctively liked Samuel Gerard. The man was old, seventy at least. That part of Dan's notion of bankers fitted, but nothing else did. Gerard was straight-backed, tall, and slender, dignified with a white beard and mustache, both very clean and neatly trimmed. He had mild blue eyes; the skin of his face was remarkably devoid of wrinkles for a man of his age. He was a gentle man with a low voice and self-effacing manner that didn't seem to fit. As Dan followed the banker through the gate and into the little cubbyhole that served as his office, he decided that bankers didn't fit a mold any more than other people.

"Now, then," Gerard said as he leaned back in his swivel chair and faced Dan who had dropped into a chair across from him, "what can I do for you?"

"There's one thing I can't get over," Dan said. "You don't look like a banker."

"I guess a good many people have preconceived ideas of what a banker looks like," Gerard said, "but whether I look like a banker or not, there was a day when this was a thriving community and I did a big banking business. As of now, however, I'm not sure I can call myself a banker." He paused, then asked: "Just how is a banker supposed to look?"

"Oh, I guess I thought they were all fat and greedy and smoked cigars," Dan said. "The truth is I never sat down and talked to a banker in my life, so I don't know what the hell I'm talking about."

"I'd say you rode for a spread near Durango," Gerard said.

"Anchor," Dan said. "Matt Clay's outfit."

Gerard nodded. "I know the sheriff. I was aware that he had a ranch somewhere around Durango, but I didn't know where or what his iron was. Back to what a banker looks like. What a banker is, too. I think we are often misjudged and hated for no reason because we control the credit in a community which makes us suspect. I believe that is generally an undeserved reputation, although I realize some fit that description. It's a little bit like teachers. We think of them as scrawny, lifeless old maids. We have one in Calamity who is not that way at all."

Dan shrugged. "I'd better get at the business I came in for. I apologize for bringing all that up about bankers. I was just surprised, when I saw you. As a matter of fact, I was surprised when I saw Calamity. I expected more of a town."

"Not much here anymore," Gerard said. "Most of us who live in Calamity are antiques left over from the old days. We've liked our homes and didn't want to move and geared ourselves to a simple kind of life. Doc Vance goes back to the boom days. Same with Jerry Moran, the blacksmith, and Mike Dugan in the store. He's postmaster, storekeeper, and bartender." He laughed suddenly and leaned forward. "But I guess the oldest one, figuring the time she's been here, is Ma Willet who has the boarding house. She came here when the strike was first made."

"What I stopped in for was to talk about my property," Dan said. "My mother died and left me her house in Durango and a small savings account. Matt Clay bought the house, but he won't pay for it until the estate is settled and he can get title to it. Judge Wren is handling the legal end and will forward the necessary papers which he said I would have to get notarized. Can you take care of it for me?"

"Certainly," Gerard said. "I'm also a lawyer, and I handle what legal business there is in the basin, so between having the bank and being a lawyer we can take care of everything right here."

"It won't amount to much," Dan said. "About fifteen hundred dollars, I think. I took what money I had saved and bought the old Chumley property. . . ."

"What?" Gerard jumped to his feet, his gentle manner leaving him. "How could you do a thing like that?"

Dan was shocked. Samuel Gerard was not exactly the man he had judged him to be. "Why, Matt told me it belonged to the county, and they'd be happy to have someone pay taxes on it. They were. I got it cheap."

Gerard dropped back into his chair. "I apologize for getting excited about this matter, but it may decide the future peace in the basin. You see, most of us are like me, old and not fighting men. We want to keep the peace because we know that if we provoke. . . ."

He paused as if not wanting to mention a name, so Dan said: "Dutch Dorfman."

"Then you've heard of our problem?"

"Matt mentioned Dorfman before I left Durango." Dan told Gerard about talking to the man and his wife at the base of the mountain and how he was received when he wanted to ask for a job. "That's enough to tell me he's a real son-of-a-bitch."

"He is and he knows it and he's proud of it," Gerard said. "He does his banking with me and he buys his supplies from Mike Dugan and he and some of his men usually eat Saturday dinner in Ma's Boarding House. It's a sort of unspoken agreement that, if we don't give him any trouble, he'll let us have his business, and he won't give us any trouble."

"What kind of trouble could you folks give him?"

"I don't know," Gerard said slowly. "I've often wondered. He's afraid of something, though."

"I still don't see what that has to do with me," Dan said, "or my buying the Chumley place."

"It's very simple," Gerard said. "He claims all of the west side of the basin along with the mountains to the west. He doesn't actually own any of it except the bottomland he bought from old man Apple. The rest is range he's acquired by claiming it's his and scaring anyone else out who might want the mountain land for summer range or maybe a mining claim."

"Where is the Chumley place?"

"In the foothills west of town," Gerard answered. "It isn't much of a place for a ranch, Mister Larsen. You couldn't possibly make a living, running cattle on it. Bill Chumley and his pa had a small spread and made a kind of a living on it, but the meadow is mostly grown up in brush now. Don't try it. You'd lose your life and stir up trouble for the rest of us."

"I don't want to do that." Dan rose, knowing there was no chance of getting a loan from Samuel Gerard to stock his place. He hadn't expected it, but it had been a possibility in the back of his mind he had not been able to overlook. "I didn't spot a livery stable, when I rode through town."

Gerard shook his head. "Ma Willet has the nearest to it. If you stay at her place, you can leave your horse in the barn back of the boarding house."

"I don't suppose there's any work to be found around here," Dan said.

Gerard rose, his gaze pinned on Dan's face. He hesitated, then said: "It depends on how bad you want a job. For a cowboy, I'd say there was no chance at all. Dorfman is the only cattleman in the basin who hires anybody, and he is very careful about the men he picks."

"I can do the work," Dan said defensively. "What do you mean, careful about the men he picks?"

"I can't prove this," Gerard said, "but it's my guess that you don't have the right credentials to suit Dorfman. If you had served a term in the pen, or had a recommendation from some outlaw he knows, he'd give you a job. The other cattlemen in the basin are little fry who do their own work or swap jobs when necessary." He hesitated again, then said slowly: "You might ask Ma Willet, but she's a booger to work for. In fact, she doesn't even know she needs a man."

"I'll have a try at it." Dan offered his hand, and Gerard gripped it. Dan turned toward the door, paused, and asked: "You know a man called Angel?"

Gerard stiffened, then said as if choosing his words carefully: "He seldom comes into town. I don't know much about him."

He knew more than he wanted to say, Dan thought, but he didn't press the matter. He nodded, said — "Good day." — and left the bank.

VI

If he was going to ask Ma Willet for a job, Dan decided he might as well do it now. Leaving his horse tied in front of the bank, he crossed the dusty street and walked up the path to the boarding house's front door. The picket fence that surrounded the yard needed paint, the yard itself was grown up in weeds, and the lilac bushes that had bloomed earlier needed trimming. The past winter had been a hard one at this altitude, he surmised, judging from the number of winter-killed branches on the lilacs.

Dan stepped up on the porch, not sure whether he should go on in as he would have a hotel, but decided he'd better ring the bell. He punched the button, heard the tinny clamor of the bell, and waited. No one came. He listened, heard someone chopping wood back of the house, and walked around it to the rear, thinking that no one was inside.

As he rounded the corner of the house, a woman came out through the back door, saw him, and asked: "You ring the bell?"

Dan's gaze touched the woman, swung to the younger one who had straightened up from her wood chopping and

182

was staring at him, holding the axe at her side. She was probably twenty, he judged, almost as tall as he was and not in any way a dainty or fragile girl. She was big and strong, but he didn't have the impression she was masculine. Her weight was perfectly distributed so that in spite of her size she was a very attractive young woman. Blue-eyed, with rich, auburn hair, she struck Dan that she was a person he would like to know. A stray lock had fallen and dangled against her forehead. Impatiently she brushed it back, her gaze remaining on Dan.

"Well, young man," the older woman said, "cat got your tongue?"

"No, ma'am." Dan turned to look at the woman as he touched the brim of his hat. "You Ma Willet?"

"I am," she said firmly.

Dan hesitated, thinking the banker was right. Ma Willet would be a booger to work for. She was bigger than the girl, taller and much heavier, but her weight, too, was not the ugly fat of an obese person. She was wide across the hips, her breasts were twin buttes, and her chin was sheer granite. Her hair was white and done up in a bun on the back of her head; her face was wrinkled, and yet she did not have the appearance of an old woman.

She was impatiently waiting for him to say what he had to say, and he knew she'd give him a curt dismissal if he didn't get on with it. He said, his words tumbling over each other once he got started: "I'm looking for a job. The banker said you could use a man."

Ma Willet's jaw jutted out an additional inch. "Oh, he did, did he? Well, Sam Gerard is a fool just like all the other men in this broken-down old camp. No, I do not need a man."

She stomped past Dan toward the woodpile and started

picking up an armload. The girl tossed the axe to the ground. She said, her voice very sharp: "We do need a man, Ma. If you weren't so damned stubborn, you'd admit it and hire this one."

Ma rose, her arms filled with stove wood. "Get on with your job, Garnet. I know what I need and what I don't need."

"Then maybe it's time you started thinking about us," the girl said, anger making her voice high and shrill. "I've been taking the place of a man ever since old Adam died. I'm finished with that, Ma. I'm a woman, and it's time I started living like one." Ma kept walking toward the back door, looking neither to the right nor to the left. Just as she put a hand out to open the back screen door, the girl said: "How'd you like to have a traveling companion, mister?"

She was looking at him hopefully, almost begging, he thought. She was using him, he knew. It was crazy because he might wind up with the girl on his hands and that was about the last thing he wanted, but he couldn't fail her. He didn't know why he felt that way, but he knew he did.

Just before the screen door banged shut, Dan said: "Fine. Saddle up and we'll be on our way."

Ma had disappeared into the house. For a moment the girl stood motionless, staring at the back screen door, then she started toward it. She paused when she reached Dan long enough to say: "I've got to see it through now, mister. Come in, while I pack a few things. I won't be a burden to you very long."

He followed her into the kitchen, not knowing what to make of it. For some curious reason he discovered he was not worried by this unexpected drama. There had been a real clashing of wills between the two women, and it would be interesting to see how it turned out. If Ma won, he'd

184

have the girl on his hands for a while at least, but that might not be a bad situation, after all.

Ma was busy filling the fire box of the range with wood as the girl stalked past her, Dan a few feet behind. She went on through the kitchen and into the dining room. Here there was a long table, covered by a white linen cloth, ten chairs crowding the table.

The girl didn't hesitate. She walked straight on into a living room that was poorly furnished with a worn-out couch and a number of chairs of various sizes and shapes, some rockers. An organ stood against the far wall. The girl made it as far as the door that led into a hall, then stopped and slowly turned to face Dan. Only then did he realize that she was crying.

Dan had a sudden urge to take her into his arms. His sympathy was entirely with her, and he didn't doubt that working for Ma Willet was as bad or worse than the banker had said. He did put his hands on the girl's shoulders and said in a low tone: "I guess I'm butting into something that ain't any of my business, but I'll do anything for you I can."

She wiped a hand across her eyes, swallowed, and said in a shaky voice: "I apologize for blubbering this way, but I can't help it. I've worked my head off for her as long as I can remember. I won't do it any longer."

"Go ahead and get your things," he said.

She whirled, her skirt flying out from the cowboy boots she was wearing, and walked rapidly down the hall and disappeared into a room. Dan cuffed back his hat and scratched his head. It was a hell of a situation he'd blundered into. He had come here looking for a job, and now he was winding up with a girl to look out for and no job. They'd have to leave Calamity. There wasn't any place in town they could go, at least as far as he knew.

185

The girl was back in a few minutes, carrying a pillowcase jammed with clothes and whatever else she could pick up in the few minutes she'd been in her room. Tight-lipped, she said: "I've got a horse in the shed. I'll saddle him up, and we'll go."

"Where to?"

"I don't have the slightest idea," she said, and went on through the living room and dining room to the kitchen.

Ma was standing at the kitchen table, kneading bread. She glanced up at the girl and Dan, then said in a conversational tone as if nothing had happened: "What's your name, young man? I've got to know it, if you're going to work for us."

"Dan Larsen."

"Where you from?"

"Durango."

"Why'd you come to a worked-out old mining camp looking for a job?"

It was none of her business, but he couldn't risk a sassy answer. It was a job that was at stake as much as the girl's future. He hesitated, glancing at the girl who was standing in the center of the room, her mouth open in sheer astonishment.

"My mom died a few days ago," Dan said. "I didn't feel like staying home, but I didn't want to get very far away until Mom's affairs were wound up. I'm getting a little money, and the lawyer, that's Judge Wren, wanted an address where he could reach me. Calamity filled the bill."

"Well, now," Ma said. "I'm right sorry about your mother. I know Judge Wren. He's honest. Would he be a reference for you?"

She was a careful old woman, Dan thought, and again he was close to telling her it was none of her business and he

186

didn't need a reference, but he glanced at the girl a second time and saw that she was about to cry again.

"I dunno if he knows me that well, ma'am," Dan said. "Sheriff Matt Clay could tell you more about the kind of *hombre* I am."

"Good, and don't call me 'ma'am.' I'm Ma to everybody around here, though goodness knows why. I never was a ma to anybody." She looked up briefly. "Go put them things back in your room, Garnet. We've got lots of work to do. You can start right in, Dan. In case you've got a prejudice about working in a boarding house, I'd better tell you what your job is. At times you'll be helping serve at the table and maybe washing and drying dishes. You'll be cutting wood in the hills and hauling it in, and you'll chop it up for the stoves. You'll be shoveling manure in the shed, and you'll keep the yard up which ain't been done for a spell. We rent the rooms upstairs. You'll have the room beside Garnet's. It's downstairs. She can show you where it is."

She started separating the dough into loaves. Garnet still stood in the center of the room as if she were rooted there. Irritated, Ma said: "You two frozen where you are? Go on, Garnet. Put them things away and come in here and start peeling potatoes. Dan, you finish the wood and work up some for tomorrow. We're going to get the yard fixed up and fence painted 'cause I'm ashamed of it, then you'll start hauling in our winter's supply of wood. We burn a lot."

"I've got business in the store," Dan said. "Give me another hour and I'll go to work."

Ma shrugged. "One hour. No more. I don't propose to pay you for a full day and have you start working at four o'clock in the afternoon." As Dan turned away, Ma added: "Oh, one more thing. I'll give you your room and board and ten dollars a month, and we'll do your laundry."

Garnet had started toward the dining room, but she stopped when Ma made her ten-dollar offer and stared at the older woman as if she didn't believe what she'd heard, then turned her gaze to Dan who was a step behind her. When she saw that Dan was not going to object, she shrugged and went into the dining room and on to the hall.

"The skinflint," she said. "Ten dollars a month. That's nothing. Why did you take it?"

"What I wanted mostly was my room and board," he said. "I don't aim to stay here very long. I'd have taken this job without any money."

"It's your business," she said as she led the way down the hall to the door of his room. "This is it, your home for as long as you live here." She shoved the door open and motioned for him to go in. "It's just a cubbyhole, but it's got a bed. Mine's next to yours. It's the same. So's Ma's room. It's the first one we passed."

The room was small, Dan mentally agreed, and sparsely furnished with a brass bed, a bureau, and one straight-backed chair. He had worried about bed bugs, thinking they were always in boarding houses, but this place was clean, and he doubted that any would be here. It was, he told himself, the first room he'd ever had that was strictly his.

He nodded. "It'll do fine."

She studied him for a moment, tears still glistening on her cheeks. "I'm wondering if you took her stinking ten-dollar offer just to save my home. You knew I'd have to go on with you, if you didn't take the job. Now you'll work a week and see that I'm all right, then you'll be on your way again."

"No, I'll be here a while."

She kept staring at him as if trying to decide whether he

188

was lying or not, then she shrugged. "I hope you will. You know, that was just like her. She raised me, and she's worked me hard as long as I can remember, and she's never said once she was sorry for anything she ever did to me or thanked me for what I've done. I wish she'd stuck to what she'd said in the first place, and I'd be gone from here by now."

"You can still leave," he said. "I'll go with you to some place where you can settle down."

She shook her head. "No, I'm ready to leave, all right, but it would be a foolish thing to do. I don't have a penny. Just my clothes and a bay mare." She brushed a hand across her face to wipe the tears away. "You took a chance on me, Dan, and you backed me up. I'll never forget that. Maybe I can pay you back someday."

"You don't owe me a thing," Dan said. "Anyhow, you took a chance on me. I don't recommend that you ride off with the next man who comes along."

"I don't aim to," Garnet said. "I wouldn't have gone very far with you."

"You'd have gone to Durango, at least," he said. "There sure ain't nothing around here to stay for."

"Well, it didn't work that way," she said, "so it isn't a problem. I've still got a home."

Impulsively she kissed him on the cheek and whirled away to disappear into her room. He stood motionless for a moment, staring at her door that she had closed after her, then he walked out of the house into the bright sunlight. He asked himself if it was possible for a man to fall in love with a woman he had known only a few minutes. It was, he decided, a crazy question.

VII

The interior of the store reminded Dan of a large, cool cave. At one time it had probably housed a prosperous business, but now most of the shelves were empty. The ones in the front of the building held an assortment of groceries. Farther back he could see various drygoods items such as bolts of cloth, thread, buttons, men's shirts and pants, a few dresses and women's hats, underclothes, and the like. That was it. Everywhere else in the cavernous room the shelves were covered only with dust.

The storekeeper was nowhere in sight. A sign over a door to Dan's right said: **Saloon**. He stepped through the door to find a similar situation. The shelves back of the bar near the front of the room held a number of bottles. A dozen or more tables, all covered by faded green felt, were scattered around the room, and again dust was over everything except the street end of the bar.

Dan shivered. He had the eerie feeling that he was looking at a weird memorial to past greatness, that he was standing amidst an army of ghosts. Certainly this place had had its share of high-stake poker games and various hectic activities and gun fights and hard drinking, but now there was only this uncanny silence. The place was haunted, he told himself, haunted by all that had gone on here and was past and would never return.

"Well, friend," a man said from the store doorway, "what do you think?"

Dan wheeled, shocked back to the world of men of flesh

and life. A florid-faced storekeeper stood looking at him, an amused smile on his lips. He was short and stocky, running to fat now in his old age, as Irish-appearing as if he had just stepped off the boat from County Cork, but he was no recent immigrant because there was little brogue in his voice.

"I think it must have been a hell of a place in its day," Dan said.

"Oh, it was." The storeman nodded. "I saw it all. I got here not long after the first strike was made, worked in the Silver Eagle Mine till the panic hit and silver wasn't worth spit. Everybody moved out, but I liked living here. I had enough savings to buy the place. It's been a living for me, nothing big, but a living." He moved toward Dan in a sort of rolling waddle and asked: "Want a drink?"

"No, but I'm hungry," Dan said. "I've been over to Ma's Boarding House, but I was too late for dinner, so I didn't ask 'em to fix anything. Thought I'd get something over here." He held out a hand. "I'm Dan Larsen. I'm going to work for Ma."

The storekeeper shook hands, a surprised look on his face. "I'll be damned," he said. "I didn't think Ma would ever hire a man. She's needed one since old man Adam died. She's just too stubborn to admit she needs anybody, or maybe too stingy."

"She's getting me for a song," Dan said, "but I wanted a place to live, so I'd have worked for nothing."

"Come on back into the store," the man said. "I'll find you something to eat. Nothing warm, but you'll make out. Oh, I'm Mike Dugan. I guess I'm about as much of a relic as this building is."

"Then you'll probably know the history of the basin," Dan said as he followed Dugan into the store section of the building.

191

"You bet I do," Dugan said as he set out a can of sardines, a handful of crackers, and a slice of cheese. "I damn' near wrote the book."

"Then you know about the bank robbery in Durango and Bill Chumley being killed."

Dugan started to reach for a can of peaches. He froze, his faded blue eyes fixed on Dan. "Yeah, I sure do. I was right here in the store when they fetched Bill's body in." His fingers closed on the can of peaches, and he set it on the counter beside the cheese. "What do you want to know?"

Dan had not eaten since early morning, and he was ravenous. He picked up the cheese and a couple of crackers and began to eat. Between mouthfuls, he said: "A couple of things. First, what sort of a man was Chumley?"

"A hell of a nice kid," Dugan said. "Well, he was more'n a kid, but he seemed to us he was still a kid. We'd all knowed him ever since he was knee-high to a grasshopper. He'd growed up on that two-bit spread of his dad's. He'd done most of the work for a year. His older brothers weren't worth a damn."

Dugan shrugged. "Don't ask me how they ever talked him into tackling the bank with 'em. None of us would have believed he done it, if they hadn't found the *dinero* right there in his cabin. But the killing . . . well, it was nothing but murder as far as I'm concerned."

"Second question," Dan said. "Do you think the posse found all the money?"

Dugan had been opening the can of peaches. He laid the can on the counter as he glanced at Dan. "Now that's a funny question. Why do you think they didn't?"

That was one question Dan had no intention of answering, so he said: "Oh, I dunno. Just seemed they didn't find much. It struck me when I heard Matt Clay tell the story that the amount of money they found wasn't much to be running a bank on."

"Yeah, we all thought about that," Dugan said, "but it ain't likely Bill would have buried the money in two different places. Anyhow, the old son-of-a-bitch who had been running the bank was a poker player, and he'd just kind o' been dipping into the bank capital to finance his gambling." He pushed the open can of peaches toward Dan. "So you know Matt Clay?"

"I worked for him," Dan said. "The reason I'm staying here a while is that I bought the old Chumley Ranch."

Dugan's mouth fell open. He swallowed, ran the tip of his tongue over dry lips, and said: "You're a surprising gent, Larsen. You're either brave or ignorant or stupid. You ever hear of Dutch Dorfman?"

It was scary the way people felt about Dorfman. The man must have horns and a tail, Dan thought. He said: "Yeah, Matt told me about him. Seems like I've been hearing about him ever since I got to the basin. Or actually before I got here."

He told Dugan about his meeting with Angel and the three Wineglass riders, then about the rancher and his wife, and finally about trying to ask for a job. He finished with: "Thinking about it now, I reckon I was a damn' fool for wanting a job working for Dorfman. I still had Reno on my mind. I never met a man who riled me the way he done and by not saying very much, either. It was a kind of instant hate. He rode in and started putting the pressure on me and making me feel I was dirt under his boots."

"That's the way he is with everybody," Dugan said. "You're right about being a fool for going in there. If the guard had let you by, they'd have stomped you to death, and nobody would ever have found your body. What most of us

193

call honor in a fight is something Dorfman and his bunch never heard of."

Dan finished his peaches and set the can on the counter. It wasn't pleasant to think of an act that had followed a sudden impulse, an act that was complete insanity as he thought about it. He could not think of any reasonable excuse.

"I guess I had a notion that if the crew was around," Dan said, "I'd have a fair fight with Reno, which was what I wanted. Last night it struck me that all three of 'em were gonna jump me."

"It would have been eight or ten instead of three," Dugan said. "Nothing's been right here in the basin from the day old man Apple left and Dorfman bought Wineglass. He gets his supplies from me and does his banking over at Sam Gerard's, but it's business we'd be happier doing without. He lords it over us, and we feel like he's doing us a favor."

Dugan stood behind the counter, eyeing Dan until he had finished eating, then he said: "You didn't buy a ranch when you bought the Chumley place. There ain't been a ranch there for years. You just bought land. What do you aim to do with it?"

"First I want to see it," Dan answered. "I don't aim to work for Ma very long, just long enough to get the lay of the land. When my money gets here, I figured I'd live up there. I guess it's in the mountains mostly, ain't it? Be good hunting and fishing around there?"

Dugan nodded. "It's up the cañon a piece. The Chumleys had a nice meadow where they raised hay. A lot of trout in the creek and plenty of deer in the timber around there. Only thing is, Dorfman ain't going to let you stay. He claims it's part of his range, which it ain't, but in this country claiming it makes it his."

Dan slammed a hand palm down on the counter. "I just don't savvy. Why is this yahoo so particular about folks riding onto his range? And why does he claim land that ain't his any way he cuts it?"

Dugan shrugged. "Who knows? We just try to get along with him."

"Sam Gerard over at the bank told me that unless I had been an outlaw or had served a term in the pen, I wouldn't have got a riding job anyhow."

Dugan nodded. "Sam gets some crazy notions, but he might be right about that. All I know is that the Wineglass crew is a bunch of hardcases."

"It's time somebody tried asking questions," Dan said hotly, "instead of just figuring to get along with the bastards."

A tolerant grin worked across the old man's face. "It's been tried, son, and them that tried it are all dead."

Dan didn't press the point. He knew very well he was talking big, that there was no point in risking his life unless Dorfman started stepping on his toes. It would be time then to decide whether he wanted to challenge Dorfman or to roll over and play dead the way everyone was doing.

"How much do I owe you?" Dan asked.

"Make it four bits," Dugan answered. "One thing. How do you aim to find out just where your land is?"

"Someday I'll have to get a surveyor up here from Durango," Dan answered, "but right now I'll try to get someone to take me up there and show me the meadow you were talking about."

"Now that's a funny thing," Dugan said as he opened a drawer and dropped the fifty cent piece into it. "You won't find nobody in Calamity who knows how to get there or exactly where it is."

"The robbery wasn't that long ago," Dan said.

"No, it wasn't," Dugan said blandly, "but it's a subject folks have a short memory about."

Dan caught the man's meaning then. He said: "I guess I'll have to find it myself."

"You won't hunt for it very long," Dugan said. "You take that Reno you were talking about. He's a mean son-of-a-bitch. He'll be on your tail the minute you try. . . ." He paused, then added in a low tone: "Talk about the devil."

Dan was not aware that a man had ridden up. Now he saw that the newcomer had left his horse tied in front of the store and had crossed the boardwalk to stride through the door. Dan retreated until he stood with his back against the empty counter on the opposite side of the store.

The man was Reno, all right. Dan had not been able to see his features clearly the night before, but this was the fellow. He gave Dugan a bare, half-inch nod as he strode past Dan to the back corner of the room that was the post office. Without hearing a word from Reno, Dan had the same impression he'd had the previous night, that the Wineglass man would simply run over anyone who was in his way.

Dugan had given Reno a polite — "Hello." — then shook his head at Dan as if warning him not to make any trouble, but Dan's intention of staying out of trouble until Dorfman stepped on his toes suddenly evaporated. He had asked for trouble last night on the mountain, and now he was bound to ask for it again, not as an act of sheer bravado, but because it occurred to him that he was going to have to challenge Dorfman in order to claim his land, and challenging Reno was one way to start.

The Wineglass man had opened a post-office box, taken out the mail, and snapped the door shut. As he turned toward the front of the room, Dan asked: "You ever find Angel?"

Reno stopped, apparently only then aware that another man was in the room. He said, surprised: "You're the hairpin who acted tough up on the mountain last night, ain't you?"

"That I am," Dan said.

"You should have kept riding," Reno said.

"I don't figure on riding until I'm ready," Dan said. "It'll take a better man than you to run me out of the basin."

Reno blinked, then grinned. Slowly he laid his mail on the counter. The big heating stove in the center of the room was between them. Reno took a slow step toward the front door. Dan knew he intended to draw. He stood waiting, right hand over the butt of his gun, but Reno never made his move. Dan heard a gun cock, then Dugan's voice: "I'll blow off the head of the first one of you who makes a move for his gun. I ain't gonna stand for your blood and guts being spread all over my store."

Reno didn't move for what seemed to Dan a long time. He remained facing Dan, his back to Dugan, his small, dark eyes flaming with the rage that was boiling up in him. He relaxed suddenly, turned to the counter, and picked up his mail.

"There'll be another day, bucko," he said. "There always is for gents like you . . . the last day."

Reno strode on to the front door, stepped down off the walk, and mounted. He left town in a cloud of dust. Dugan took a long breath as he laid his shotgun on the counter. "I just kept you from committing suicide, friend. You stay out of my place the next time any of the Wineglass bunch is in town."

"Thanks," Dan said.

He left the store, thinking that Dugan might have been right about keeping him from committing suicide. Still, he didn't regret doing what he had.

VIII

Dan rode to the shed behind the boarding house and stabled his horse. He saw three other horses — two blocky work animals and a slim-legged bay mare. There were several other stalls. A pen at the far end of the shed held a black-and-white milk cow.

When he had left Durango, Dan had wrapped his shaving gear, a pair of socks, and a clean shirt in his slicker, and tied the bundle behind the saddle. Now he carried it to the woodpile, laid it down, and, picking up the bucksaw, tackled the wood. He worked for two hours, sawing and splitting, before Garnet came out of the boarding house and announced supper. Then she stood, admiring the pile of stove wood.

"Dan," she said, "I've had to do that ever since old Adam died, and I'm sick and tired of it. I'm glad you're here."

He dropped the axe, thinking she had reason to rebel. As he picked up his bundle, he said: "I'm glad to be here."

She nodded as she turned toward the back door. "Come in. You've worked up enough wood to last a week."

He looked ruefully at his hands as he fell into step with her. "Guess I'll have to get some gloves. I'm not used to an axe handle and a bucksaw."

"You'll need gloves, if you stay here," she agreed. "It'll

198

get worse, going into the mountains after our winter's supply of wood. We'll be hauling hay before long, too."

"I won't be waiting on the table much with that kind of work ahead of me," he said.

"Just Sundays," she said. "That's a big day for us. Or maybe on Saturdays, if Dutch Dorfman and some of his crew come in for dinner."

"Dorfman here? For a meal?" Then he nodded. "I remember now. Somebody told me he came here on Saturdays."

"I guess you've heard of Dutch Dorfman. It's true. Usually he brings a man named Reno with him. Sometimes several others. They go to Dugan's place and drink, then come here and eat, and finally get their mail and pick up anything at the store they want, then head back." She shook her head. "You wonder why they ride into an old mining camp like Calamity."

So he'd be seeing Dorfman, Dan thought. Reno, too. He didn't want to kick up a row under Ma Willet's nose, but anything might happen the next time he ran into Reno.

"Doesn't make sense," he said. "Not much in Calamity to go on a toot about. Why don't he ride into Durango and turn his wolf loose?"

"It's a funny thing," she said as she stepped through the back door into the kitchen. "It seems that none of the Wineglass bunch ever go to Durango. Maybe they don't need to. Dorfman has women out there. Liquor, too. It's a terrible place from what we hear. They have some brutal fights."

"Maybe they don't ride into Durango because they're wanted men," Dan said.

Ma was stirring gravy at the stove. She glanced up as she said: "You hit it right on the head, young man. I've thought for a long time that the sheriff could fill his jail if he'd come out here and look around. Wash up. It's ready."

Dan tossed his bundle into a corner, pumped water into a wash basin, and scrubbed. It had been a long time since he had put his feet under a table and had sat down with women for a meal. After he had run a comb through his hair, he picked up his bundle and carried it through the dining room and on into the front room. He paused briefly and nodded at two people who were sitting there, an old, white-haired man and an attractive young woman whom he judged to be about thirty. He went on along the hall to his room and tossed his bundle on the bed, then returned to the front room where Garnet was waiting for him.

"Come and sit down," she said.

The woman and the old man were seated at the table. Garnet introduced the woman as Vera Manning, the schoolteacher. The old man was Fred Murray. He held out a claw-like hand and muttered: "Howdy."

Dan shook his hand as Ma brought a platter of roast beef from the kitchen and took the chair at the head of the table. The food was good, better than Dan had expected. They ate in silence for a few minutes, then Fred Murray began to chatter, first about the weather, then the condition of the cattle on the range, and finally about the old, glory days when Calamity was a roaring mining camp.

He was eighty or more, Dan thought, with crêpe-like skin and faded blue eyes. His right hand was so shaky that he had trouble lifting food to his mouth from his plate. All the time he sat listening to Murray's talk, Dan kept trying to remember where he had heard the name Fred Murray. Then just as Ma lost patience and snapped — "Fred, shut up!" — it came to him. Fred Murray was the man who had recognized the Chumley horses when the Durango Bank was being robbed, the Fred Murray who had been with the posse that had murdered Bill Chumley.

The old man lowered his head, his face showing his hurt. He said: "Well now, Ma. I was just talking. Nobody else was saying nothing."

"I know, Fred," Ma said. "A little talk is fine. A whole lot of talk gets on a person's nerves."

"I'd like to ask a question," Dan said, looking at Ma who shrugged and nodded. Dan turned his gaze to Murray, not sure he was doing the right thing, but very sure that the sooner his reasons for being here were known, the better. "Mister Murray, I have bought the old Chumley place. Do you think you could show me where it is?"

There was the usual stunned silence that he had come to expect when he told anyone he had bought the Chumley property. The others stopped eating to stare at Dan as if what he had just said could not possibly be true.

Murray was as stunned as the others, then he remembered he had been asked a question. "Why, sure I can, Mister . . . Mister . . . ?"

"Call me Dan."

"You bet." He swallowed, glancing at Ma, then said: "Of course, I can show you where it is. Just find me a horse, Dan. I ain't owned a horse for a long time."

Ma had laid her fork down. "Dan Larsen, do you have the slightest notion what you've done and what will happen if you try to settle on the Chumley place?"

"I reckon I do," Dan said. "I'm getting tired of hearing what Dutch Dorfman will do to me. I know he's claiming land that belongs to me, but I do aim to live up there."

"Better order your coffin the day before you move up there," Ma said. "There ain't nothing up there to move into. You know that?"

"I know." Dan nodded. "The trouble is, I don't know where it. . . ."

"I told you I can show you," Murray broke in eagerly. "It ain't more'n an hour's ride from here. Just find me a horse, like I said."

"You can't ride that far, Fred," Ma said. "You might just as well quit dreaming about it."

Murray stabbed a piece of meat, lowering his gaze. "I reckon Ma's right, Dan. I ain't been on a horse for ten years. I was just running off at the mouth like usual."

"Maybe you could draw me a map," Dan suggested.

Murray looked up. "Sure, I can do that. You bet. I will, too. I'll have it here tomorrow evening."

Ma rose, went into the kitchen, and returned with part of a two-layer chocolate cake. She passed it as Vera Manning said: "Mister Larsen, don't try to move up there right away. Please wait a few weeks. Maybe a few months. I don't know how long you'll have to wait, but I do know this situation is not going to last forever."

"How do you know that, Vera?" Ma asked.

The teacher flushed and looked away, not answering. Murray cackled. "You oughta know, Ma. Angel told her."

Silence then, a tense silence that puzzled Dan who looked from one face to another, ending with Vera Manning who was busily eating her piece of cake.

"I'm sorry, Vera." Ma said. "I shouldn't have asked. It was just that . . ." — she hesitated, glancing quickly at Dan, then hurried on — "it's just that I'm sick and tired of living this way." She looked at Dan. "Do you know what I'm talking about?"

"I think I do." Dan told about his meeting Angel, Reno and his friends, and his talk with the rancher and his wife. "I wanted to see what Dorfman looked like, so I tried to go to his headquarters and ask for a riding job, but I got shot at. A guard turned me back."

"A stupid thing for you to do," Ma said sharply. "Nobody goes to Wineglass except the crew and a couple of women he keeps out there, but I guess you didn't know that."

"I knew it was stupid," Dan said. "A sudden impulse when I saw the gate, and I didn't stop to think. After I got here, I talked to Sam Gerard and Mike Dugan. They said about what you folks are saying." He shook his head. "I can't figure it. How can Dorfman make his own laws up here?"

"Ask Matt Clay," Ma said harshly. "Maybe he can tell you why he's stayed out of it like he has."

"Maybe Matt don't know how bad it is," Dan said.

"He knows," Ma said. "We've told him often enough."

Vera shoved her plate back. "I think I know why Clay doesn't do anything. So far Dorfman has not done anything that bad. Mostly it's been a bluff."

"Reno killed two ranchers right here in the street." Ma shook a finger at Vera. "Sure, they called it a fair fight, but I call it murder when a hardcase like Reno guns a man down who works for a living."

"But the sheriff couldn't have made it stick if he had arrested Reno," Vera said. "The rest of us have been intimidated by Dorfman. Besides, arresting Reno wouldn't have got rid of Dorfman."

"He's run several ranchers off their spreads," Ma said belligerently. "What do you call that?"

"They were bluffed off their places after Reno killed those two men," Vera said. "That's why it's hard to change anything here in the basin. Fear is contagious. It has spread all over the valley. When something happens that is so outrageous that it forces everyone to stand up and be counted, we'll get a change."

"Moving onto my land might be that something," Dan said.

203

Vera shrugged. "It could be, but please don't make your-self the sacrificial lamb. I said Dorfman was a bluffer, but when a bluffer gets his bluff called, he has to prove himself. It would be that way with you because the Chumley prop-erty is the key to what he's doing."

Dan slammed a hand palm down on the table top so hard that the dishes rattled. "Just what the hell is he doing? It's plain he's doing something he don't want anybody to know about, but what is it?"

Vera looked as if she could have bitten off her tongue. She rose. "I've got to get home," she said, and left the dining room.

Ma got up, too. "Dan, you help Garnet with the dishes. I'm going to bed. Fred, you'd best get along home."

"Sure, Ma, sure," the old man said, and rose and left.

Garnet smiled as she turned to Dan. "I'll wash, and you can dry. Help me carry the dishes into the kitchen."

"There are some mighty queer things going on around here," Dan said. "What's this about Angel? Nobody seems to want to talk about him."

"It's partly because nobody but Vera knows anything about him," Garnet said as she lifted a stack of dishes and carried them into the kitchen. "She and Fred take their sup-pers here. She can't afford it, she says, but she gets lone-some when school's out, so she eats here for the company. Usually she stays and talks."

"What about her and Angel?"

"It's a kind of unspoken scandal," Garnet said. "I guess they knew each other before Vera started teaching here a year ago. We don't know when Angel got here. I think he was with Dorfman at first, but he's on his own now. He hides out most of the time. He comes to Vera's place after dark and leaves before daylight."

Garnet hesitated as she lifted the tea kettle and poured hot water into a dishpan, then said: "He's like a shadow. Vera won't talk about him. Old Fred knows that, and, if he had any sense left in his dried-up little head, he wouldn't have said what he did."

"Why does he eat here?" Dan asked. "Has he got any money?"

She nodded. "He eats here because he can't cook. He fell into some money a few years ago. A bachelor brother died and left him several thousand dollars. Sam Gerard talked him into putting it in the bank. Sam doles out some each month. The meals he gets here are about the only decent grub he gets."

"He's the man who put the posse on Bill Chumley's trail, wasn't he?"

"So you heard about that," Garnet said. "You know, Dan, you're just adding one mystery on top of the others."

He laughed. "I'm not very mysterious. I just want the land I bought and don't want Dorfman killing me for doing what I've got a right to do."

"I don't want you killed," she said quickly. "Neither does Vera. That's why she said as much as she did. I don't know what Angel's told her, but I suppose he's got a notion about putting Dorfman out of business." She dropped a plate into the rinse pan, her gaze on Dan. "I may regret it the rest of my life, but I'll show you where your place is. I've been there lots of times . . . before Dorfman came to the basin."

"You know where the cabin stood?"

She nodded. "I used to fish in the creek right below where it was. Nothing there now, but when I was little, there were a few old logs lying there, some rocks from the chimney, and things like that."

Dan patted her on the back. "When can we go?"

"Later," she said, "after you've worked here long enough to talk Ma into letting us have a day off. We'll take a picnic lunch and fish. You can't push Ma. And you've got to promise not to get yourself cornered and get killed. I'd feel responsible."

"I promise," he said, and knew it was a promise he would have trouble keeping.

IX

The next day Dan bought paper, envelopes, and stamps from Mike Dugan and wrote to Matt Clay. He told the sheriff that there was a reign of terror in the basin, that Dorfman had driven people from their homes, that everyone was scared of him, including the businessmen. In the last line he asked the question that had been bothering him, the question everyone in the basin was asking: why hadn't the sheriff looked into the situation?

Dan read the letter through three times before mailing it. He knew the question was too blunt, that Matt would resent it, but he decided that if Matt wanted to get sore about it, he could. Somehow Dutch Dorfman had to be cut down to size, and Matt was the only one who could do it legally. After the third reading Dan added a postscript, that the way things stood he'd get killed, if he tried to move onto the land he owned.

Clay's reply came by return mail. It was brief and to the point. First, Dan and everyone else in the basin ought to know that until a criminal act had been committed, the law could not do anything. As far as Matt knew, no criminal act had been committed. Second, he had offered Dan a deputy's badge, and Dan hadn't wanted it. The offer was still open.

Dan didn't show the letter to anyone, but it put a burr under his saddle. Even if he had a deputy's badge, he couldn't touch Dorfman. It would take a posse to do that. He thought about it a short time, then wrote back to Matt to that effect, adding that if he ran across evidence that pointed to what Dorfman was up to, he'd let the sheriff know.

Dorfman and Reno did not come to dinner the following Saturday, but a number of ranchers and their wives did. "We never know how many's gonna be here for dinner," Ma told Dan, "but we've got to be ready for a tableful."

Afterward, when Garnet and Dan were cleaning up the kitchen, Garnet said: "If Dorfman comes, the rest will stay away. They see each other in the store and saloon, but they don't mingle. None of the ranchers is looking for trouble, so they head home as soon as they buy what they need. Dorfman is always in town well before dinner time, so if he's not anywhere in sight, the crowd moves in on us right about noon. Judging by the way they act, it's the only meal they get all day."

"Don't you waste a lot of food on the days the crowd doesn't come?" Dan asked.

"Yes, but Dorfman savvies how it is. That's surprising, considering the kind of man he is. He always overpays when he's here, so Ma doesn't lose anything." She started washing dishes, then asked: "You learn anything from the talk at dinner?"

"One thing struck me," Dan said. "Nobody mentioned Dorfman or Wineglass, but it seemed to me everyone was kind of boogery."

Garnet nodded. "They are. Maybe it's like Vera says. He's a bluffer, but enough real things have happened to make folks uneasy."

"Like Reno killing two men?" Dan said.

"That's right," Garnet agreed. "Now everyone stays away from Reno because they are afraid he'll work them into a fight like he did the two he killed."

"Maybe he won't do it any more," Dan said. "Whatever Dorfman's up to, he don't want anyone watching him. The way it stands now, no one can get close enough."

"What do you think he's doing?"

"I don't have a good guess," Dan answered, "but whatever it is, it's against the law. Maybe he's kidnapped somebody and is holding him for ransom. Or he might be making counterfeit money." He had been drying dishes as fast as Garnet was washing them, but now he stopped and looked at the girl. "You think Vera knows?"

Garnet nodded. "If Angel knows, Vera knows, but she'll never tell you. If you've got a notion about asking her, save your breath."

"I'm going to try," he said. "If she'll tell me, it may be enough to get Matt Clay up here."

Garnet shook her head. "You might get it out of Angel, if you can find him, but not Vera."

"I've gotta try. If she won't tell me, maybe she can get me a chance to talk to Angel."

That evening, when Vera left the boarding house after supper, he caught up with her. He asked: "Mind if I walk along with you?"

"I do mind," she said. "Does that make any difference?"

"No," he answered. "I've got to ask you some questions which I know you wouldn't answer at the table."

"Like what Dorfman is doing?" she suggested.

"That's exactly what I want to know."

"And it's why I mind you walking with me," she said. "If you just wanted my company, I'd be delighted, but to take the opportunity to ask some questions which I can't answer is another matter."

"I do enjoy your company," he said. "The questions are just an excuse to walk with you."

She laughed. "You're lying, but I can't get rid of you, can I?"

"Not yet," he answered. "I didn't really expect you to tell me what Dorfman's up to. I don't expect you to admit that you're seeing Angel occasionally, and I don't give a damn what your relationship with him is. It's your business. All I want is a chance to talk to him."

She studied him as they walked, her face unsmiling. "Well," she said finally, "I get more consideration from you than from most of the people who live in Calamity. Even Ma, who used to run a brothel, looks down her nose at me. . . ."

"Now just hold on a minute," he broke in. "How do you know that?"

"It's common knowledge," she answered. "She doesn't deny it. Ask her. Ask Garnet. Ask your friend Matt Clay. I don't hold it against her. A human being, man or woman, can change the direction of his or her life, and Ma has. I just can't understand a person being so critical of another person who is doing what she used to do. As a matter of fact, I'm not as bad as she was. I don't sleep with ten different men in one night."

Her eyes sparkled in fury, her face turned red, and her lips quivered. He had never seen her angry before; he had never heard her talk that much before. He didn't blame her, not if what she said about Ma was true.

He was silent for a moment, not knowing what to say, but her fury left her and she smiled. "I'm sorry to take it out on you, but Ma is such a Puritan, and of all people she has no right to be. Now you said you wanted to talk to Angel. Why?"

"I don't know why he's so elusive," Dan answered. "Or mysterious. You'll remember I told you he stopped at my camp the night before I got to the basin. I figured the way he talked that he wasn't exactly fighting Wineglass, but was having fun with them and making fools out of them. I don't know what his game is, but I'm thinking we're on the same side. Maybe the two of us could do more than either one of us working alone."

They reached the door of the teacherage and stopped. She stood, looking thoughtfully at him in the thinning light. Finally she said: "I respect you, Dan. You're honest, but I can't decide whether you're very brave or just running over with the audacity of youth which isn't always very intelligent."

He grinned. "That's me. Trying to ride in to ask for a job at Wineglass was nothing but that. I did learn something, though. I'm not going to take Dorfman on by myself. That's why I want to see if Angel and me could do something together."

"Give me a little time," she said. "That's all I can say now."

She opened the door, went into the teacherage, and shut the door behind her. Dan slowly walked back to the boarding house, thinking that Vera had neither admitted nor denied that she ever saw Angel, but he was sure she did and that she would contact the man. Then Angel could decide whether he wanted to see Dan.

His mind turned to Ma and what Vera had said about

her running a brothel. She had lived here a long time, and she had never said how she made a living before she started running the boarding house. Vera probably was right. It didn't make any difference to him, either way. Garnet did. She could not have been one of Ma's girls. She was too young, but he wondered how Ma had got hold of her. She had told Dan that Ma had raised her. Beyond that, he knew nothing of her origin or why Ma had given her a home in the first place.

He would ask Garnet, when he had a chance, but Sunday was as busy as Saturday had been. The long morning was filled with the work of getting dinner ready. Chicken was the meat dish on Sundays, Ma told him, and gave him the job of preparing two young roosters.

When Dan brought the chickens to the kitchen, ready for cutting up and frying, Garnet said: "This is a different crowd than we had yesterday. We'll have town people. It's a sort of community get-together."

"Saturdays and Sundays must be the days that keep you and Ma solvent," Dan said.

"That's right," Ma broke in, "but I don't know how long I'll be doing it. It ain't like the old days. Sometimes it gets to be a kind of wake, with so many of us having lived here for twenty years or more. We get to thinking about the ones who ain't here."

Dinner was always set for one o'clock, Garnet said, but the diners came early just to sit in the living room and visit. When it was time, Ma called them into the dining room and seated them at the table. Garnet introduced Dan to people he had not met before, Mrs. Gerard first. She was a petite, white-haired woman, and the thought crossed Dan's mind that she might have been one of Ma's girls.

Mike Dugan nodded at Dan and said they had met, then

the blacksmith, Jerry Moran. The preacher and his wife sat next to Dugan, the Reverend Frank Faraday and Julia. Faraday was a small man with a big voice, but after Dan got used to that he found himself liking the man. Perhaps the reason he felt that way was because Faraday brought Dorfman's name up and thoroughly denounced him.

"He's a monster," Faraday declared. "After he drove those families out of the basin, I told him what I thought of him. It was in Mike's store. I think Dorfman's right-hand man, that despicable Reno, would have killed me if Mike hadn't picked up his shotgun and interfered."

Dugan grinned. "It was a mite touchy there for a minute. The Reverend kind o' got carried away." His face turned grave, and he added: "I don't propose for Reno to kill any more men here under our noses like he done them two."

Ma had taken the chair at the head of the table. Now she leaned forward. "I don't, either. We can all help, and that includes you, Sam. I hope you've got a shotgun or a Winchester in the bank. We may get ourselves killed, but we're old, and we've lived our lives. We owe something to what's left of this town."

To Dan's surprise, Gerard nodded agreement. "I've got a double-barreled twelve gauge, and it's loaded with buckshot. I couldn't put it to better use than blowing Reno's head off."

His wife stared at him, shocked. "Sam, you couldn't."

"Oh, yes, I could, my dear," the banker said. "Dorfman has always been courteous, when we've had any business dealings, but Reno. . . ." He shook his head. "I won't go into that."

Faraday stopped in the process of devouring a drumstick. He said: "I understand you are a friend of Matt Clay's."

Dan nodded. "That's right."

"Ask him to come to the basin," Faraday urged. "Have him talk to us. He'll know then that Dorfman is an outlaw, a killer, and a tool of Satan."

Mrs. Faraday sighed. She was a large, bosomy woman who had probably raised a large family of children and now spent her time mothering her husband. She said: "Frank, you're upsetting yourself again. You know what it does to your stomach."

Dan, on impulse, said: "Maybe you've all heard that I bought the Chumley place from the county. I plan to find the gold he hid."

The remark had the effect he expected. Everyone stopped eating to stare at him, then Fred Murray burst out. "There ain't no gold up there, Dan. Me 'n' the rest of the posse dug it up and brought it down the day we got Bill Chumley."

Dugan nodded agreement. "I don't know where you got that cock-and-bull story about the gold, but if you bought the place to hunt for it, you wasted your money."

"I'm afraid so, young man," Sam Gerard added.

"Well, I aim to hunt for it, anyhow," Dan said, "if Dorfman don't kill me."

"He may do exactly that," Faraday said. "I told you he's a murderer. Or his man Reno is. Same thing."

The talk changed to some church business that Faraday brought up. A few minutes later the diners finished their custard pie and left the boarding house.

"Well, Dan," Ma said, "you done it up brown, telling everybody you're after the gold. I think they're wrong about it not being there. I always thought so, but after all this time you ain't gonna find it. Now Dorfman will hear about it, and he'll be here next Saturday. You can count on it."

"I figured he'd hear," Dan said. "I aim to push him, and, if that don't bring results, I'll have to think of something else."

"Are you plumb daft?" Ma demanded. "You can't whip that bastard by yourself."

"I don't aim to," Dan said. "He's been scaring everybody to death. It's time somebody stood up to him. Maybe we'll find out how much of a bluffer he is."

She shook her head, smiling. "Yes, I'm afraid *you* will."

"I've heard a lot about Bill Chumley," Dan continued. "What sort of fellow was he? I guess you knew him."

"Oh, I knew him," Ma said. "I knew all the Chumleys. Their pa was all right . . . nobody to set the world on fire, but he never bothered nobody. The two older boys weren't worth nothing. They left home, and I don't think their pa or Bill missed them one damn' bit. But Bill?" She stirred her coffee, staring down at the black liquid. "It's kind o' hard to figure how he ever came from that family. Him and his brothers were as far apart as strangers could be. A fine young man. Anybody who knew him will tell you that."

"But he was a bank robber," Dan said.

"Yeah, I guess he was," Ma admitted, "but why and how he ever got into it is more'n I can say."

He'd heard nothing new, Dan reflected. He knew why Bill Chumley had helped rob the bank, and yet it didn't add up. But maybe Bill was in love with Ann Larsen so much he was willing to do anything for her. It was something Dan thought he could not understand, but, when he looked at Garnet who had started to pick up the dishes, he realized that maybe he could understand it.

He had never met a woman like Garnet before, and he wished he had some inkling about how she felt toward him. All that he knew was the simple fact that his few days here in Calamity had been the happiest days of his life. He wished they could go on forever, and that, he knew, was the wildest of fantasies.

Ma rose. "I'm going to take a nap. Dan, help Garnet with the dishes." She walked to the door leading into the living room, then stopped and turned back. "Oh, Garnet says you want a day off to inspect your property. Tomorrow's Monday. I can manage, if you get back in time to help with supper. Just see to it that you don't get yourself or Garnet killed." She smiled again. "You're a good worker, Dan. I didn't want to hire you because I never seen a cowboy before who was worth a damn for anything but cowboying."

She went on toward her bedroom. Garnet stood motionless beside the dishes she had stacked. "She likes you, Dan. It's kind of queer because she's always hated cowboys, Bill Chumley being the one exception. I didn't think we'd get away for another month."

"At least, I'm going to get a look at my land before I thought I was going to," Dan said. "You sure you know where it is?"

"I'm sure," she said. "I don't know where your corners are, but I know where the meadow was and where the Chumley cabin stood."

"That's all I need," he said.

As he started picking up the rest of the dishes, he told himself she didn't know how important the position of the cabin was. He'd have to tell her sometime, but not yet. He wanted to know her better, although he had a strange feeling that he knew her very well, that he had known her for a long time.

X

Dan and Garnet left Calamity Monday morning, their long shadows moving ahead of them. Miles to the west were towering peaks with patches of snow that would linger through the summer. As Dan stared at the saw-toothed range in front of him, it seemed to him that only a mountain goat could possibly find its way across or through those mountains.

"There's only one way into the basin, ain't there?" Dan asked. "The road that comes in from Durango?"

"That's the only way you can bring a wagon or stage-coach in," she answered, and nodded at the peaks in front of them. "We're on an old Ute trail that comes in from the west. It follows Calamity Creek on this side. When the Chumleys lived there, they could drive a wagon to town, but some of the road has fallen into the creek since then."

"But horses can still get into the basin this way," Dan said, "which means they can get to Wineglass from here?"

She gave him a questioning look. "You think that's what's behind Dorfman being so ornery?"

"It's worth thinking about," Dan said. "It doesn't tell us what he's doing, but it sure is part of the pattern, him putting out guards and building a barbed-wire fence and raising hell with anyone who trespasses." He paused, glancing at the girl. "I don't feel right about fetching you up here."

"Well, I'm not going back, if that's what you're getting at," she snapped. "I see you brought your Winchester and your Forty-Five. If we get into trouble, I guess you're fixing to fight our way out."

"No," he said. "If we run into trouble, we're heading back. *Pronto!* You savvy that?"

She smiled impishly. "I hear you talking."

"Which means you ain't listening," he said. "You know, I've got a notion you'd be a hard woman for a man to control."

"Well," she said indignantly, "I don't aim for any man to control me. I don't think you or any other man wants a woman he can control."

"I guess control was the wrong word," he admitted.

"It sure as hell was," she said. "Maybe I'm pig-headed. Ma will tell you I am." She paused, staring thoughtfully at the row of willows that lined Calamity Creek ahead of them. "I guess my trouble is that I don't know how a marriage ought to be, but I've watched several couples like the Gerards. They've been married almost fifty years, and they're still in love. Sam doesn't control her, and they're very happy."

He held his hands up. "I surrender. I'm in about the same fix as far as knowing how a marriage ought to be, but I don't think loving each other is enough. I think two people have to work at their marriage."

"And control is not a part of it," she said firmly.

"Oh hell," he said, irritated. "I told you I had surrendered."

"I couldn't let that pass," she said. "We've never had a man around the boarding house except old Adam. But I know one thing. If it comes to control, no man ever controlled Ma Willet."

"Is it true that she ran a brothel back in the boom days?"

Her mouth dropped open as she stared at him. "Now, who told you that?"

"Vera. I didn't believe her, but she said to ask you."

217

"It's true," Garnet said. "The old-timers remember, but they don't talk about it. I don't know how Vera heard it. Anyhow, it was before I was born. Or about that time."

"Vera says Ma is a real Puritan now."

"She is," Garnet admitted. "She's like a drunkard who takes the pledge. She's the greatest reformer in the country. Ma doesn't try to reform Vera. But she thinks it's terrible that the schoolteacher sleeps with Angel. I wouldn't be surprised if Vera is fired next year, but she is a wonderful teacher, so maybe her mortal sin will be overlooked."

"Maybe Ma's the only one who cares what Vera does."

Garnet shrugged. "Oh, there are some others, but nobody makes much of a fuss about it. Maybe it's better to let sleeping dogs lie."

They reached Calamity Creek a few minutes later. Here it took a slow, meandering course across the basin, but ahead of them the land tilted upward, and the hills on both sides began crowding in and soon became cliffs, the water now boiling downstream in a series of pools and rapids.

Garnet pointed to a sign beside the trail: **No Trespassing**. She said: "The last time I was by here that sign wasn't there."

"How long ago was that?"

"Last summer," she answered. "I didn't get to fish much last fall or this spring. After old Adam died, Ma said there was too much for me to do to waste time fishing." She shook her head. "Ma's been on her good behavior since you came."

Dan rode up to the sign, twisted it off the tree it had been nailed to, and tossed it into the creek. "I don't guess I can be accused of trespassing on my own land. What you said about Ma may explain something. I've never savvied why you got so mad, when I showed up and wanted a job.

218

You were hell-bent on pulling out."

"I was just damned tired of being overworked," she said bitterly. "You don't know how good it feels to be out here, riding with you and leaving all that work back there in Calamity. It's a sort of reprieve, I guess." Then she giggled, adding: "You know, Dan, if you try anything funny with me, Ma will fire you if she can't trust you. We were just talking about Vera. Well, Ma's told me more'n once that she'll throw me out if I ever let a man take advantage of me."

"I'll behave," he said, "not wanting to get shot. I don't want to get fired, either."

The cliffs had closed in on them so that the trail, barely wide enough for a horse and wagon, hung between the creekbed and the granite wall on the right. White water roared by with a steady pounding, then suddenly the noise died down as the land leveled off and what had been a cliff on the north side became a ten foot dirt bank. Beyond a wide meadow stretched out for more than half a mile.

"This is the Chumley meadow," Garnet said as she put her horse up the steep bank. "I don't know just how the land lies, but I do know that all of the meadow belonged to the Chumleys. They had a quarter section, but the meadow isn't that big, so you must own some of the land on the other side of the creek and part of the hill to the north."

They rode slowly along the edge of the bank, Dan savoring the sight of the land he had bought, the land that had belonged to his father. Most of the meadow was covered by brush so that anyone trying to make a ranch out of it would have to do some clearing. Large pines were scattered along the edge of the meadow and up on the slope to the north. To the west the land tilted up once more, and the cliffs closed in on the creek.

"You say this was an old Ute trail?"

Garnet nodded. "It's not a hard trip on horseback," she said. "The trail follows the stream on this side until it gets almost to the top, then it drops down and goes along another creek to the bottom. When you get out of the mountains, you're in sagebrush country. Utah isn't far off, when you get down off the pass."

"The trail's been used a lot," Dan said.

"Sure. Dorfman uses it. Some say outlaws who are on the run come in from Utah and have a place to stay until it's safe to go on." She reined up and dismounted. "Here's where the cabin was. I couldn't be more than a few feet off because I'd come up from the creek and play around here when I got tired of fishing. Some of the fireplace was still standing. You'll locate the base, if you dig around a little. I used to find rusted pots and pans, parts of a mattress, and legs and backs of chairs."

Dan stepped down, leaving his horse ground-hitched. He motioned to a nest of boulders to the north. "Is that how you know this is the place?"

She nodded. "A lot of things change with time, but those rocks have been there for a few thousand years, and they'll be there a few more thousand."

Dan walked toward the boulders, kicking at the grass as he walked. He overturned a rusty frying pan that had been covered by a thin layer of dirt. He held it up, and Garnet nodded. A moment later he found a mass of mortar and rocks that had to be the base of the fireplace. His heart began to pound. The hearthstone would not be more than a few feet away. Now he believed he knew exactly where the gold was.

He kept walking, saying nothing to Garnet. He reached the boulders and stopped, thinking it was a beautiful setting for a small ranch. If the meadow was cleared and the irrigation ditches cleaned out, the quarter section would again furnish hay and grass for a few head of cattle.

For several minutes he imagined his father — the notion shocked him because he still had trouble thinking of Bill Chumley as his father, living here, a poor living but a living from this tiny piece of land, dreaming his dream of bringing Ann Larsen here, of raising a family. For the first time Dan had some understanding of how an honest young man, very much in love and wanting his future wife to have more than he could give her, might be lured into robbing a bank.

He walked back toward Garnet, who was watching every move he made as if trying to understand what was going on in his head. Again he stopped beside the base of the fireplace, knowing that the hearthstone must be directly in front of him.

A wild sense of exhilaration flowed through him. He was standing within three feet of the gold. He had never really been convinced he could find it. He had come here, partly to know about his father but mostly because he needed something to take his mind off the loss of his mother, something to look forward to, yet it had never been more than a dream. He used to be too practical to take much stock in dreams. Now he did. He knew where he would find the gold.

"Let's catch our fish and eat lunch," Garnet said. "I'm a little uneasy. I don't want to stay here any longer than I have to."

It took a moment for him to bring his mind back to the present, from the hard but probably pleasant life that Bill Chumley had lived here until the morning the posse showed up. He moved toward Garnet, the nostalgic aura that had enveloped him still shielding him from the hard truth that he and Garnet would probably be killed if Dutch

Dorfman found them here.

"What's the matter?" Reaching toward him, Garnet gripped a forearm. "Are you seeing ghosts or something?"

"That's right," Dan answered. "I was thinking of Bill Chumley. He lived all of his life here, so it seems like he's still around."

"Oh, you are a crazy one," she said, tugging at his arm. "Come on. It won't take long to catch our fish. I always caught all I wanted in half an hour. Nobody else ever fished up here."

He was still in a daze as they staked out their horses and carried a frying pan, coffee pot, and sack of sandwiches down the bank to the creek. Upstream was a waterfall that made a steady, pounding sound. Here where Dan stood, the stream flowed past them in a deep, black pool before it widened and ran swiftly in a long riffle over a pebble-covered bed.

They took only moments to cut two willow poles, tie a string, leader, and hook to one end, and bait the hook. Suddenly Dan's mind snapped to the present moment with a strike that bent his pole. He hadn't been prepared for it and lost the fish. He stood swearing at himself softly as Garnet laughed.

"I told you," she said. "It doesn't take long to catch fish here. This was the place I always came to when I wanted to find fish to take back to Ma."

The fish had taken Dan's worm off the hook. He dug the tobacco can out of his pocket that they had filled with worms before they left the boarding house and baited his hook again.

"How'd you find this spot in the first place?" Dan asked.

"Old Fred Murray used to bring me here," she answered. "He was a pretty good man, when he was younger, and Ma always trusted him to take me fishing. He spent more time fishing and hunting than he did working. I guess he knew all the fishing holes within ten miles of the basin. He'd tell me every time we came here about how he led the posse up to Chumley's place and how they all waited until Chumley came out of his cabin and how they shot him and Matt Clay was so mad he threatened to jail all of them for murder."

"He's so old and doddery now that it's hard to think of him any other way," Dan said.

"He's failed a lot in just the last year," Garnet agreed. "Like that map he was going to draw for you. You'll never see it. We all look out for him. I don't know how much longer he can get along by himself."

Dan baited his hook again, cast upstream, and, before the bait had floated to the lower end of the pool, he had hooked a ten-inch cutthroat. He landed this one. In a matter of minutes they had caught enough for themselves and some to take back to the boarding house.

Dan gathered dry driftwood for a fire, cleaned the fish, and fried two of them. After they had eaten and the fire had died down to the bed of coals, Dan lay back on the grass at the edge of the water and closed his eyes.

"This is all a man could ask for," Dan said. "A warm day, a full stomach, and the company of a pretty girl."

Impulsively Garnet reached out and took his hand that was the nearest to her. "Dan," she said softly, "you don't know how much it means to me to have you here. I guess you know that the day you walked in was a bad day for me."

He sat up. "I figured that, but I've been wondering why you wanted to pull out. It was more than being overworked, wasn't it?"

"Yes," she answered, withdrawing her hand. "You don't know Ma. She's different since you came. Easier to get along with. Before it seemed that nothing satisfied her."

She picked up a rock and tossed it into the water. "I'm going to tell you something I've never really talked to anybody about. I think you'll understand how it's been. You see, Ma is my real mother, but she's never admitted it. She's always told me one of the women who was staying in her place was my mother, and the woman went off and left me, so Ma raised me. I know different because the midwife who delivered me told me Ma was my mother. I've never told her I knew. She'd just get mad. She's never in any way showed the slightest bit of affection for me. I've just been a hired girl to her from the time I could help with the work."

He saw the stricken look on her face, more misery than he had ever seen on any person's face in his life. In a sudden rush of affection for her, he reached out and, putting an arm around her, drew her to him. His lips had barely touched hers when a rifle cracked from across the creek, the bullet sending the coffee pot kiting off the coals, the coffee pouring out through the bullet hole raising a cloud of steam from the hot ashes at the edge of the fire.

A second slug hit the gravel in front of them. The next instant a man holding a rifle stepped out of the brush on the other side of the creek. He yelled: "Mount up and get to hell out of here before I blow your brains all over the creek. Move."

XI

Dan's first impulse was to draw his gun and start shooting, but there was no cover within fifty yards. He had Garnet to think of, too. Then he realized that, if the rifleman had intended to kill them, he would have done it before now.

Dan pulled Garnet to her feet, calling: "We're going." As he climbed the bank beside Garnet, he said softly: "Let's ride before he changes his mind."

She nodded, saying nothing, but he saw from the expression on her pale face that she was terrified. They walked across the meadow to their horses, but they heard nothing from the rifleman until they rode back down the trail. When they reached him, he called: "Hey, you're the hardcase who wanted a job riding for Wineglass, ain't you, and gave us some lip on the mountain that night?"

"That's right," Dan said, and kept on riding.

"It's damned funny how you keep turning up," the man yelled at their backs. "You've been told to get out of the basin. Now you'd best do it."

Dan didn't take a deep breath until they were in the cañon and out of sight of the rifleman. Then he said: "We were lucky. I figured Dorfman had given orders to shoot anybody his guard found up here."

"I was never so scared in my life," Garnet said in a quavery voice. "That fellow was Ace Bradley. He's with Reno a lot. He's not as bad as Reno, but I don't trust him. I thought he might shoot us in the back."

"That notion went through my mind, too," Dan said.

225

They were silent until they were out of the cañon. Suddenly Dan motioned to Garnet as he said: "Pull up." She obeyed, throwing him a questioning look. He didn't give an explanation for more than a minute, but sat his horse, his head cocked as he listened.

"A bunch of horses are coming," he said. "I want a look at 'em. You go on to town and keep ahead of them."

"I'm staying, if you are," she said stubbornly.

He started to argue, then shrugged. "All right," he said, nodding at a thick grove of aspens north of the trail. "Let's get over there. We won't be clear hidden from 'em, but they're not going to be looking around much. They've got enough horses to keep 'em busy."

"You've got better ears than I have," Garnet said as she turned her mare toward the trees.

"I've been expecting something like this," Dan said. "I doubt that Dorfman keeps a guard here all the time. I figured that guard being in the cañon today meant they were doing something they didn't want anybody to see."

By the time they reached the aspens, the sound of hoofs was a steady beat. A few minutes later the horses pounded out of the cañon and into the valley, thirty or more of them, with four riders keeping them moving at a fast pace. Dan couldn't get a clear view of them through the trees, but judging from what he did see the animals were good stock. Some of them were bays, with a good proportion blacks. He saw one buckskin and one sorrel.

They raced by in a great cloud of dust, their manes streaming in the wind. As Dan had guessed, none of the riders looked in their direction. They were too intent on keeping the horses moving, and probably didn't know that Ace Bradley had driven two strangers out of the cañon.

Dan waited until the horses had turned south toward

226

Wineglass, then he said: "I reckon we can go now."

"What do you make of it?" Garnet asked.

"Looks like one of our guesses was right," Dan said. "I'd say Dorfman's into a big horse-stealing operation. They likely steal them from Utah ranchers, drive them here, change brands, then sell them to horse traders in New Mexico or Arizona. They probably plan to hold them on Wineglass range until they figure it's safe to move them out."

"What are you going to do now?" she asked.

"I'll write to Clay tonight," Dan answered. "This ought to be enough evidence to bring him up here."

When they reached the boarding house, they took care of their horses, but, before they left the shed, Dan said: "We were interrupted back there before we finished what we were starting to do."

She smiled as she turned to face him. "Then we'd better get busy and finish. I never like to leave anything until tomorrow that I can finish today."

He put his arms around her, and she tipped her face up for his kiss. When he let her go, she didn't stir from his arms, but remained motionless, her lips inches from his. She said: "I've wanted you to do that from the day you rode in. I don't think we'll ever finish it, Dan."

"Remember what you told me about Ma firing me or shooting me if I got funny with you?"

"You haven't got that funny," she said, and raised her arms and brought his lips down to hers again.

It was a long kiss, a kiss that warmed and stirred him with feelings he'd never had before. When she released him, he said: "Maybe I've been pushing you too fast, but I had a feeling about you that first day. Like we weren't strangers. I guess that's pretty crazy."

"I had the same feeling," she said. "Crazy, all right. What's it been . . . a week?"

"Just about," he said. "Well, we'd better get in or Ma will be out here to see what we're doing. She might fetch her shotgun."

She nodded and stepped away from him reluctantly. She remained silent until they were halfway to the house, then she took a long breath and said: "Dan, I'm scared. Now that I've got you, or at least I think I have. . . ."

"You've got me," he said.

She refused to be diverted. She hurried on. "I'm worried about you. You're so damned stubborn and you don't seem to be afraid of anything."

"Oh, I'm afraid, all right," he said, "but I've got something invested in this country, and I sure as hell don't want to lose it because a greedy son like Dorfman aims to keep me from having it. The gold's up there, Garnet. I'm going to get it."

"Even the gold's not worth dying for," she said doggedly. "Let's go somewhere else so you'll be safe. You never will be safe here as long as Dorfman's in the basin and you try to move onto your land."

"No." He shook his head. "I'm not leaving until this is cleared up."

"That won't be easy or safe," she said as she opened the screen door.

"I don't figure it will be," he said.

Ma was rolling out pie crusts, when they entered the kitchen. She glanced up, frowned as she looked from one to the other and back, then she said sharply: "What have you two been up to? I never saw you look like this before in your entire life, Garnet."

"I never felt this way before," Garnet said. "We almost got killed."

Ma sighed. "You always were one to exaggerate, but I . . ." She stopped, then demanded: "Didn't you catch any fish?"

"Yeah, we sure did," Dan said, "and we had 'em laid out on the bank to bring, but we didn't have time to pick 'em up."

He told her what had happened. She muttered, scowling: "That damned Dorfman! What are you fixing to do now?"

"I'll write to Matt tonight."

"For all the good it'll do," Ma grumbled. "Well, get busy. Now that you're back, Garnet, there's potatoes to peel. Dan, you'd better. . . ."

He was already halfway to the back door. She didn't finish her sentence, but waited until the screen door banged shut, then she glanced at Garnet as she said: "He's a good man, Garnet. He's the first one I haven't had to push every time I wanted to get some work done."

"I know," Garnet said softly. "I love him so, Ma. I'm going to marry him."

"Does he know?"

"Of course he knows," Garnet said as if she considered it a stupid question. "We haven't made any plans yet, but I'm worried about him. He won't give up his land, and you know Dorfman won't let him use it."

"He's got a lot of sand," Ma said as she laid a thin section of the dough across a pie pan, then picked up a knife and trimmed the dough around the edge of the pan. "Trouble is one man ain't enough against Dorfman and the crew he's got."

"I know," Garnet cried. "I asked him to leave here and go somewhere else so he'd be safe, but he wouldn't listen."

"You wouldn't have wanted him to," Ma said. "You worry about a man like him and you cry over him, and all the time you love him because he's the man he is. I never found a man like him. You're more lucky than you know."

Ma turned her back to Garnet, and for a moment the girl thought she was crying. She had never seen Ma cry; she had never seen her show any emotion except anger. For a moment she hesitated, wanting to say something but not knowing what, even wanting to hug her and tell her she knew how lucky she was, but, before she could do either, Ma wiped a hand across her eyes and snapped: "Go on, girl. We've got a supper to cook."

Garnet turned away, wondering.

XII

Dan told Matt Clay about his trip to the Chumley place, when he wrote to him. He emphasized that Ace Bradley had fired two shots at them, but he didn't say they had been warning shots. Matt could come to his own conclusions. He also emphasized the horse herd he had seen the Wineglass men drive into the basin, and theorized that they had come from Utah. He signed his name, then added a postscript, saying it was a hell of a note when a man wasn't allowed to go fishing on his own property without being shot at.

He mailed it the following morning, but he was disappointed when Mike Dugan told him that the stage wouldn't be back in Calamity for a couple of days, so Dan wouldn't receive an answer until the end of the week or the beginning of next week.

He walked home with Vera Manning that evening. As soon as they were out of the boarding house, he asked: "You get word to Angel about me?"

She was silent for a time, then she inquired: "What makes you so sure I know Angel?"

"I'm assuming you can get a message to him," Dan answered. "I don't see any sense in beating around the bush. It seems that everyone in the basin knows you know him very well."

Again she was silent. When they reached the teacherage, she stepped up on the porch and sat down in a rocking chair as she motioned toward another chair a few feet from her. She frowned, her gaze on Calamity's deserted Main Street. He didn't take the chair, but remained standing on the ground waiting for her answer.

"Garnet told me about your trouble yesterday," Vera said. "I don't know that Angel will be of any help to you, but if you'll take a ride this evening, you may find him. Go east until you reach the trees . . . close to the place where the road turns south." She glanced at the mountains to the west, the sky beginning to color above them, the sun almost down. "Better get started." She waggled a finger at him. "Remember I have not promised you anything."

"I savvy," Dan said and, turning, strode back to the boarding house.

He saddled up and rode around the boarding house to the street, then headed east. He felt the way Vera did, that Angel might not be of any help, but it was worth the trouble. He needed all the help he could get if he was going to whip Dorfman, and Angel seemed to be the only possible help. Right now he wasn't counting on any help from Matt Clay. He simply could not understand how Matt in good conscience could have ignored the basin for the last year.

Ahead of him a long spine of timber ran down from the mountains. He reached the first scattered trees in less than an hour. The road started to make a wide turn to the south as he passed an old mill, the roof caved in, the machinery badly rusted. In the thin light he made out a ranch to the north, the only one he had seen since leaving Calamity.

From what he had heard, there were a number of ranches on the east side of the basin and a few on the south end, and Dan wondered if these ranchers were as worried about Dorfman as the others he had met since coming here.

The timber made a solid mass in front of him, and, as he began the turn to the south, he saw a small campfire. He rode toward it slowly, his gaze searching the area around the fire, but no one was in sight. A coffee pot was on the fire and a small frying pan was on the ground beside it, so Angel was probably not far away.

Dan pulled up a good twenty feet from the fire and called: "Hello, the camp."

No one answered. Anger began to stir in Dan then, because this didn't seem right, and he was afraid. Here he was out in the open, a target a man couldn't miss, if he had any murderous intentions. Still, he could not think of any reason for Angel to kill him.

Dan swore and started to rein around, cursing both Vera and Angel, when a man appeared out of the shadows, calling: "Light, and have a cup of coffee."

Dan saw that it was Angel, as thin and tall as he remembered from the few seconds he had talked to him more than a week ago. Dan swung down and walked to the fire, asking: "Why all this mystery, and why keep me out here in the open, wondering if I'm about to get shot out of the saddle?"

"I told you once to keep riding," Angel said, "and that you'd find nothing but trouble in the basin. Now I hear you're crazy enough to think you can whip Dorfman single-handed and move onto the land you bought."

"I'm not crazy enough to play games with Dorfman's outfit the way you're doing," Dan snapped, "and I didn't figure on whipping Dorfman single-handed. I thought you might help."

Angel picked up a cup and filled it with coffee, then held it out to Dan. He filled another cup and squatted beside the fire, his black eyes on Dan. He had cuffed back his hat, and a lock of hair was showing below the brim that was straight and black. His skin was dark, not black or brown but darker than the average white. Suddenly it struck Dan that the man was part Indian.

"All right," Angel said. "I'll try to answer a few questions, most of them ones you haven't asked. The game I'm playing ain't just for fun, and I'm not as crazy as you seem to think. I'm trying to push Dorfman into doing something that will bring the sheriff up from Durango. Maybe I can get the ranchers to fight. If they'd work together, they could beat Dorfman, but some of them will get killed, and they ain't convinced Dorfman will do anything to them."

He sipped his coffee, his gaze still fixed on Dan's face as if sizing him up. Finally he said: "About the mystery. For one thing, I don't know much about you, and I've learned not to completely trust anyone. For another thing, being mysterious has some advantages. Folks don't know what to make of me, so they are afraid to talk much about me. I don't suppose you learned much in town about me."

"That's right, I didn't," Dan admitted.

"They don't know much," Angel said. "The way it is, Dorfman doesn't learn anything from them." He paused, then added: "Vera tells me I can trust you, but she can be fooled as well as anybody else, although she's a damned smart woman. Just now, I stayed out of sight simply because I wanted to look you over."

233

"How do you survive, with Dorfman chasing you like he does?"

Angel laughed softly. "I'm a hard man to catch, and I guess I'm enough of a kid to enjoy the game. I've got a few caves where I hole up. Some prospectors' cabins, too. In cold weather I use 'em and move around enough so Dorfman never catches me. They keep trying."

"And when they ain't chasing you," Dan said, "you're over on their side of the basin teasing 'em as you called it the other night."

"That's right," Angel said, "and it makes 'em so damned mad they just about go loco. I laugh in their faces. I aim to make 'em suffer, and Dorfman suffers because he can't stand being made a fool of. I inherited some qualities from my Cheyenne ancestors that may help in a fight like this. I've been right down at their headquarters, listening to their talk. One time when the crew was gone, I walked into the main house and caught Dorfman and one of his women having a hell of a good time in bed."

Angel slapped a thigh and laughed. "Dorfman hates me. God, how he hates me. Well, I hate him, too, but that time I had him, both of 'em naked as jay birds. Dorfman couldn't believe I'd walked into his house like I done. Other times I've put a few slugs through the windows. One time I opened up, when they were branding some horses, and you should have seen 'em scatter."

He flipped his coffee grounds toward the fire. "Sure, I've had some fun, and the hell of it is I haven't accomplished a damn' thing so far. What I'm doing ain't rational, but that's the very reason I'm still alive. Dorfman don't know when I'll hit 'em or where. I've made a fool out of him and Reno. Dorfman's a cool bastard, but if I can keep the pressure on him, I'll get him."

"You got anything personal against Dorfman?" Dan asked.

Angel untied the bandanna that he wore around his neck and pointed to the red scar on his throat. "I joined up with his outfit, but I hadn't been on Wineglass more'n a week when Reno caught me in a lie about a train robbery I said I was in and I wasn't. So they figured I had lied about some other things. They put a rope around my neck and damn' near strangled me to death. Then they told me to get out of the country. That was a mistake. They should have killed me."

The fire had died down, and the twilight was too thin to see Angel's face clearly, but Dan sensed the hatred that was in the man. Still, there had to be more to it than Angel was saying. He tossed his cup to the ground beside the fire, thinking there was no sense in asking more questions.

"Well, now," Angel said. "That's enough about me. What do you have in your sights?"

"I want to talk to you," Dan answered. "I figured we could work on Dorfman together."

He told Angel about the fishing trip with Garnet and that he knew where the gold was hidden, but he didn't know how he could dig it up without getting shot. Angel drew tobacco and papers from his pocket and began making a cigarette.

"You ain't as crazy as I thought," Angel said. "That is, providing you do actually know where the gold is. I guess you won't know that for sure until you dig it up." He fired his cigarette, then asked: "When do you figger on trying for the gold?"

"I'll wait a few days till I find out if Matt Clay is gonna take a hand in the game," Dan answered. "I think he will, but folks around here don't have much confidence in him.

So far, he hasn't done anything, but I've known him all my life, or thought I did. I guess I'll find out how much man he is."

"Get word to Vera when you want to try it," Angel said. "I'll go with you. I can keep 'em off your back while you dig."

"For a share of what's buried?"

"Hell, no," Angel said angrily. "I don't want any of your damned gold. All I want is to clean Dorfman's plow. I've had chances to kill him. I don't want to do that. Not yet. I want him to suffer, and the best way is to disgrace him, humiliate him. That's why I've been playing tag with him the way I have." He paused, his head bowed, then he said slowly: "I've hated a lot of men in my life, but none of 'em the way I hate Dutch Dorfman."

"I know one thing," Dan said, "this basin won't be safe until Dorfman is dead."

"Then, by God," Angel said, "we'll kill him, but not for a little while. He's got to suffer some more, and taking his pride away from him is the best way to do it." He rose and held out his hand. "I'll hear from you by the middle of next week?"

"That's right," Dan said as they shook hands. "Or let me hear from you if anything turns up."

He mounted, and, by the time he reined his horse around, Angel had disappeared.

236

XIII

When Dan finished cleaning up around the boarding house, work that had been neglected for a long time, Ma admitted that the place looked better than it had for months, then she told Dan to harness up the team and go with Garnet to cut wood.

"You'll be hauling wood for the next month," Ma said.

Through the rest of the week Dan enjoyed being with Garnet, but he hated the work. He had never used a crosscut saw or an axe, and he found himself pitifully inadequate. The first loads they brought in were skimpy because Dan wasn't doing his part, but Garnet didn't complain, and Ma didn't say anything if she noticed how small the loads were. By the end of the week Dan had developed considerable facility with both tools and had collected some sore muscles in the process.

While they were eating their lunch under some tall pines on Friday, Garnet told Dan that the odds were Dorfman and Reno would come to the boarding house on Saturday for their dinners. She said they seldom missed two Saturdays in a row, and they had not come the previous Saturday.

"I've never met Dorfman," Dan mused, "but I've heard enough about the man to make me feel I know him."

"You'll be surprised when you meet him," Garnet said. "He's not a bully as you'd expect. He's smooth, he's handsome, and you think you'd just have to like him."

"Well," Dan said, "I won't like him. I don't know what I'll say when I meet him. I'd like to punch him in the nose,

237

but for Ma's sake, I guess, I'll take it easy."

"She wants you to wait on the table," Garnet said. "She'll sit with the boarders, so it will be up to us to take care of the serving. She thinks she can keep the lid on, if she's there at the table all the time."

"I guess I'd rather have it that way," Dan said. "I don't want to shake hands with the son-of-a-gun, so I'll stay as far away from him as I can."

"Vera and Fred Murray will be there," Garnet said. "Maybe several of Dorfman's crew. We have to be ready for a full table, but we never know how many we'll have on Saturday."

Dan had not told Garnet about his talk with Angel. He'd thought about it all week, and he still felt there was something about the man he couldn't put his finger on, something that was important. He finished his sandwich and lay back on a carpet of pine needles. The ground was covered with them, and he thought that, if a fire started up here, it would be out of control immediately. There had been no rain for weeks, and needles and twigs crackled under foot.

"We need rain," he said, "and we'll get lightning when it does rain."

"Then we'll get fires," Garnet said.

But his mind wasn't on the weather or fires. It always circled back to Angel, and he had a growing feeling that the man would turn out to be the key to what was happening. He asked a question that had been prodding him for days. "How did Angel and Vera get acquainted?"

"We don't know," Garnet said. "She applied for the school last summer after Dorfman had bought old man Apple out. She was hired and moved into the teacherage. We're a long ways from anywhere, and the pay is low, so nobody else wanted the job. Angel showed up that fall. It wasn't long until folks began noticing that he'd come late at night to see Vera, mostly on Friday and Saturday nights. He never comes to school affairs or to dances or even to town except at night."

"Didn't anybody . . . the school board or anybody . . . ask Vera what he was doing there?"

She laughed. "Sure they did, but Vera is a tough woman and as independent as they come. She told them it was none of their business. By that time it was the middle of the winter and there was no way they could get a new teacher to come and take the school. By May, when school was out, they all knew Vera was a good teacher, and no one wanted to fire her, even if she was living a life of sin."

"They'd known each other before," Dan guessed.

Garnet nodded. "That's what we think, but we don't know which came first. That is, did Vera apply for the job here because she knew Angel was coming, or did Angel come to the basin because he knew Vera was here?"

Dan began seeing Vera in a different light. She was, on the surface, a pleasant, polished woman who, from what he had heard, satisfied everyone with her teaching. That, he knew, was not easy in a small country school. The thought had occurred to him that Angel was an outlaw, that what he had told Dorfman about robbing a train was not as much of a lie as he had pretended. Maybe he was really hiding from the law by staying in the basin.

"Does she keep the kids under control?" Dan asked.

"You never saw anything like it," Garnet answered. "I don't know how she does it, and she's got boys twice as big as she is, but they're afraid to turn a hand in school."

"It's a gift," Dan said. "I've had tough teachers like that, and the funny thing is that we all liked them better than the easy ones."

239

"They love her," Garnet said.

She finished eating and fitted the lid back onto her dinner pail. She sighed. "You changed our lives the day you rode in here," she said. "It's been wonderful. Ma hasn't had a temper fit for almost two weeks. She says I'd better marry you."

"We've got to think on that," he said, and put out a hand to her.

She took his hand and leaned down and kissed him. "What are your intentions, sir?"

"Honorable," he answered, "but I've got to decide if I want to build a ranch up there on the Chumley place. Doesn't seem like a good idea right now. It would take a lot of work to clear the meadow and put up some buildings and clean out the ditches. I wouldn't ask you to go through all of that with me. Maybe Bill Chumley could face it, but I can't."

"I know," she said gravely, "it wouldn't really give a couple a living after you did all of that work."

"I bought it cheap," he said, "so I won't be out much."

She nodded. "I guess so, but we can always go fishing up there."

"If we can get Dorfman off our backs."

"We will," she said as if there was no doubt about it. She hesitated, then asked: "You said you didn't have a father when you grew up?"

"That's right," he said. "My ma raised me. It must have been that way with you, too."

"Not exactly," she said glumly. "That's why I don't feel right about Ma. My father might have been any of a dozen men she slept with, but after she turned her place into a boarding house, she became the most straight-laced woman in town. She raised me that way, always worried about some man touching me and what I'd let him do."

Her face turned grave, and she looked out across the basin that stretched out for miles below them. "That's what's funny about the way she thinks of you. She hasn't known you very long, but she says she's a good judge of men. I guess she's had enough experience to be a good judge. She's failing, too. You've noticed she takes a nap or goes to bed early. She never used to do that. I think she's got something wrong with her heart that she hasn't told me. . . ."

A rifle cracked from somewhere up the hillside above them, the bullet sending Dan's lunch pail spinning down the slope. For an instant Dan froze, unable to believe what was happening. He did not have either his .45 or his Winchester. He had not thought that Dorfman wanted him killed badly enough to send a dry-gulcher after him.

"Get to cover," he yelled, and dived toward the log they had been working on.

He bellied down on the lower side, turning his head enough to see that Garnet was down behind the log a few feet from him. It was not adequate cover, but there wasn't any other close enough to get to without being cut down.

The hell of it was he couldn't fight back, he couldn't risk showing himself by running, so the dry-gulcher could keep them pinned down for hours. He'd simply wait until Dan got so tired of lying here that he'd make some kind of stupid move, and he'd be a sitting duck for the man.

"He's after me," Dan said, "but if he thinks you got a glimpse of him, he'll beef you, too. This is a hell of a fix I've got you into."

"You didn't get me into it," she cried. "What are we going to do?"

"Nothing, right now," he said. "We may have to wait until it's dark."

"We can't do that," she said. "I couldn't lie here that long without moving."

"If you move," he said, "you'll get a slug."

"Why?" she demanded. "You haven't done anything for Dorfman to want to kill you."

"Maybe it's Reno up there," Dan said. "He sure wants me dead. Or maybe Dorfman figures I'm dangerous now that I own the land on both sides of the creek."

He lay motionless, trying to think of some way out of the box they were in. He worried more about Garnet than he did himself. He had no way of measuring the meanness and brutality of a man who could murder another man from ambush.

He reached for a stick, placed his hat on one end, and lifted it above the log. His action brought another shot, the bullet driving through the crown of his hat. Dan lowered the stick, a sense of helplessness rushing through him.

A second rifle cracked from farther up the hill, then another shot. It was too much to have expected, but some other man had taken chips in the game. He said — "Don't move." — and tried again to lure the killer into taking another shot, but nothing happened.

A minute or two later a man called: "It's over. You can get up."

Dan took a moment to identify the voice, then he realized it was Angel who had called. He rose and, looking up the hill, saw that Angel was lifting a man's body onto a horse. He watched Angel tie the body down and give the animal a whack with his hat. The horse loped down the slope as Angel mounted and rode to where Dan and Garnet waited.

When he reached them, Dan said: "How do you thank a man who saves your hide?"

"Don't try," Angel said. "It's all part of the game. Dorfman's got one less hardcase." He paused, staring at the horse that was disappearing into the timber below them. "As soon as Dorfman sees his man, he's gonna go loco. He'll guess it was me, so he'll try again to run me into a corner."

He rode on.

Dan called: "If Matt Clay shows up and goes after Dorfman, do you want to go with us?"

"No," Angel called back, and kept riding.

Staring at his back, Dan had the thought that maybe Angel had good reason not to have anything to do with a lawman.

XIV

A few minutes after eleven o'clock Saturday morning, Garnet, looking through a front window, called: "Dan, Dorfman's in town." When he reached the window, she said: "That big roan tied in front of the store belongs to him. The bay is Reno's horse."

Dan took a long breath, wondering if he should strap on his gun belt, then decided it wouldn't be the thing to do. Ma would object, and maybe Reno would take it as a sign Dan was on the prod. He was, he told himself, but he didn't want to make trouble under Ma's roof.

He had never met a man he could call a thoroughly bad man, but Dutch Dorfman, judging from what he had done since coming to the basin, was a bad man. Dan was not one to condemn a man he had never seen, but he condemned

243

Dorfman simply on the basis of his record. He had no doubt that Dorfman had ordered his killing, and only bad shooting on the part of his ambusher had kept Dan alive. There would come a day when he would face Dorfman with that accusation, but today he would try to keep the peace.

Ma was more concerned about what was going to happen than Dan was. The meal was ready long before twelve. As the three waited in the kitchen, Ma said: "Dan, just see that they have coffee and water when they need it. Otherwise, I want you to sit down and enjoy your dinner after everything is on the table." She hesitated, then added sourly: "I don't need Dorfman's business, and many's the time I've thought of telling him not to come here anymore, but I was afraid I'd make things worse."

She stopped, her features twisted into a worried scowl. "Maybe you've heard of the business I used to be in?"

"Yes, I have," Dan said.

She studied him intently. "It don't make any difference?"

"Hell, no."

She sighed. "Like I told Garnet, you're a good man. I haven't met any that I considered either good or bad. Most men don't cut the ice either way. Dorfman now, he's a bad one and no mistake. I've had men who beat up my girls. I'd gun 'em out of the house. I even shot one man. He didn't die, but I wish he had. Dorfman is that kind, but to just be around him you'd never know it."

She stared through the dining room door into the front room where Vera and Fred Murray were already seated. "Here he comes with Reno. I've always been uneasy when they're here, but I'm downright worried today." She turned to Garnet. "I'll call them to the table. You finish cutting the roast. Dan, you fetch it to the table."

She stomped out of the kitchen and went on through the

dining room into the front room. Garnet, slicing the roast, said softly: "She's wound up tighter'n I've ever seen her. Sometimes she seems to know what's going to happen. I think she knows something now that worries her."

Standing beside the kitchen range, Dan watched Vera enter the dining room, a stranger beside her who was talking animatedly, his big hands in constant motion. He would be Dorfman, Dan thought, and, as Garnet had told him, he was surprised at the man's appearance. Dorfman was not big and broad-shouldered and rough of features as Dan had mentally pictured him. Rather, he was medium height, fine-featured, and handsome. He wore a brown broadcloth suit, white shirt, and a black tie, with a gold watch chain across his vest.

Dorfman had taken off his broad-brimmed Stetson and had hung it on an antler rack in the living room. He wore cowboy boots that were scuffed and had manure dried on them. Still, he did not look like a rancher, even though the skin of his face was lined and wrinkled from countless hours in the saddle.

Fred Murray and Reno followed Dorfman and Vera. Ma, who had stepped back into the dining room, took a chair at the head of the table and motioned for the others to sit down. Dorfman sat around the corner from Ma, Vera on the other side of him. Fred Murray had the chair across from Dorfman, Reno beside him.

Garnet took a plate of biscuits from the warming oven and, carrying it into the dining room, set it on the table in front of Dorfman, then seated herself near the foot of the long table.

Reno, smiling at her, patted the chair next to him. "Sit beside me, Garnet."

"Thank you," she said, her tone carefully neutral, "but I

have to be next to the kitchen."

Ma had told Dan to take care of the serving if anything was needed, but the answer Garnet gave Reno was a logical excuse for her not to sit beside him. Dan grinned, noting the expression of dislike on her face, but he told himself that Reno wasn't a man to notice anything that wasn't as plain as the nose on his face.

Dan carried the platter of roast beef into the dining room and handed it to Ma who passed it to Dorfman. Dan returned to the kitchen for the gravy. Reno was staring at Dan as if he thought he ought to know him, but it was not until Dan started back into the dining room that recognition flooded his face.

"Well," Reno shouted, "look at our waiter, Dutch. A tough *hombre*, wearing an apron and carrying grub into the dining room." He lifted a hand and waggled his fingers at Dan, a sneer curling his lips. "That apron fits you to a T, kitchen boy."

Dan had started down Dorfman's side of the table, expecting to hand the gravy boat to Ma just as he had the roast beef, but when he heard Reno's derisive words, he reversed himself and walked along Reno's side of the table, the gravy boat held in front of him. Reno sat with his face tipped up, a grin stretching his meaty-lipped mouth across his face.

Again Dan gave way to impulse. When he reached Reno, he held the gravy boat over Reno's face and turned it upside down, the hot brown gravy running down his face and onto his shirt. The gravy had been off the stove long enough to cool, so it didn't actually burn Reno, but it hurt, and he let out a squall of agony as he clawed at his face. He tried to get up out of his chair, cursing in a wild rage, but somehow he lost his balance and fell backward to the floor, making a terrific thump that set the dishes dancing on the table. He lay there twisting and cursing and trying to wipe the gravy off his face.

Garnet jumped up and, running into the kitchen, grabbed a towel that hung beside the washstand and ran back into the dining room. She knelt beside the man to wipe the gravy off his face. Dan coolly set the empty gravy boat on the table and strode into his bedroom. When he returned, he was wearing his gun. By that time Garnet had Reno on his feet and was leading him into the kitchen to wash his face and hands.

Dan picked up the empty gravy boat and, going back into the kitchen, poured what was left of the gravy into the dish and returned it to the dining room. Without a word he handed it to Ma. Once more he went back to the kitchen and returned with dishes of potatoes and turnips. Then he sat down at the end of the table.

Dorfman sat staring wide-eyed at Dan, his expression less friendly than it had been. He said: "You must be the Dan Larsen I've been hearing about."

"That's exactly who I am," Dan said, unable to keep the hot anger out of his voice that boiled up in him. Then, because he knew he couldn't be any worse off than he was as far as Dorfman was concerned, he added: "I bought the old Chumley place from the county. When I got here, I found out that you claim that land and won't let anyone else on it."

Dorfman smiled tolerantly. "Quite so."

"Damn it, I own that property," Dan said hotly. "I have a right to live on land that belongs to me."

"Not in the basin, you don't," Dorfman said blandly. "I don't give a damn about the law in Durango. The law here in Calamity is something else. You'd better accept reality, my young friend, if you want to die of old age."

Fred Murray cackled, his wrinkled face filled with the pleasure of being able to tell Dutch Dorfman something he didn't know. "Young Larsen here says he's going to find the gold Bill Chumley hid up there. I told him there wasn't no gold. We found all of it twenty years ago, but he thinks he knows. He's a damned young whipper-snapper, Mister Dorfman."

The Wineglass man nodded, speculative eyes on Dan. "That's true. In case you do find anything up there, it belongs to me."

"Oh, hell," Murray said in a high-pitched voice of excitement, "he can't even find out where the Chumley place is. I told him I'd draw him a map, but I never got around to it."

Reno returned from the kitchen, his face red from the scrubbing it had just received. Dorfman said pleasantly: "Now are you going to settle down and eat this fine dinner, Reno, and be polite to everyone?"

Reno opened his mouth to say something, then closed it and glared at Dan, but he did sit down, mumbling: "Yeah, I'm going to eat."

"Everything is getting cold," Ma said plaintively. "Please dig in, Mister Dorfman."

"Of course, Missus Willett," Dorfman said as he helped himself to the meat. "I guess I just kind of got carried away by the excitement. We have never had this kind of thing happen at our table, Missus Willet. Perhaps you will want to fire this fellow."

"Perhaps not," Ma said, her tone icy, "but you might think of firing Reno. He started the whole business."

"I'll make up my own mind who I fire," Dorfman said.

"So will I," Ma said.

There was little talk after that. Everyone ate hurriedly

and silently, Dan sensing the tension that gripped the diners. Dorfman obviously had not expected Ma to answer him as she had, and Dan wondered if she realized she had put herself into a dangerous situation. Dorfman would certainly try again to kill him, but regardless of what happened to him Ma was in trouble. He couldn't tell how much trouble. Dorfman, for all of his suave and cool manner, was a maniac. He probably had logical reasons for controlling the basin, but regardless of that he simply was not a man who could bear being defied.

There was no standing around talking when dinner was finished. Dorfman moved to the door, but Reno stood motionless for a moment, staring at Dan, then he turned and walked into the living room. Garnet hurried past him and disappeared down the hall.

Ma shook her head at Vera who moved toward her, saying: "Stay out of trouble."

"I'm already into any trouble that concerns Dorfman," Vera said. "I think I can find Angel. He'll help."

"We'll be all right." Ma glared at Murray. "You always were an idiot, clear back to when you brought the posse down on Bill Chumley. You still are. Just once I'd like to see you keep your damned mouth shut."

"Yeah, sure, Ma." He swallowed, lowering his gaze. "I didn't aim to hurt nobody."

"You never do," Ma said grimly. "Now get to hell out of here before I forget I'm a lady."

Murray shoved his chair back and left the dining room as fast as his rheumatic legs could carry him. Dan had started to stack the dishes, fully aware that Reno would not let this go. He was also aware that he was no match for the man, if it came to a gun fight, but he didn't see how he could avoid it. His bravado had backed him into a corner. He had found a woman he loved, a woman he wanted to marry, and now the chances were he'd be dead in another ten minutes.

Dan carried a stack of dirty dishes into the kitchen. When he returned, Vera was gone. Ma still sat at the table, her face pale. She said: "Vera's hell-bent on getting hold of Angel. Well, I don't think he can do anything to help." She swallowed, then flung out a hand. "Damn it, Dan, don't let that son-of-a-bitch call you out. He's already done that with two good men, and he killed them. He'll do it with you, if you let him."

Dan didn't say anything, but began piling the rest of the dishes that were left on the table.

Ma went on: "I ain't blaming you for what you done, though it sure was a waste of good gravy. It's the first time I ever saw anybody get the best of Reno, and it was the first time I ever talked back to Dorfman. I've always been polite to him, but many's the time I've felt like punching him in the nose. But I've done it now, and I guess I'm finished in the basin."

"Maybe not," Dan said. "We'll hang and rattle. If Vera can get hold of Angel. . . ."

Garnet's yell from the hall — "Let me go!" — interrupted Dan.

He started out of the dining room on the run as he heard Reno shout: "You can't stay here. You'll be killed, if you do. Come out to Wineglass. We'll take care of you."

Dan plunged through the front door and made the turn into the hall, his hands fisted, then he stopped, flat-footed. Garnet was backed against the wall, Reno's hands on both sides of her, but, just as Dan turned the corner, Garnet succeeded in squirming around enough to have room to swing a foot. She gave Reno a savage kick just above the top of his boot. She was wearing cowboy boots, and the sharp point of her toe apparently sent a spasm of pain up Reno's leg. He stumbled back against the opposite wall, cursing as he raised a hand to hit her, but by that time she was halfway down the hall to the front door.

Dan laughed as Garnet ran past him. He said: "You're having a bad day, Reno. You get a baptism of gravy, now a girl gives you a bunged-up leg. You'd better get on your horse and head for home."

Reno dropped a hand to the butt of his gun, then drew it away. He said: "I ain't having half as bad a day as you're going to have. I'll give you thirty seconds to come outside. I don't want to spill your blood on Ma's carpet."

He stalked past Dan and went out into the bright light of midday. Dan, staring at his back, knew there was no way he could back out of it, and now, facing death, he realized how much he wanted to live. He had been asking for trouble from the moment he had defied Reno and his two friends on the mountain, but that had been before he had met Garnet, and that made all the difference in the world.

Dan drew his gun and checked it carefully, then eased it back into leather, the thought in his mind that, even if he was lucky enough to down Reno, he hadn't solved the problem. Dorfman could always replace a man like Reno who would pick up the fight where Reno had dropped it.

He glanced up in time to see Garnet dart out through the front door and run across the street to the store. Ma was there, her hands on her hips.

"Don't go out there, Dan," she said. "Nobody says you have to. Dorfman's holding a pat hand. I don't want you dead, for Garnet's sake, if not yours. I've seen Reno use a gun. He's fast."

Dan stepped around her and walked slowly toward the door, Ma's words beating at him: "You're a fool, Dan

Larsen. All men are fools when it comes to honor or whatever it is you're trying to prove." She grabbed his arm.
"Damn it, Dan . . . !"

He jerked free and stepped through the door and went
on across the boardwalk, then his boots bit into the dust of
the street. Reno stood on the other side of the street,
waiting, a triumphant grin on his face.

XV

Dan stopped after taking three steps into the street, remembering that he'd heard an old-time gunfighter say that one of
the best ways to upset an opponent was to stall. "Take a lot of
time," the man had said. "Let him think about what's going to
happen. The more time you take, the jumpier he's going to be,
and the worse shooting he's gonna do."

He stood motionless, aware that Dorfman was watching
from the front of the store, but he kept his attention riveted
on Reno who now began to move toward the middle of the
street, his right hand close to the butt of his gun. Still Dan
didn't move. Suddenly Garnet rushed out of the store and
ran to the bank. Irritated, Dan wanted to shout at her to get
off the street and stay off. *Why wasn't she in the boarding
house where she belonged?*

Reno's patience frayed and broke. He snarled: "Get out
here into the street, damn it. Or are you going to run back
into the boarding house?"

The old gunfighter had been right, Dan thought. Slowly
he took another step forward, watching Reno closely for the
first hint that he was going to draw. The Wineglass man

would make his move sooner or later, if Dan didn't, but he knew Reno preferred to wait. It would look better, if Matt Clay ever investigated the killing. Self-defense, Reno would say. It was what he had said when he had killed the two men.

Dan took another step, very deliberately, then he realized how tense he was and that nothing was going to work for him. He saw Garnet run out of the bank and across the street behind Reno. He tried to yell at her, but no words came. Diverted for an instant from his own danger, he felt a rush of anger. If he had got off a shot then, she would have been in the direct line of fire.

"Come on, pilgrim," Reno taunted. "Don't you want to die?"

Dan took two steps and faced Reno, his self-control leaving him. He knew this was the moment. He felt a cold stone in the bottom of his belly; he saw the grin on Reno's face, the hungry, wolf-like expression telling him that taking a man's life was the very mountain peak of pleasure for Reno.

But Reno, ready to draw, never moved his hand toward his gun butt. Ma's bellow broke in the tense silence. "I'll blow your head off, if you touch your gun, Reno. We've had two good men killed in our town by you. We don't aim to have no more."

Dan and Reno froze, heads swinging toward the boarding house. Ma stood in front of the door, a cocked, double-barreled shotgun in her hands, the gun aimed squarely at Reno. For a moment it seemed to the astonished Dan that all life had stopped, that they had been turned into stone statues here on Calamity's Main Street. Ma's face was red, her mouth hard-set, and Dan, staring at her, knew she would do exactly what she had said. Reno must have known it, too.

"If you think I might miss your ugly carcass," Ma yelled, "just take a look at Mike Dugan. And Sam Gerard. And Jerry Moran behind you. The same goes for your boss. I've got no more use for him than I have for you. Now get on your horses and vamoose. Both of you."

Dan turned his head to see Mike Dugan standing in the doorway of his store, a shotgun in his hands. The same was true of Sam Gerard who was behind Reno. And Jerry Moran was on the other side of the street in front of the blacksmith shop.

"Well, by God, pilgrim," Reno said, "you always seem to have someone pulling you out of the fire before you get burned. I had a chance to beef you that night on the mountain. I should have done it."

"Let's drift, Reno," Dorfman said.

Slowly Reno turned toward his horse. Dorfman had already untied his mount and now stepped into the saddle. He tipped his head at Ma as he said: "You've just committed suicide. You and your town, too. You were a hell of a lot smarter when you were a whore. You'll get no more business from us."

Reno swung up, then jabbed a forefinger in Ma's direction. "She's still a whore, Dutch. She always will be. Now she's playing nursemaid to her serving boy."

For a moment Dan had felt the tension that had built up in him beginning to fade; he was alive, and he would go on living a little longer, but, when Reno called him a serving boy, a wild rage roared through him and beat at him. He started toward Reno, intent on pulling him out of the saddle and beating him into a bloody pulp. He wasn't great with a gun, but he knew what he could do with his fists.

"No, Dan," Ma shouted. "Let 'em get out of town. That's all we want. Dorfman, we don't need your business.

254

I've been wanting to tell you that for months, but I've been afraid to. I'm glad I've got the guts to do it now."

For a moment Dorfman sat his saddle, his gaze on Ma. He said in a low, fury-filled voice: "This stinking little town has been a useless pimple on the face of the earth too long. We're going to wipe it out. Get out of town, all of you, if you want to live."

Dorfman reined his horse around, dug in the steel, and left town on the dead run, Reno a few feet behind him. Dan heard Ma's sigh of relief, then Gerard, Dugan, and Moran all moved forward to stand around her. Garnet appeared from the blacksmith shop and walked rapidly along the street to the boarding house and disappeared inside.

Dan stood motionless. His hand had fallen away from the butt of his gun, and his shoulders sagged. He was relieved, but he was angry, too. He glared at Ma, wanting to tell her she had no right to butt into his business even it had meant saving his life. She was looking at him as if expecting him to tell her exactly that.

Gerard nodded at Dan as he said in his gentle voice: "I know how you feel, Larsen. Right now, you're thinking you're less than a man for having a woman interfere in your life. It's not true. Maybe Ma wanted to save you for your own sake, but I was thinking of myself and this basin. You've had the guts to stand up to Reno ever since you had the set-to on the mountain. That meant standing up to Dorfman. You're the best chance we've got to whip that bastard. You'll get plenty of opportunity to show how much you've got in the way of guts before this is over."

"That's right," Dugan added. "I was scared to death. I still am. That son-of-a-bitch will be back with his whole crew."

Jerry Moran nodded. "They'll kill us and burn the town.

If we had a lick of sense, we'd be on our way out of town, but I reckon we won't be doing no such thing."

"No, we won't." Ma was still holding her shotgun on the ready as if she still needed it. She was pale-faced, shaking as she looked at Dan. "I apologize for what I done, but we" — she motioned to the three men surrounding her — "talked it over. We decided we were not going to have any more of Reno's killings. Murders, they were. No ordinary cowhand is going to beat a professional gunslick like Reno. It's like Sam said. We did this for our own sakes, not just yours."

Dan didn't have anything to say to that. He looked from one to the other and on around the circle back to Ma, not sure he was hearing the truth, but, truth or not, he could not argue with it. He said — "They'll be back, all right." — and turned and walked into the boarding house.

Garnet was standing just inside the doorway. She had been crying, and, when Dan reached her, she threw her arms around him and hugged him, a wet cheek pressed against his. "Oh, Dan, I thought I'd lost you. I died a thousand times while I was running to the store and the bank and the blacksmith shop. I kept expecting to hear gunshots, and I'd look around and see you lying in the street. I couldn't stand it. To have found and lost you was more than I could stand."

She kissed him, holding onto him as if she was never going to let anything take him from her. He knew, then, for all of his injured pride and anger at Ma's butting into his fight, that the older woman had been right. It would have been a foolish and useless way to die. He knew, too, and it was a good feeling, that he would have his chance. The choice was clear. Get out, or stay and fight, and maybe die.

When she gave him a chance to talk, he said: "They were saying that Dorfman will be back with his crew. I guess a man with pride can't do anything else. Anyhow, it ain't just me. It's everybody. I think you'd better go to Durango. You'd be safe there."

"Me?" She was angry as she drew back to stare at him. "What do you take me for? I can shoot."

Stubborn women, Ma and Garnet. Ma had just come in. As she brushed past them, she said: "I think we need a bracer."

Dan and Garnet followed her. She went on into the pantry and returned with a whiskey bottle and three glasses. She said: "I'm not much of a whiskey drinker, but I figure we all need this." She poured their drinks, then turned her gaze to Dan. "Am I forgiven?"

Some of the anger was still in him. He kept telling himself that what she had done was right, that she had, indeed, saved his life, and yet for some irrational reason he found it hard to accept the fact that he owed his life to a woman's interference. He barely nodded, knowing that he would be fighting himself for a long time over this.

Ma lifted her glass as she said: "To a long and happy life for both of you. I could not let you die, Dan. For Garnet's sake."

They touched glasses and drank, and slowly the warmth of the whiskey washed through Dan's body and dispelled the chill that possessed him. He relaxed and was able to bring a small smile to his lips as he turned his gaze to Garnet.

Ma had dropped into a chair and leaned forward, her elbows on the table. "God, I'm shaking and I'm tired and I'm ashamed of myself for all the times that I let Dorfman and Reno eat here when I hated 'em and knew what they'd do sooner or later. I likewise knew we had to do something. I thought about putting poison in their food, but that ain't my way." She heaved a long sigh, and added: "I'm glad it's come to a head."

Dan wheeled to the door, calling back over his shoulder: "I'm going to chop some wood."

He left the kitchen and crossed the back yard to the woodpile, but he didn't pick up the axe. He sat down on the chopping block and stared at the mountains that formed what appeared to be an impassable barrier, blocking his way to the gold his father had hidden. It wasn't impassable, of course. If anything barred his way, it was Dorfman and his crew.

He didn't move for a long time. The early afternoon sun warmed him, and he was comfortable except for the rat that was gnawing at the inside of his stomach. Overhead a few cottony clouds drifted toward the rim of mountains to the east. He'd had his look at death, his pride had been injured, and suddenly he wished Matt Clay was here.

XVI

Dan had his wish before he expected it. Matt Clay rode in late that afternoon. Dan was carrying an armload of wood into the kitchen when Clay rode around the boarding house toward the shed. Dan dropped the wood and let out a whoop as he ran toward Clay.

The sheriff dismounted and shook hands with Dan, then slapped him on the back. "Well, son," Clay said, his expression grave, "from what I hear, you've been having some fun since you got here."

"I guess you could say that," Dan said as he led Clay's horse toward the shed. "A little more than you've heard."

As he off-saddled, he told Clay what had happened early that afternoon. "They'll come in here, fixing to shoot the men, maybe the women, too, if they give 'em any trouble, and burn the town. If Reno had beefed me, which he figured on doing, they probably would have left the town alone, but with Ma and the businessmen taking chips in the game, well, Dorfman's got too much pride to let it go."

Clay filled his pipe and fired it, listening to what Dan had to say, then nodded. "You're right about that. I've been writing around to other sheriffs, trying to find out all I can about Dorfman, but I didn't learn a damned thing. I don't know where he came from or what he did before he showed up here. Maybe he's changed his name, and maybe this is a long ways from his stomping ground, but I'm reasonably sure his crew are wanted men." He pulled on his pipe, eyeing Dan as he finished watering and feeding his horse, then he said: "I figure on riding out to Wineglass in the morning. Want to go?"

Dan stepped out of the stall and stood staring at Clay. He said: "Sure, I'll go, which ain't saying I want to. We'll never get out of there alive."

"Yes, we will," Clay said. "I don't know Dorfman that well, but I'll give him credit for being smart. He'll know it was no secret where I've gone, so he'll know my deputies will be up there with a posse, looking for me, if I don't show up in Durango."

Dan didn't want to argue with Clay, but he didn't think it would work the way the sheriff had said, simply because Dorfman figured his will was the law in the basin. Dan said: "He's smart, I'll give him that." Her jerked his head toward the boarding house. "Let's go put the feed bag on." As they started toward the kitchen door, he added: "Me 'n' Garnet are getting married."

259

"I'll be damned." Clay stared wide-eyed at Dan who was picking up the sticks of wood he had dropped. "You've been busy."

"I reckon." Dan grinned. "Don't make sense, knowing her as short a time as I have, but, Matt, she's one hell of a woman. I'll tell you all about it when I get time."

"How you getting along with Ma?"

"Good." Dan straightened up, the wood in his arms. "I'd heard some bad things about her. Even from Garnet. I guess she cottons to me because I work hard. That's one reason she stuck her nose into my fight with Reno today, though she didn't say so. She was fighting with Garnet something fierce when I came, but Ma thinks a lot of her even though she never says so, and Garnet don't think so."

Dan opened the screen door and stepped into the kitchen, calling, "We've got a customer for supper."

Ma looked up from the kitchen stove, where she was stirring gravy. "Why, you old horse thief. Where'd you come from?"

"Just dropped out of the sky," Clay said, grinning broadly. "Got an extra plate for me at your table?"

"Oh, I dunno about that," Ma said truculently. "You took a hell of a long time getting here."

Garnet, standing in the pantry doorway, said: "Of course, we have. I apologize for Ma's bad manners."

"Don't apologize for me, girl," Ma snapped. "He has been a long time getting here."

"Guilty," Clay agreed.

Ma motioned toward the washbasin. "Go ahead and clean up. Supper'll be ready in a minute."

After they were seated at the table, Ma said: "I reckon Dan told you what happened today?" When Clay nodded, she demanded: "Well, you gonna do anything about it?"

260

"I dunno what I'm going to do . . . or can do," Clay said. "I'm going out to Wineglass in the morning with Dan. I don't know if I can get Dorfman to listen to anything I say or not." He hesitated, then added: "I'll stay here, if you think he's gonna make his play right away."

"Who knows?" Ma shrugged. "It's my guess he'll wait a while. He knows we'll be expecting an attack, so he'll probably hold off till he figures he can catch us off guard."

Clay nodded. "I still can't figure this out. He knows a raid like this will bring me and a posse into it. So far he's stayed within bounds, so I haven't done anything. I couldn't make a charge stick on anything that's happened so far, so why does he threaten to do something now that he knows will stick?"

"You've heard of Angel?" Ma asked.

Clay nodded. "Not much. Just that he plays with Dorfman, and that Dorfman's been trying to catch him."

"Vera Manning . . . she's the schoolteacher and Angel's woman . . . Vera thinks Dorfman never took over Wineglass with the idea of making a ranch out of it." Ma sliced her steak, frowning thoughtfully. "Sometimes I think nobody has any sense but me. I sure don't think Dorfman was smart to come in and run Wineglass for a year, then walk off and leave it."

"That's exactly the way it's sizing up," Clay said. "He made his down payment to old man Apple and nothing since. He was to pay the note off by the end of the year. Apple waited, thinking he'd come through, but he hasn't, so now Apple's gonna close him out, and I've got to tell him he's lost his spread."

"If you can get him off Wineglass," Ma said. "Vera told me that Dorfman had the idea that an out-of-the-way place like the basin would be perfect for a ranch they could bring

261

stolen horses to, change the brand, then sell 'em somewhere else. He's been doing that, I guess."

Clay nodded. "We were guessing that was his game."

"The other thing is that he wanted a place where men on the dodge could come and hole up," Ma went on. "He thought he could charge these men a lot of money and make a fortune, but it didn't work out the way he expected. Nobody much showed up, so now he's restless and ready to move on. I suppose that's why he hasn't paid old man Apple. He don't care if he does lose the spread."

"That could be," Clay conceded.

"Dorfman's made some money," Ma said, "no matter what he does now. He sold off all of the Wineglass cattle." She waggled a finger at Clay. "There's something funny about Dorfman. He ain't normal. He's so proud he's wacky. He can't stand any criticism. He can't bear to have anyone defy him, so he's gonna hit us before he pulls out."

"If he's moving," Dan said, "why has he built the fence, and put out a guard to keep everybody off Wineglass, and run some of his neighbors off their places? And tried to keep me off my property?"

"He intended to run the spread as a horse ranch," Ma said. "For stolen animals, that is. Naturally he wanted privacy. As for your place, it controlled the only way into the basin where he could drive his stolen horses without folks seeing 'em."

It seemed to make sense, Dan thought. Then he asked: "How did Vera happen to tell you all this? She was a clam, when I talked to her."

"She's been that way with me, too," Ma said, "until this afternoon. I think she opened up because she knows it's gonna be a showdown." Ma picked up her cup of coffee. "One thing I don't know. Why does Angel keep plaguing

Dorfman the way he does?"

"He told me he wanted to kill Dorfman," Dan said, "but not until after he's made him suffer."

"He's vindictive," Garnet said. "He'll be on his way as soon as Dorfman's dead, and it's my guess Vera will go with him."

Clay had finished eating. He sat back and dug his pipe and tobacco out of his pocket. "We're all crazy in one way or another. Mostly in little ways that don't matter much, but I've always noticed that lawbreakers are crazy in big things. Sure, they're rational enough to get along, but there's always a part of their makeup that ain't right. It strikes me Dorfman's that way. So's Angel."

"He is," Dan agreed. "I've only talked to him a couple of times, but I sure had that notion."

Ma rose. "I'll let you off tonight, Dan. Go ahead and visit with Matt."

"I'd like that," Dan said, and led the way through the front room to the porch.

They sat down, Clay puffing on his pipe. Dan stared off across the basin, the sun almost hidden behind the granite peaks to the west. Neither spoke for a time, both enjoying the companionable silence. Dan glanced at Clay's face, his expression grave, and he realized more than ever that Clay had functioned as a father, that Bill Chumley's blood relationship had nothing to do with his life, with his sense of values, with what he was as a man. He wanted to tell Clay that, but he couldn't find the words, so he remained silent until Clay tapped his pipe out on the porch railing.

"Looked for the gold yet?" Clay asked.

"I haven't started digging," Dan answered, "but I'll get at it in a day or two."

"It's as safe up there as anywhere." Clay cleared his

throat. "I've got something to say to you, son. I've missed you, and I've thought about you every day since you left Durango. I knew you were walking into a hornet's nest up here. I knew it as soon as you told me you wanted to buy the Chumley place." He reached for his can of Prince Albert and dribbled fresh tobacco into the bowl of his pipe. "What I didn't know, of course, was that Dorfman was the wild man that he is." He tamped the tobacco down, then struck a match and held the flame to his pipe, his gaze on Dan. "Your letter sounded like what the basin people have been saying for a long time, that I was derelict in my duty, that I was afraid to come up here and tackle Dorfman."

He puffed for a moment, then went on. "I ain't sore, and I ain't being critical. I just want you to understand how it is. I reckon any man who says he's never afraid is a liar, and I'm gonna be scared when we ride onto Wineglass range tomorrow morning, but I've done a lot of things that scared me since I pinned on a star."

He took the pipe out of his mouth and pointed the stem at Dan. "I wasn't afraid to come up here. I just knew there wasn't any use. You can't arrest a man because you know he's going to commit a crime. You've got to wait till he's done it, and you've got to know you've got enough evidence to stand up in court.

"Reno killed two men, but both were so-called fair fights, and I'd never get a conviction on either one. Some families were run off their places, but they were long gone before I heard about it, and I couldn't get 'em into court to testify if I had arrested Dorfman. I don't know that I can get him convicted now unless I find some evidence that will hold up. I don't have it yet. Maybe I can stop his raid on Calamity. I'm sure gonna talk turkey to him."

He shook his head. "Any crime I hold him for will give

the district attorney a weak case. The real nub of the thing is no one will go to Durango to testify. I found that out a long time ago. The basin people scream about me not doing nothing, but they don't have the guts to do their part."

Dan felt sick. He had known he shouldn't have written that last letter, but he had done it anyway. He had heard it said so often that Clay wouldn't do anything to stop Dorfman that he had come to believe it.

"I'm sorry, Matt," Dan said, his head bowed as shame flooded through him. "I'm damned sorry, and I apologize. I'm no hero. I sure don't have no business pointing the finger at you after you've made the record you have."

"That's the way I felt," Clay said. "But about being a hero. Maybe you are. Garnet thinks so, judging by the way she looks at you. Facing Reno says so, too. Stupid, maybe, but then I guess you could say a lot of heroes are stupid. In my book, it's always stupid to buck the other man's game."

Dan, staring at the floor, said nothing. Matt was right about his being stupid, but he was dead wrong about the hero part.

XVII

Dan and Matt Clay ate breakfast by lamplight the following morning. Garnet got up and cooked the meal for them in spite of Dan's assurance he could do it.

"It's a woman's job to cook for her men," Garnet said, wrinkling her nose at Dan. "We don't have anybody staying in the rooms upstairs except Mister Clay, so I can go back to bed after you leave." She brought the coffee pot from the stove and filled their cups. "You know, I'm worried about Ma. She used to work her tail off. Mine, too. But she's let up. Like this morning. If this had been a few weeks ago, she'd have got up to see that I did it right. Here she is, staying in bed and letting me go it alone."

"I guess you don't mind that," Dan said.

"Heavens, no," Garnet said quickly. "It's just not like her . . . that's all. She's fallen apart since you came. She gives out when she didn't used to."

"Does she talk about what's wrong with her?"

"Not much," Garnet answered. "If I ask her, she puts me off, although the other day she did say that the doctor told her that her heart wasn't good."

"All this excitement with Dorfman ain't good for her, if that's the case," Dan said.

"No," Garnet agreed, "but just try to keep her out of it."

"I know her pretty well," Clay said. "Back to the days before you were born. She's always been a fighter. Too much so, sometimes. One thing's sure, though. When her time comes, she'd rather go out with a heart attack than to lie in bed and die slow-like."

"I know," Garnet said. "She won't change, either. Not really change, but she does seem different. Easier to get along with. I think it's because she doesn't have the strength to fight anymore."

"She had it yesterday," Dan reminded her.

"Oh, she'll fight when she has to," Garnet agreed, "but not with the everyday run of things." She hesitated, staring at her plate, then she said slowly: "Sometimes I've hated her and wanted to be anywhere but here, but then I know she's been concerned about what would happen to me after she was gone. I guess your coming is what made her ease up. She figures you'll take care of me."

"I figure on doing that," Dan said.

Clay rose. "Time to move." He nodded at Garnet. "I won't be here tonight. I'm going back to Durango as soon as we leave Wineglass."

She looked at him questioningly, but she didn't put her question into words. She only nodded and said: "There'll be a room for you, when you get back again."

Clay went upstairs and returned with his Winchester, his Colt in his holster. Dan had brought his guns from his room and stood waiting beside the back door. Garnet hesitated, looking at him as if she were afraid she'd never see him again, then she cried — "Dan, don't go." — and ran to him and threw her arms around him.

"I've got to," he said, and kissed her.

Clay stood by the back door, smiling, until Garnet drew back and said: "Be careful, Dan." She swallowed, and added: "I mean, as careful as you can. I know now how women feel when they send their men off to war."

Dan turned from her and strode out through the back door, not saying anything until they reached the shed. The early morning light was still very thin, so he lighted a lantern and hung it from a nail near the door.

"You've got yourself a fine girl," Clay said as he saddled up. "I've watched her grow and always thought well of her, but she's become a woman since I was here the last time. It hasn't been so long, either."

Dan blew out the lantern, then mounted, and they rode around the boarding house to the street. Garnet stood on the front porch, waving. Dan waved back, then made the turn south toward Durango with Clay.

"There's something queer with Ma," Dan said. "Garnet says she knows Ma is her mother, but she's never told Garnet that she was. I'm sure she loves Garnet, but she's treated her like a slave. She's never given her any wages."

"You'd have to know Ma to understand that," Clay said. "She ran a whorehouse for several years before Garnet was born. She'd had others in different mining camps before she came here. The first time I saw her I thought she was a fine-looking woman. Tall and slender and sort of regal-looking. I think that's the right word. Sounds good anyway.

"She didn't sleep with many men. Real choosy about the ones she did. I think she hated men, but she took all the money she could get from them. Then about the time the mines started petering out, a man showed up here she took a shine to. He was a lawyer. Handsome. Smooth. A slick son-of-a-bitch. Don't ask me why she didn't see through him. She knew enough about men that she should've, but she didn't. He asked her to marry him, she said yes, and the next thing she knew he was gone, and she was pregnant.

"She was bitter as hell. If she hadn't hated men before, she sure did then. Changed her place into a boarding house. Had a change of conscience and thought a woman should never sleep with a man unless they were married. I reckon it don't make any sense, but she seemed to feel it was a disgrace to admit she's had a baby, though everybody who lived here then knew. There's still a few people around who know, but they probably keep their mouths shut."

He paused, looked at Dan thoughtfully. "How'd Garnet find out?"

"The woman who was midwife when she was born told her."

Clay sighed. "She's a bitch. Garnet would have been happier not knowing."

Dan shrugged. "Maybe so, but I don't think Ma's ever going to tell her."

They rode on in silence for a time, Dan's thoughts turning to what lay ahead of them. He wondered what Clay intended to do. Finally, just before they reached the turnoff to Wineglass, he burst out: "How do you figure to work this?"

Clay's lips formed a tight grin. "Dunno. I'll play it according to what happens when we get there. Just one thing. Don't go off half-cocked. Follow my lead."

"I'll do that, all right," Dan said. "Suppose Dorfman gets his back up?"

"I'll be surprised, if he does," Clay answered. "Anyhow, old man Apple aims to come up here next week with a herd of cattle to restock Wineglass. He wants Dorfman off the property before then. If he ain't, I'll have to come up here with a posse and move him off."

Dan sucked in a long breath. Dorfman wouldn't leave until he was finished here in the basin. Not if Dan had him pegged right. He'd leave in his own good time, which might mean a hell of a lot of blood-letting if Clay really pushed him.

"Looks to me like Dorfman's a sick man," Dan said.

"Sure he is," Clay said as if that was a plain fact. "There's a lot of sick men running around that nobody knows are sick until they get their tail in a crack. Dorfman's just worse than most of 'em."

When they reached the gate in the barbed-wire fence with the sign **Wineglass** above it, Dan dismounted and opened the gate, then closed it after he had led his horse through with Clay riding ahead of him. Dan remounted, and rode on toward the ranch buildings beside Clay. They had gone fifty yards or more, about the same distance Dan had gone the first day he had been in the basin, when a rifle spoke, the bullet striking within three feet of one of the hoofs of Dan's horse.

Clay and Dan reined up, hands lifted above their heads. A man yelled: "Can't you read, you idiots?"

"That's the same greeting I got," Dan said in a low voice.

"Yeah, we can read," Clay yelled back, "but that sign don't apply to us. I'm the sheriff, and I have business with Dutch Dorfman. Now cut out this fooling around and let us by."

The man moved out from behind the boulder, rifle on the ready as he stared at Dan. He was Ace Bradley, the man who had stopped him before, one of the men who had been with Reno the night they had jumped him on the mountain, the man who had held a gun on him and Garnet and had ordered them to get off the Chumley place.

"I'm running into you all the time," Dan said. "Are you the whole crew?"

"Well, by God," Bradley said, "I was just thinking you turn up everywhere I look." He nodded at Clay. "What's he doing with you?"

"He's my deputy, if it's any of your business," Clay snapped, lowering his hands. "Get out of the way before I ride you down."

Bradley laughed, his rifle cocked and lined on Clay. "Now you are a tough rooster, ain't you? Well, I always figger that *hombres* who ride around with tin stars on their shirts are full of spit and no bite." He shrugged and stepped aside. "It's no skin off my nose. Go on in and see how Dutch likes doing business with a lawman."

Dan lowered his hands and sighed in relief. The problem wasn't solved, but this had been in his mind as the first hurdle to jump, and he'd been afraid that Clay wouldn't turn back and Bradley would shoot if he were backed into a tight situation.

Clay rode on past Bradley, not giving him as much as a

nod. It was still early in the morning, the sun now a round, red ball above the eastern peaks. Their long, thin shadows moved ahead of them across the grass. Dan told himself that as of this moment they were alive. What they would be in another ten minutes was something else.

Dan saw a group of men standing at the corral gate. As he came closer, he saw that Reno was talking to them, maybe giving them their orders for the day. Then Reno swung around and faced Clay and Dan, right hand on the butt of his gun. The other men, six of them, made a solid wall behind Reno. If it came to a showdown, Reno would step aside, and there would be seven guns against two.

None of the men moved as Clay and Dan rode up. Reno demanded: "What do you want? Must be something big for Ace to let you ride in."

"It is," Clay said. "Ask your boss to come out. I have business with him."

Reno didn't say anything for a moment. His gaze moved from Clay to Dan, then his lips curled in distaste when he saw who it was. "So the apron boy rides along with the sheriff. You're hard up for company, Sheriff."

"Keep the rest of 'em off my back, Matt," Dan said as he swung down.

"Damn it, get back on your horse," Clay said roughly. "We didn't come here, itching for a fight. Reno, go get Dorfman like I told you."

Reno still didn't move, his insolent stare on Dan's face. Finally he said: "You know, Sheriff, that pup is living a charmed life. Every time I see him and figure on stopping his clock, somebody steps in and saves his no-good skin."

Dan had not stepped back into the saddle as Clay had ordered. He didn't now. At the moment it didn't occur to him that the Wineglass man was trying to goad him into going for his gun. He never gave a thought to trying to outdraw Reno. He simply drove at the gunman, his fists swinging.

Clay bellowed some angry words at him, but Dan didn't hear him. He was on Reno before the gunman had a chance to make his draw, his right fist slamming into the Wineglass man's stomach. Instinctively Reno pawed at Dan, a blow that had no real power to it. Dan's second punch caught him on the nose and flattened it, bringing a shower of blood, then caught him with an uppercut to the jaw that knocked him flat on his back. He lay still while a murmur ran the length of the line of men.

"Damn' fool," one of them said. "Why didn't he figure out what the kid was gonna do and use his gun when he had a chance?"

"I'd have nailed him for murder if he had," Clay said hotly. "Now, you go fetch Dorfman, or I'll go into the house after him myself."

The man who had spoken shrugged and, stepping around Reno, strode toward the house.

"Dan," Clay said impatiently, "you've had your fun. Now will you get back on your horse?"

Rubbing the knuckles of his right hand, Dan grinned and said: "Glad to."

By the time Dorfman came stomping out of the house, Reno was sitting up and wiping a shirt sleeve across his dripping nose.

Dorfman said sourly: "Go poke your head into the trough. Maybe it'll stop that bleeding." Dorfman tipped his head back and gave Clay an arrogant stare. "You are as welcome around here as a case of smallpox. State your business and git."

"I understand you have been bringing in stolen horses,"

Clay said. "Then you alter the brands and sell 'em. I want to look your horses over."

"It's a damn' lie," Dorfman said as he jerked a thumb at the corral. "But go ahead and look."

Dan, back in the saddle, glanced at the corral and saw there were no more than eight or ten animals there. These certainly wouldn't be the stolen horses, and it was evident that these were not the ones he had seen driven in over the trail from Utah.

"I see," Clay said, making no effort to ride toward the corral. "One more thing, Dorfman. Old man Apple tells me you made the initial down payment to him when you bought Wineglass, but nothing since. The balance is long overdue, and he says he has reminded you about the matter a number of times. Is that true?"

"Why, I don't know," Dorfman said blandly. "I never pay much attention to things like that."

"You're going to pay attention now," Clay said. "Old man Apple has taken legal steps to close you out, and he's moving a herd in next week. I want you out of here, bag and baggage, by the end of this week."

"I'll tell you how it is, Sheriff," Dorfman said in a carefully controlled voice. "I'm the law in the basin. You may be the law in Durango, but not up here. According to my lawyer" — he paused and patted his gun — "I don't owe the old man another nickel. If he moves any cattle onto my range, they become my cattle. Tell him that."

Clay stared at Dorfman, shaking his head. "I don't believe what I'm hearing. I don't know what kind of world you live in, but it sure as hell ain't the real world. You've been warned. Now it's up to you."

He reined his horse around, then pulled him to a stop. "I understand you have made some threats against the people

273

of Calamity. If you harm any of them . . . man, woman or child . . . I'll see you hang so high they won't find you in time to bury you."

Dorfman laughed. The cowhands snickered. Even Reno, standing beside the horse trough, holding a bandanna to his nose, grinned. Dorfman said: "You scare me, Sheriff. Indeed, you do."

Clay jerked his head at Dan, and they rode toward the gate. Neither looked back, but prickles ran down Dan's spine all the way to the gate. It wasn't until after he had opened the gate and closed it behind Clay that he felt safe.

"That son-of-a-bitch," Clay said between gritted teeth. "He believed what he said."

"He acted like it," Dan said. "I figured they'd shoot us in the back."

"If we'd gone sashaying out across his range," Clay said, "nobody ever would have found our bodies. That's what he wanted us to do, but he just didn't have the guts when we rode right up to his headquarters and faced him." Then he grinned. "I'll admit I felt a mite squashed when we rode off. Well, I'm heading back to Durango. Keep your eyes peeled. I can't believe they'd actually raid the town, but you can't judge what he'll do by what another man would do."

"You're bringing a posse back?"

"I'm gonna bring an army," Clay said grimly. "The trouble is I don't know how long it will take me to get 'em together, but I'll get here as soon as I can, maybe tomorrow evening."

He swung his horse and touched the steel to him, heading south toward Durango. Dan watched him for a moment, wondering if Dorfman might send Reno and some others after Clay to kill him before he could reach Durango. He was certain of one thing. Dorfman would raid Calamity.

XVIII

Dan reached the boarding house shortly before noon. When he put his horse away, he discovered a horse he didn't recognize in the stall next to the one he used. He was uneasy as he strode to the kitchen door, wondering if Dorfman was tricky enough to plant one of his men here, perhaps a newcomer who would be a stranger to Ma and Garnet.

When he entered the kitchen, he saw that Garnet and Vera were cooking dinner. Ma was not in sight. When Garnet looked up from the range where she was frying steaks, she saw who had come in and cried out: "Dan, you're all in one piece. Thank heavens!"

"Sure am," he said as he went to the stove and hugged her. "Who's here?"

Vera looked up from the pie she was cutting. She said: "Angel. He wants to see you."

It was surprising to have Angel show up here in the middle of the day, but he didn't question Vera about it. He washed and dried his hands and face, then asked: "Where's Ma?"

"In bed," Garnet said worriedly. "Her chest pains are worse."

"You go after Doc Vance?"

"Yes, but he's somewhere in the east side of the basin delivering a baby," Garnet answered. "He probably won't be back in town until tomorrow."

Dan went into the dining room, uneasiness growing in him. Even in the short time he had known Ma, she had be-

275

come more than an ordinary person to him. If she died, no one could ever fill her place. When he entered the living room, he saw Angel lifting a bar from the front door. Angel turned when he heard Dan, nodded, and said: "Howdy, Larsen. I was just trying out this bar to see if it would fit the door, but it don't make a hell of a lot of difference. This house is a damned poor fort. The doors are solid enough, but the walls are like paper. Slugs will rip right through 'em. I can't see any place in the house where we'd be safe, if they start pouring lead at us, and they will."

Dan stared at him scornfully.

"I know what to expect. Soon as Dorfman gets his outfit together . . . I'd say sometime tomorrow afternoon . . . he'll ride into town and blow it off the face of the map."

"I figured that," Dan said, "but I hadn't thought about us holing up here. You're right about the walls. You hear what happened yesterday?"

Angel nodded. "That's why I'm here. Something like this was bound to happen sooner or later. That's why I'm done playing games with Dorfman, and I'm showing myself in town. We've got maybe twenty-four hours to figure out what to do. That is, if we're lucky." He paused, frowning. "I hear you left this morning with Clay."

"Yeah, we paid Dorfman a visit," Dan said. "Clay will be back with a posse, but probably not in time to do us any good."

"He was a fool for going out there," Angel said scornfully. "I don't know how he's lived as long as he has. I'm surprised that Dorfman let you ride off. Maybe he ain't ready to make his move and figured he'd nail you when he hits town." He pointed a forefinger at Dan, pistol-like. "You're a dead man same as me, if he catches us. We can ride out of the basin and keep going, but I want to nail his mangy hide to his barn door too much to do that. You could, though . . . you and Garnet. Take Vera if you do."

Dan shook his head. "That ain't my style. If we've got twenty-four hours, we'll figure something out."

"I can't guarantee we've got that much time," Angel said. "All I know is that he'll want his whole outfit when he rides in here, and it'll take a little time to get 'em together. Several of his men are a long ways off with that last bunch of stolen horses he brought in. He's too smart to keep 'em where Clay was likely to find 'em. It's my guess he's run his string out here, and he's ready to move on. He'll hit the town, kill anybody who gives him trouble, rob the bank, take what he can get in the store and here at Ma's, get his horses, and light a shuck out of the country."

"I guess you know his habits," Dan said, hoping Angel would say something about his past association with the man.

Angel disappointed him. He said: "Yes, I know his habits. He was never one to work any game very long. He gets bored. This one didn't pay off as well as he'd figured." His face darkened as a sudden burst of fury boiled up in him. "I'll tell you one thing, Larsen. He's not leaving the basin alive. I'm sorry I played tag with him as long as I did. I wished I'd killed the bastard the day I walked in on him and his woman. Now I'm worried what he'll do to Vera, if he gets me."

"Dan," Ma called from the bedroom.

"I'd better see what she wants," Dan said.

He found Ma sitting up in bed, wearing a red robe over her nightgown. She was looking better than he had expected.

"I'm glad you got back alive, son," she said. "What happened?"

277

He told her, ending with Angel's remark that Matt was a fool and it was a wonder he was still alive. She said slowly: "Matt's smarter'n Angel thinks. He's always been a gambler when he's working at his job, but he knows the odds. I'd say he'd thought it over and figured that Dorfman wouldn't shoot him in the back. If he'd started looking for the stolen horses, Dorfman would have killed him. I've known Matt a long time, and I've seen him handle some real hardcases, so I've decided, with him living as long as he has, that he's either smart or lucky, and I guess of the two it's better to be lucky."

"How sick are you?" Dan asked. "In case you don't know, we're worried."

She dismissed the question with a wave of a hand. "Don't worry about me. I'm old, and I've had a good life. Not a life the preacher would hold up as an example, but it was the life I wanted at that particular time, so let's have no regrets. I've got to live a little longer because I know something that you and Angel don't know. I heard enough of your talk to know you're worried about forting up here in the house. Well, you won't have to. When the time comes, you'll be safe, though it'll boil down to how well you and Angel can shoot."

"You'd better tell me about it," Dan said.

"No." She shook her head. "I ain't kicking the bucket until we clean Dorfman's plow for him."

"Just how can you tell how long you're going to live?" Dan asked.

"I don't know," she admitted, "but I'm going to live long enough. I know something that nobody else knows except Dugan. A lot of men used to know it, but they're all gone now."

She closed her eyes for a moment. Dan, staring at her

rough-hewn face, thought she was an old, stubborn woman who might have some stratagem up her sleeve that could save their lives, and she'd die right there in bed without telling them what it was. Being stubborn to the point of foolishness as she was, she would not be persuaded by anything he said, so he didn't try to change her mind.

"I've made a lot of mistakes," she said, opening her eyes. "There's things I'd do different, if I could live my life over. I guess we don't always know what's right, when we're young. We can change when we get older, but we can't undo our mistakes. We just have to live with 'em, hating ourselves and feeling guilty, and going to hell without being able to forgive ourselves." She swallowed, then added in a low voice, "Sometimes you can't even say the things you need to say when you're still alive and have the opportunity to say 'em. Like with Garnet. I love her, Dan, but I can't tell her. Don't ask me why. I just by God can't." She waggled a forefinger at him. "I want her to have a good life, and I expect you to give it to her. Make her happy, or I'll come back and haunt you. Your showing up here that day was an answer to a prayer I'd been praying for a long time. I think I knew when you walked in that you were the right man. Sounds foolish saying it, but things like that have happened to me before."

Garnet appeared in the doorway. "Dinner's ready, Dan."

"If you think I'm gonna lie here and rot and miss my dinner, you're loco," Ma said angrily. "Dan, help me into the dining room."

She'll have her spirit, Dan thought, *right down to the end. A mean spirit, maybe, but she'd have it.* She threw back the blanket that covered her and swung her feet to the floor. She stood up, swaying a little, her face turning pale as Dan gripped her arm. Then she nodded and started toward the door, Dan walking beside her. They went through the living room and on into the dining room where Dan pulled her chair back at the head of the table and eased it into place after she was seated.

Ma gave Angel a hard stare. She said: "I'm glad you're here, Mister Angel. I think we're going to need you."

"I know you will," he said. "I'm going to hang and rattle. Not because I give a damn about your hide, or any of the rest of you except Vera, but for some reason she likes you. I've got an old debt to settle with Dorfman. I aim to get the job done before I leave the basin."

"You're an honest man," Ma said. "Not many men are. They pretend they like you, but they don't really give a damn about you. Now we know how we stand with you."

"That's the way I want it," Angel said. "As soon as I eat, I'm heading for Wineglass. Not all the way, but close enough to see what's happening. I'll be back in time to warn you, so you can clear out and go somewhere else."

"We ain't leaving here," Ma said. "We'll be safe. I'll tell you how when it's time."

"I hope you know what you're talking about," he said. "We're in a hell of a tight."

When Angel finished eating, he rose and said: "Vera, I want you to stay here."

He turned and strode out through the back door. Garnet said: "He's kind of abrupt."

"Just a little," Vera said in disgust. "I don't know why I love a crazy man, but I do."

"So you're stuck with him," Ma said. "He'll make you happy, or he'll make you want to kill yourself. That's the way men are. Dan, help me back to bed."

Dan pulled her chair back and walked beside her to her bed, one arm around her waist. She dropped onto the bed as if her legs had suddenly given way under her.

than he had thought he was. The meal was a meager one: cold roast beef, warmed-up biscuits, boiled potatoes, and coffee, but there was plenty of everything.

When they finished eating, Vera leaned back in her chair, holding her cup of coffee in front of her. She said slowly: "I'm going to tell you about Angel. He hasn't wanted me to, mostly because he doesn't want other people to know. He doesn't want anyone's sympathy. Says he can stomp his own snakes. He thinks about it all the time. Torturing and then killing Dorfman is a compulsion in him. He won't be free of it until Dorfman is dead. He wanted to humiliate the man, and he knew that what he was doing would torture Dorfman more than any physical suffering would. Dorfman has always been a man to pride himself on being smarter and tougher and I guess meaner than anyone else. Angel has showed him repeatedly he's not that superior."

She paused and went on. "We used to live in Montana, close to the Canadian line. Dorfman had a legitimate business buying and selling horses, but he also had an organization that stole horses, brought them across the line, altered the brands, and sold them. He had the qualities that he has now, but he's much worse. Angel worked for him, and I guess was part of the horse-stealing gang. He got too ambitious and tried robbing a bank. He was arrested and sent to the pen. While he was there, something happened. We don't know what exactly, but Angel's family found out what Dorfman was doing and told the sheriff. He nailed the whole bunch. At the trial Angel's father was the state's principal witness, and Dorfman and his bunch were convicted, but before they got to the pen, they escaped. Before they left Montana, they raided the ranch where Angel's family lived. They were all murdered, but one brother lived long enough to tell who did it.

"Dorfman and his men not only killed everyone on the ranch, stole what they could, and burned the buildings, but tortured and raped the women before they left, including Angel's eight-year-old sister who was the apple of his eye. When Angel heard about it, he went crazy for a while, then swore he'd even the score.

"I was teaching in Cutbank, when Angel got out of prison. He came to see me. We'd been in love ever since we were kids. I gave him all the money I had, and he bought a horse and saddle and guns and started out on the owlhoot trail. I guess he robbed some banks, although he never told me much about those years. He kept drifting south, and somewhere along the way he heard that Dorfman was here in the basin. He's using a different name than he used to go by, but Angel heard enough about him to know who he was.

"Angel wrote to me to come down here and live, to get a job in the basin so I'd be able to keep track of Dorfman. Later on he rode in, pretended he didn't know who had murdered his family, and said he wanted to throw in with Dorfman. Dorfman agreed, laughing up his sleeve, I guess, because Angel was working for him and not knowing what had happened. Everything went fine for a while. Angel was thinking up ways to get at Dorfman, when he got drunk enough one night to give a hint that he knew about his family. Apparently Dorfman didn't know that Angel's brother had lived long enough to identify him. Dorfman went into a rage and almost hung Angel." She nodded at Dan. "You've seen the scar on his neck?"

Dan nodded. "He showed it to me."

"Why Dorfman didn't finish him is anyone's guess. That would have been the rational thing to do as we know Dorfman, but whatever he is or isn't, Dorfman isn't rational. Maybe he was so drunk on his sense of power and his notion of his superiority that he wasn't afraid of Angel and got some kind of satisfaction out of letting him go. There's always been this quirk in Dorfman's makeup. He defies the odds. He's that sure he can handle anything that comes along and enjoys proving his superiority, so I guess it amused him to have Angel working for him and letting him go, thinking he didn't have anything to fear and that Angel would leave the basin."

Vera paused, fingers tapping on the table, then she went on. "Angel likes you, Dan, and he's willing to help out today in return for your help with Dorfman. Sometimes I think he's about as crazy as Dorfman is. Don't tell him I've told you all of this. He'd be furious. I guess he's enjoyed his so-called games with Dorfman and being a mystery man here in the basin. He's loved taunting Dorfman, but now he just wants to finish it and start over somewhere. Maybe in Arizona."

"What will you do when he leaves?" Garnet asked.

She shrugged. "Go with him. Like I told you, I love him. I don't know why, but I do."

"And leave your teaching job?"

She nodded. "I've enjoyed it here and met a lot of people I like, including both of you," Vera said, "and I guess it's really pretty foolish to say this, but where Angel goes, I go."

Dan hadn't heard Angel ride in, but apparently he had put his horse in the shed. Now he slammed the back door open and burst into the kitchen. "They're coming," he said. "Right behind me. About ten of 'em. If Ma's got a miracle in her head, it's time to trot it out."

Dan rose and ran into Ma's bedroom. He said: "They're close."

Ma threw back the blanket that was covering her. She said: "Help me into the dining room."

Ma dropped into a chair as soon as she reached the dining room. Dan, who had held an arm around her all the way from her bedroom, saw the gray pallor of death in her face, and he thought with a sudden rush of dread that she had better produce her miracle in a hurry. Still, she kept a tenacious hold on life, and maybe she could dictate the moment of her passing.

Ma motioned to the dining room table. "Move it," she said. Dan hesitated, thinking there was no sense in her order. She said impatiently: "Do what I told you, damn it."

Garnet pulled several chairs back from the table, and Dan, taking hold of one side of the table, pulled it about six feet toward the west wall. When he stepped away from the table, Ma said: "Now roll the rug back."

She had always done the cleaning in the dining room, and Dan had paid little attention to the big rag rug that covered much of the dining room floor. He lifted one edge of the rug and rolled it back against the legs of the table.

"Now the trap door," Ma said.

Angel had stepped out on the front porch to watch Dorfman's men ride in. "They're here," he called. "They're riding in behind the store and bank. No use of us barring the doors. They'll knock out the windows in the store and bank and fill this place full of lead."

"Come here, Angel," Dan shouted.

He had lifted the trap door. Below, it was a black hole with a short ladder leading down from the dining-room floor. "Get your sacks of money and drop 'em down there,"

Ma said. "Let 'em fill this house full of flying lead. You'll be gone before that happens. When you get to the bottom, you'll find a tunnel that crosses the street and comes out in Dugan's store room. There's another ladder on that end. It takes you up into Dugan's store room. If he ain't forgot and left some sugar sacks on top, all you've got to do is to shove the trap door open. Dorfman sure ain't gonna figure on you coming up out of the floor."

Angel stood staring down into the opening below him, a slow grin crawling across his face. "You done it, Ma. You pulled a miracle out of your head."

"I've lived here all my life and never knew about that," Garnet said. "I always wondered why Ma insisted on doing the sweeping and mopping around the edge of that rug."

"I didn't want you to know about it," Ma said. "The tunnel was dug in the old days, when I had the best house in Calamity and the prettiest girls. My customers were all A-Number-One men . . . bankers, lawyers, storekeepers, and one doctor. Their wives got on to where they were spending their evenings and waited outside for 'em one night. The women had rolling pins and brooms and the like, and they chased the men home, beating them every jump. I figured my business was done for because those men weren't coming back after that, but one of the mine owners had taken a fancy to one of my girls, and he wasn't going to let that stop him, but he didn't want to lose his wife, either, so he brought some miners into town that nobody knew and lodged 'em here in my place. He had 'em dig the tunnel. Nobody knew about it but me and the men who used it. After the tunnel was finished, he shipped the men out of town.

"The wives never figured it out. They knew their men were staying out most of the night, so they'd come and wait for 'em out in front until they got so cold they had to leave. When they got home, they'd find their husbands in bed and asking where their wives had been. Finally they gave up and took the men's word for it that they'd been playing poker all night."

She laughed, a strained sound that ended in a spasm of coughing. She slumped in her chair, holding to the sides as if keeping herself upright by the sheer power of her will.

Dorfman's shout reached them. "Come out with your hands up, Angel. Larsen, if you're there. All of you. I'll give you three minutes. Not a second more."

"He'd gun us down as soon as we showed ourselves," Angel muttered.

"You've got three minutes to get down into the tunnel," Ma said. "You go first, Dan. There's a lantern at the base of the ladder. You go next, Angel. Then Vera. I'll lower the trap door as soon as Garnet's down the ladder."

Dan tossed the flour sacks to the floor of the tunnel. Then he said: "You're coming."

"No, I ain't," Ma said. "I couldn't drag myself through that tunnel, and you know it. The tunnel ain't big enough for you to carry me. I'm safer right here. I'll go into the kitchen and lie on the floor. I won't get shot."

For an instant Dan stood motionless at the edge of the hole, his gaze upon Ma. He didn't want to do it this way, but he knew she was right. She didn't have the strength to crawl the length of the tunnel. He knew, too, that there was no use to argue with her. Sick or well, Ma was not a woman to be changed by anyone else's argument. He glanced at Garnet who nodded as if to say that, if Ma wanted it that way, they'd better do it.

Dan descended the ladder, found the lantern, and, jacking up the chimney, struck a match and held it to the

298

wick. He eased the chimney back into place, noting that the light would be dimmed because the chimney was blackened by soot. He also saw that the tunnel roof was too low to stand fully erect, but by keeping his head down he would not have to crawl as he'd been afraid he would.

He picked up his flour sacks of money and moved away from the foot of the ladder, so Angel could descend.

"Some woman," Angel said, when he stood beside Dan. "By God, she delivered all she said she would."

Dan moved deeper into the tunnel to give Vera and Garnet room to stand, then the trap door banged shut and the slim shaft of light that had fallen from the dining room was blotted out. Holding the lantern as high as he could, so the women would have some light, he edged forward.

The air in the tunnel was bad, the smell musty, and Dan had a feeling it would not be safe to linger here any longer than necessary. In several places he ran into dirt slides that forced him to get down on his hands and knees. He called a warning back, when he reached one of the slides, and knew it was almost a matter of feel for the others to climb over them because very little of the lantern's murky light reached back to them, but he moved slowly, waiting at times for the women to keep up.

He had no idea how far they had come. Their pace was so slow that it seemed they took a long time to reach the south end of the tunnel and there was no possible way to measure the distance they had covered, but no one complained. Then, suddenly, a black wall appeared ahead of them in the dim light of the lantern. A ladder was there just as Ma had promised. Now the crackle of gunfire came to them distinctly.

"We're here," Dan said, holding the lantern high so the others could see.

Angel ran one hand up and down the ladder. "Looks like it will hold us. I'm going up."

The women were huddled close together, their dresses covered with dust, their faces grimy. For a moment Dan wanted to argue about who went up first, then he remembered how Angel felt about Dorfman, so he said: "Don't start the ball till I get there. Garnet, you and Vera stay here. I'll get you when it's safe."

"Where are the sacks?" Garnet asked.

"I dropped 'em halfway through the tunnel," Dan said. "I figured nobody would find 'em there. I didn't want to leave 'em here because Dorfman might look at the end of the tunnel, but he wouldn't be likely to go through it."

"Good," Garnet said. "I'd rather that nobody found them than for Dorfman to get them."

Angel had climbed the ladder as far as he could without opening the trap door. "All set, Larsen?" he asked.

"You bet," Dan answered, handing the lantern to Garnet.

"There's nothing on top of the trap door," Angel said. "Here we go."

He shoved the trap door back and over. It fell with a floor-shaking crash as the light from Dugan's store room filled the opening. Angel was up and off the ladder in an instant, Dan scrambling up beside him. He lifted the trap door and dropped it back into place. Dugan lay next to the back wall, hands and feet tied.

"I figured Ma would send you this way," Dugan said. "Cut me loose."

Neither Dan nor Angel paid any attention. The sounds of rifle fire from the front of the store was a constant hammering at their ears. Both men had their guns in their hands.

300

"If Dorfman's here," Angel said, "he's my meat."

"Then Reno's mine," Dan said.

Angel nodded. "Fair enough."

They eased toward the door that led into the store part of the building. There was no danger of their steps being heard by Dorfman's men, but they moved cautiously until they were through the door and into the store proper. Three men were standing close to the windows, firing their Winchesters as fast as they could pull the triggers and lever shells into the chambers of their rifles.

Dan and Angel moved side by side toward the front of the store. Dorfman and Reno, their rifles empty, turned to the end of the counter where a box of shells had been laid out. They loaded their Winchesters, then looked up. Dan wished he could have taken a picture of them in that instant. Expressions of absolute shock crossed their faces. They must have thought they were seeing ghosts of two men they had just killed.

The shock lasted no more than a few seconds. Dorfman and Reno reacted by raising their rifles, but neither got off a shot. Dorfman was hit by Angel's bullet that shattered his right arm and sent his rifle flying. Dan cut Reno down, his bullet smashing into the man's chest, hammering him back against the wall. He hung there a moment, his boot heels digging into the floor, then he toppled sideways and sprawled to the floor. Angel was in no hurry to finish Dorfman. His second bullet broke the other arm. The next ripped through his belly and put him down.

Dan covered the third man who had stood next to Reno. It had taken him several seconds to realize what was happening. When he did wheel around, he was staring into the muzzle of Dan's gun. He dropped his Winchester and raised his hands. Dan recognized him then, Ace Bradley, and was reminded of his words: "You turn up everywhere I look." This, Dan told himself, would be the last time.

The men in the saloon were firing steadily. Dan jerked his head through the door that opened into the saloon. "Tell 'em they're wasting their ammunition. They've got no reason to keep on fighting."

Bradley looked at the two dead men, nodded, and turned to the saloon door. He yelled above the rifle fire: "Hold up, boys. The fight's over."

They faced him, saw his hands in the air and Dan behind him with his cocked Colt in his hand, then dropped their rifles. "Bradley, you 'n' me are going to the bank," Dan said. "Angel, take these tough hands who ain't very tough right now and put 'em on their horses. Hold 'em till I get back with the others."

For a moment Angel didn't move or act as if he had heard. He dug a toe into Dorfman's body, staring down at the dead man, and for an instant Dan had the strange feeling that all reason for Angel's existence had left him.

"Angel, you hear me?" Dan yelled.

The man jumped as if he had suddenly been yanked back into the world of reality. "Sure, Larsen," he said. "I'll take care of 'em."

As the sullen men walked past Dan, he said: "Pick up that carrion and take 'em outside and tie 'em on their horses. Do whatever you want with 'em. Just get 'em out of town."

They carried Dorfman's and Reno's bodies back through the store room to the alley, Dugan yelling for them to untie him. Again they ignored him. Dan and Bradley went on to the bank, leaving Angel to see that the dead men were tied face down across their saddles.

It took only minutes to go through the back door of the

302

bank to where four of Dorfman's crew were still firing. When Bradley told them that Dorfman was dead, they dropped their Winchesters. One of them, glaring at Dan, said: "I don't know how you done it, but you are a lucky son-of-a-bitch."

Lucky? Maybe so, Dan thought, as he cut Sam Gerard loose, *lucky that Ma Willet had stayed alive long enough to show them the tunnel.*

"I'll be back and tell you what happened," Dan told Gerard. "Right now, I want to get this bunch out of town."

By the time he marched Bradley and the others to the rear of the store, the men Dan had left with Angel were mounted, the dead men lashed across their saddles. As Bradley and the four others mounted, Dan said: "Pick up your women and whatever you want from Wineglass and light a shuck out of the basin."

For a moment they stared at him, beaten, miserable men with the fight drained out of them, then they touched up their horses, and rode out of town at a gallop.

"Cut off the head of a snake," Dan said, "and you don't need to worry about the rest of it."

Angel didn't say anything, but wheeled and strode back into the store. Dan caught up with him and cut Dugan's ropes, ignoring the man's curses and his question: "What took you so long to cut me loose?"

Dan didn't answer. He lifted the trap door and called: "Come on up." He gave Vera a hand, then Garnet. Angel had strode on through the store to the front door and on out into the street.

"Dorfman?" Vera asked.

"Dead," Dan answered.

"Then it's over," Vera said. "We'll be leaving. I don't know where to, but we're going."

She kissed Garnet, then Dan, and whispered — "Thank you." — and raced after Angel.

Dan opened his arms, and Garnet ran into them, and for a long moment they stood that way, their lips pressed together, holding each other as if they would never part and completely ignoring Dugan who was screaming: "Damn it, Larsen, I could have helped if you'd cut me loose in time."

Garnet finally drew back from Dan, patted his cheek, and whispered: "I'm just glad you're still alive." Then she turned to Dugan and said: "Mike, Dan didn't think you'd want to help since you wouldn't believe me when I told you what was going to happen."

They walked through the store and across the street to the bullet-riddled boarding house. Dan shook his head as he looked at the front of the building. "Ain't that a mess? I'll go down and get that money pretty soon and take it to the bank. Maybe we'll use some of it to fix this building up. There ain't enough glass left in them windows to know there ever was any."

"You think Ma might still . . . ?" Garnet began.

"Not likely," Dan said, "unless she went out through the back door."

They crossed the living room, window glass grating under their feet. Ma's body was not in the dining room, but the rug had been rolled into place and the table moved back so the trap door was covered. They found her body on the floor in the pantry. There were no bullet wounds. Her heart had simply given out at last.

Dan picked her up and carried her into her bedroom and laid her on the bed. For a moment he stood beside Garnet, looking down at Ma's body, an expression of peace on her face, an expression he had seldom seen when she had been alive.

"I never met another woman like her," Dan said, "and I don't figure I ever will. She knew for a long time she was going to die, but damned if she didn't fight it off long enough to do what she had to do."

"I'll never understand her if I live to be a thousand years old," Garnet said. "Just before I went down the ladder, she said . . . 'Good bye, daughter.' I started to go to her and kiss her, but she motioned for me to go. It's the only time she ever acknowledged I was her daughter."

"She told me she loved you, but she couldn't tell you," Dan said. "I don't know why."

Garnet was silent a moment, then she said slowly: "I think it was because she was so ashamed of having me. It was the last thing she ever wanted to do."

She drew a blanket over Ma's body, then left the bedroom, Dan following. She said: "I'll see Preacher Faraday about the funeral. We'll probably have it tomorrow."

Dan reached for her hands and turned her to face him. "We'll get married as soon as you can manage it. Matt told me something I haven't told you because I wanted to be sure I lived long enough to marry you. He said old man Apple was going to offer me a partnership in Wineglass. It won't be a big operation for a while, but it'll be a living. What do you think?"

She smiled. "What do I think? I think it's a great idea, and as to when I can manage to marry you, would tomorrow be too soon?"

"Just right," Dan said, and knew it was the way Ma would have wanted it.

About the Author

Wayne D. Overholser won three Golden Spur awards from the Western Writers of America and has a long list of fine Western titles to his credit. He was born in Pomeroy, Washington, and attended the University of Montana, University of Oregon, and the University of Southern California before becoming a public schoolteacher and principal in various Oregon communities. He began writing for Western pulp magazines in 1936 and within a couple of years was a regular contributor to Street & Smith's *Western Story Magazine* and Fiction House's *Lariat Story Magazine*. BUCKAROO'S CODE (1947) was his first Western novel and remains one of his best. In the 1950s and 1960s, having retired from academic work to concentrate on writing, he would publish as many as four books a year under his own name or a pseudonym, most prominently as Joseph Wayne. THE VIOLENT LAND (1954), THE LONE DEPUTY (1957), THE BITTER NIGHT (1961), and RIDERS OF THE SUNDOWNS (1997) are among the finest of the Overholser titles. THE SWEET AND BITTER LAND (1950), BUNCH GRASS (1955), and LAND OF PROMISES (1962) are among the best Joseph Wayne titles, and LAW MAN (1953) is a most rewarding novel under the pseudonym Lee Leighton. Overholser's Western novels, whatever the byline, are based on a solid knowledge of the history and customs of the 19th-Century West, particularly when set in his two favorite Western states, Oregon and Colorado. Many of his novels are first person narratives, a technique that tends to bring an added dimension of vividness to the frontier experiences of his narrators and frequently, as in CAST A LONG SHADOW (1957), the female characters one encounters are among the most memorable. He wrote his numerous novels with a consistent skill and an uncommon sensitivity to the depths of human character. Almost invariably, his stories weave a spell of their own with their scenes and images of social and economic forces often in conflict and the diverse ways of life and personalities that made the American Western frontier so unique a time and place in human history. THE OUTLAWS will be his next **Five Star Western**.